About the Author

Dan Kussart has self-published three novels set in Victorian England. His short story, *Hiraeth*, was selected for the 2017 edition of *Creative Wisconsin*, the literary journal of the Wisconsin Writers 'Association. He lives with his wife, Bonnie, in Sheboygan, Wisconsin.

Eddie & Iggy

Dan Kussart

Eddie & Iggy

Vanguard Press

Vanguard Press is an imprint of
Pegasus Elliot Mackenzie Publishers Ltd. www.pegasuspublishers.com

First Published in 2024

Vanguard Press
Sheraton House Castle Park
Cambridge England

Printed & Bound in Great Britain

To Bonnie and to my childhood friends: the Eddies to my Iggy

One

Call me Iggy.

The full name's Ignatz Tomas Silver, but no one calls me that, except a couple of aunts everybody ignores anyway.

This whole thing started when I was eleven, in 1924. Now, in 1926, I'm a lot older, and can write the whole thing down better. Got a little help from a couple of grown-up friends with some of the tough words, but mostly this is me. Anyhow, I've always been a lot better at reading and writing than my best buddy, Eddie. More on him in a bit.

It was... let me *think!* It was a Friday—December 19th—day before the long Christmas vacation at school. The classroom where we were taught by crabby old Miss Postlethwaite was decorated with paperchains and a small Christmas tree, and a few other doo-dads and whatnots. Lots of kids were excited about Christmas, and I guess so was I, but I'm kinda old for all that Santa Claus rigmarole. Mind you, I played along for my folks 'sake. We're Jewish, so we celebrate Hanukkah, but that doesn't keep old Kris Kringle from stopping at our door. My household is a little confused when it comes to religion.

Anyhow, like I said, Miss P's classroom was decorated to the gills with Christmas, and there was a lot of chatter going on, and even Miss P allowed it for a while. Then she clapped her hands, and the chatter stopped, liked she'd snuffed out a candle.

Miss Postlethwaite is tall, and skinny as a green bean. She wears her hair in a real old-fashioned do, not like the short curls most gals wear now. No mystery there (she has to be at least thirty years old). Anyhow, she's an okay sort if you don't mess up on purpose. Honest mistakes are fine, but she isn't big on goof-offs. Eddie is sort of one of those goof-offs, so he didn't care much for Miss P. I was okay in her book, mostly.

"Now class," she started. "I've a little assignment for you over the Christmas vacation".

You'd have thought she'd announced Santa had been shot. An *assignment?* Over the *vacation?* Didn't she know we had candy to eat and toys to break? Not to mention all the pressure that came from visits to and from relatives we didn't know or didn't like. Why, the annual visit from the Meiselwitz family alone would make strong men weep. Their kids were terrors, and *loud!* I can shout with the best of them, but those kids could shatter porcelain – from a distance.

"Now, now," Miss P said over the top of our groans. "This will be fun! And you can start this afternoon."

On her desk, she had a stack of newspapers, a couple of feet high. She put a hand on the top. "I am good friends with the city's head librarian." Of course she was. "Every three years, the library discards its old newspapers. I asked her if I might have a few dozen. These," she patted the stack like it was an obedient kid, "are from 1921. Three years ago."

Miss P added that last sentence because she could see some of the kids mentally subtracting 1921 from 1924 and coming up with all sorts of answers.

"Now, I want you to break up into pairs. Groups of two." She held up a hand because most of us started to move. "Wait! Wait!" That didn't work. By now, nearly everyone was already sitting next to or across from their best friend. Eddie had already moved his desk across from me and grinned. Seeing the cause was hopeless, she said all right, we could pair up now and she would explain the assignment.

When we were all paired up, Miss P signaled for silence and mostly got it.

"Very good. Now, I will give each of you two editions. You are to go through them and select one article, one story that sounds interesting to both of you. Then, over Christmas vacation, you will write a report about that article." She went to the blackboard and wrote:

Who? What? Where? When? Why?

"Answer those questions," she said as some scribbled them down. "Tell us what went on. When we return from vacation, you will each read your report to the class."

She went to the blackboard again.

No comics! No advertisements! Must be an article!

"I do not want *The Katzenjammer Kids* or some advertisement for Stu's Meat Market!" There were a few giggles about that. "Any other article will be fine. Yes, David?"

David Gooch was a big, lumbering, future prize-fighter type. Dumb as a stone. "Kin we write about sports?"

To everyone's surprise, Miss P nodded. "If you can answer those five questions about it, yes, you may."

Seeing no other questions, she grabbed a handful of papers and began distributing them. She knew better than to let us pick our own, (there'd be newspapers all over the place).

Best now I tell you all about Eddie. His name's Edwin James McDonald. He's big, with dirty yellow hair and spit in his eye. He's a little on the slow side. Not stupid, certainly in Gooch's league. Just… well, it takes him a sight longer to figure something out than it does me. He also isn't much for books; reads when he has to, is about it. Well, he does read his adventure magazines, like *Amazing Worlds* and *Slash Danger, Detective*.

One important thing to say about Eddie: a fellow couldn't have a better friend. If you're on his good side, he will stick by you no matter what. More than once he's pulled me from the soup. See, I sometimes say things without thinking. Where Eddie's a bit slow, I'm too quick, and my big yap has gotten me in trouble a few times. Good old Eddie has saved me. We've been best friends since we were toddling, and a fellow couldn't ask for a better pal.

I knew Eddie would want me as a partner, not just because we're buddies, but because he knew I'd do most of the work on the report. Miss P knew it too, but didn't say boo about it. She hadn't said who we could team up with.

We sat at our desks, facing each other, looking over the newspapers like bankers reading the financial pages.

"What you got?" I asked Eddie, seeing he was actually reading an article. "This story," he said, tapping the paper, "about Hippo Vaughn."

"Who?"

Eddie was stunned by my ignorance. "*Hippo Vaughn!* You've heard of him. Pitcher for the Cubs? Only one of the best baseball players in the history of the game."

"Oh. What about him?"

Eddie rolled his eyes like I was as dim as a tulip.

"Look," I said. "I suppose Happy Vaughn is a great pitcher—"

"*Hippo*. His name is Hippo." Like Hippo had been christened that.

"Right. Hippo. Anyhow, I suppose he's great but," I pointed to the blackboard," can you answer any of those questions from the article except *who*? We've got to have a story with some teeth in it."

"Okay, okay. You think Miss P would let me tear out this picture of Hippo, though? It'd look great on my wall."

"You can ask her later. Meantime, I've found something that maybe would work for our report."

Eddie looked mildly interested. I could tell he was still thinking about Hippo's picture on his wall. He asked what I had, and I handed over the newspaper and pointed to the article I'd found.

Now, before I go on with the article, I have to tell you something: Eddie and I like detective stories. I mentioned those magazines Eddie reads, but the fact is we both enjoy a good mystery. The only books Eddie will read for pleasure are Sherlock Holmes collections. Except *A Study in Scarlet*. He was bored to tears on that one. Anyhow, a couple of years back we got pretty excited because a real detective moved into the neighborhood. His name's Tom Delancey, and you'll meet him eventually.

So here is the article I showed Eddie. I cut it out of the newspaper later (because Miss P said we should take out the story we wanted to do) which gave Eddie license to cut out his picture of Hippo Vaughn, so he was one happy sparrow.

Strange Discovery

A very strange discovery was reported at the home Miss Agnes Hogwood, 1711 North 5th Street. Miss Hogwood, who lives alone in the large house—with the exception of a housekeeper, maid, and cook—had long ago shut off a great portion of the house, as it was no use to her.

One of the rooms closed off was the former study of her late father, Mr John Hogwood. This past Thursday, the maid and housekeeper entered the study to do some cleaning.

The maid, Miss Gladys Schmidt, discovered the mortal remains of a woman, dead for some time, according to the coroner. The body was in a mummified state, as the room had been closed off for so long.

There were signs of violence upon the body, but the police do not wish to release more details as yet. It is hoped that the identity of the deceased woman may be established, and clear up the mystery of how the unfortunate soul came to be in the sealed room.

This is a great tragedy," said Inspector John Klein, and we shall not rest until the poor woman is identified and the person responsible brought to account."

"Well?" I asked Eddie when he'd read the article. It took him a bit. Eddie's slow, but he's thorough. "Do you think we should take this article for our report?"

Eddie rubbed his chin. He sometimes does that because he thinks it makes him look like Sherlock Holmes. "Maybe. But this story don't say much. I mean, take that first question on the board: who? I mean to say, we can't even answer *that* one, can we? At least with my article, we know it's about Hippo Vaughn."

"Would you give Hippo a rest, Eddie? We can't do that one. I just want to know if you want to do my article or not. If you don't like it, we'll keep looking."

More chin rubbing. Suddenly, Eddie did the unthinkable, something I don't believe Eddie had ever done his whole life. He raised his hand. Miss P looked like she'd spotted the *Flying Dutchman* on the horizon.

"Yes, Eddie?" she asked, coming forward.

Others looked up at the strange sight of Eddie McDonald with his hand up in class. "Miss Postlethwaite, I have a question," Eddie said, polite as you please. He can be a real gentleman when he sets his mind to it. "We have this article Iggy found, and I'm not sure it's enough to answer your questions, but maybe it is. I wondered if we could look into it some more and maybe do a report on the whole story, instead of just this little bit."

The whole class was listening now. I don't think I've ever seen Miss P so stunned. She was shocked enough when Eddie raised his hand; now, she looked ready to faint. To think Eddie not only had an actual question that made sense, but was actually suggesting he could do more work than necessary. She just had to see this article for herself.

It didn't take her long to read the story, of course. I could tell she wanted to judge it as too horrible, dead bodies and such, but on the other hand, she didn't want to put the kibosh on Eddie's willingness to work. So she compromised.

"How would you go about it?" she asked. A perfectly good question, so I started to answer, figuring Eddie wouldn't be able to. But no, he cut in.

"We know a guy," he said. "He investigates stuff, and he knows a police inspector, and he could find out some more for us."

Boy, Miss P wanted to say no! She chewed her lip and fiddled with a cuff on her dress. But you know what Eddie did? He put on these big wide innocent eyes and waited so patiently for her answer, and she just couldn't say no. She did manage to wring one concession out of him though.

"Very well. You and Iggy may choose this article. But if the two of you cannot answer those five questions on the blackboard, you'll have to choose another. And I still expect it by the time you return from Christmas vacation."

"We've got another article all lined up," Eddie said, and I thought he might mention Hippo Vaughn by name, but he didn't; just tapped the newspaper knowingly. I think even Miss P might have preferred Hippo to a dead body in a big house.

Two

Tom Delancey started his detective business a few years before. Eddie and I met him the summer of 1923 when we ran into a bit of trouble and he got involved in the case. Though we hadn't spoken his name in class, Eddie and I both knew who he was talking about when he mentioned someone who might help us.

Not that Delancey (he always goes by just his last name) owed us. I mean, we did help him with that case, and he probably earned a good fee, but we're buddies, him and us, so we figured he'd do us a favor. All he had to do was call his friend, Inspector Jacob Fenrow, after all.

So when school let out that day, Eddie and I headed for Delancey's office instead of home. Eddie lives alone with his mom, who is a waitress at the local department store lunch counter. She's usually gone to work by the time Eddie comes home from school. Eddie's old man cut out when Eddie was a baby, and good riddance to bad rubbish, my friend says.

Delancey rents a two-room office on the second floor of an old building. The place has an elevator that works sometimes. Most folks take the stairs because the elevator looks like it's ready to die.

The outer office is a reception room where sits Mrs Beulah Willows, a young widow who Delancey helped way back when. Don't say I told you this, but Eddie thinks Mrs Willows is the bee's knees. I admit she's not bad looking, with brown hair and eyes, and a nice smile, but come on—she's old enough to be his mother. Besides which… well, leave it at that. Mrs Willows is really nice and tells us to call her Beulah, so we do. She was wrapping Christmas gifts at her desk when we walked in, and smiled sweet as pie when she saw us. That made Eddie all drooly, naturally, and I had to do the talking, which happens a lot around Beulah.

"Is Delancey busy?" I asked. "We want to see him on something."

"Come in, boys," came a call from the next room.

Eddie gave his best movie star smile to Beulah as he walked off… and bumped into the doorframe. Poor drip, he's got it bad.

Delancey is not real tall, but he's pretty strong, and kind of wiry; dark hair that won't comb; sort of a round face that's nice and friendly, which must help in his line of work when folks come to him with a problem. As we walked in, he was picking up the playing cards and the hat he'd been tossing them into.

"Have a seat," he said, nodding to two chairs across from his desk. "What can I do for you? All set for Christmas?" Delancey knows I'm Jewish, but he also knows I don't make a deal about it, and that my family celebrates Christmas, too.

"I guess," we both said. What else could we say? It isn't as if we bake cookies or actually buy presents or something.

"So what's up?"

Beulah entered then and Eddie started stammering like a chucklehead so I explained about the assignment. Eddie took the newspaper clipping from me and handed it to Delancey, saying, "I found this." It was a lie, of course, but it's best not to argue when Eddie's trying to impress a girl. Even a girl nearly three times his age.

"So," Delancey said when he and Beulah had read the article and handed it back, "what do you want me to do?"

"Well," I said, rubbing my nose, "it's this way. We thought of Inspector Fenrow when we read the article, and we know you know him, and we wondered if maybe you could find out whatever happened with that dead body. Who was it? Did they catch who did it? Stuff like that."

"I dunno, boys," Delancey started.

"He'd be happy to," Beulah cut in.

"Now, wait a minute…"

"Come on, Delancey. It will take a telephone call. Inspector Fenrow probably remembers the case and can tell you what happened without even looking it up. You could do it right now."

"Please?" I asked.

No adult can resist a kid who says please without even being told. Well, almost no adult. (I had an old aunt who figured all kids were liars and after her jewelry.)

Beulah handed the telephone receiver to Delancey. He took it, shot her a warning glance, and started to dial.

Eddie suddenly blurted out, "Anything the inspector remembers about the case would help."

Delancey stopped dialing, glared at Beulah some more, and finally completed the number. We waited. Someone Delancey knew answered. He asked for Inspector Fenrow and looked disappointed when he was told the inspector was in his office and Delancey should hold a moment. Soon, the old friends were talking, and after a little light exchange, Delancey got down to business. He explained what he was calling for, but left our names out of it; just said he was doing it for a client. After a long pause, Delancey said, "Yeah, we'll be here. Okay. See you then."

Delancey cradled the receiver and took a deep breath before saying, "Now look, boys. I like you, and went out on a limb for you on this one. Inspector Fenrow's a busy man, and he's offered to come here in an hour, to talk about the case. When he finds out it's a school assignment, he's gonna have kittens. So you've got two choices: either you can stay here and get hollered at by a senior police official, or you can take off and I can fill you in on Monday."

"Might we confer?" Eddie asked. Sometimes he likes to act the high-handed gentleman in his speech, especially around Beulah.

Delancey nodded and we went to Beulah's office to talk.

I gotta admit, I was scared. I mean, who knows what Inspector Fenrow would do to us? Better to have him holler at Delancey, than to have us get run into the pokey. My mother would cry herself into conniptions.

Eddie was all for staying, but I think part of that was to show Beulah how brave he was. We debated a bit, but I finally won out. We returned to the office, and told Delancey we'd take off, and maybe could come see him the next day.

"I don't work Saturday," Delancey said flatly. He was lying, because we know that when he's got a case he'll work whatever hours it takes, but of course we weren't paying customers, so it looked like Monday would be the day we'd learn what Fenrow had to say. Seeing our disappointment, Delancey sighed and glanced at his wristwatch.

"The inspector will be here in around forty-five minutes. He'll probably stay an hour. Come back here around six."

That worked for us. We could go home and have supper first, then head out.

My family lives above Dad's jewelry shop. It's not what you'd call spacious, but there's enough room for our little family. That afternoon, Mom was in the kitchen, fixing something delicious. Dad was still in the shop, but would be up soon, after closing. So I washed my hands, then sat in the living room. A menorah was prominently placed on the mantel, though we never go through all the routine most Jewish families do at Hanukah. Basically, we light the appropriate number of candles and then listen to the radio while Dad reads the paper.

The previous year, Dad had given in to my whining and bought a small Christmas tree. Of course, we had no decorations for it. We had vague ideas of how the tree should look, but that was all. So for several days, it just sat there, like Mom's African violet on the windowsill. We finally put some paperchains on it. My folks 'more orthodox friends frowned at the tree, but said nothing. A few of them shook their heads and muttered something in Yiddish. Didn't matter; we've had a small tree with paperchains every year since.

After supper, I met Eddie outside Delancey's office building. We went up together, and found him alone. To Eddie's dismay, Beulah had gone home.

"Did the inspector come?" Eddie asked as we sat in his dark office. Delancey seldom works late, and all the lights were out except a couple of feeble lamps.

"Yep. And it was all I could do to keep him from getting the names of my 'clients'. I tell you, boys, this is best left alone."

"Well at least tell us what he said," Eddie insisted.

Delancey sighed. He sighs a lot around us. He sat back and his chair creaked something awful. Delancey's not that heavy; his chair is that old.

"To start with," he said, "the tale goes back more than just three years—to 1919. There was a guy named James Clapham."

"Of Clapham Jewelers?" I asked. I'd taken out a pencil and notebook, and was scribbling names and dates and such for our school report.

"Who's telling this story?" He looked miffed. "But you're right, Iggy. He owned—still owns—Clapham Jewelers. Well-respected and not a little on the rich side. Anyhow, at the time he was doing just okay, financially. I guess this whole story brought him lots of publicity, and folks discovered his shop because of it.

"Anyhow, his wife's name was Millicent. Millie to her friends. Liked by most. A housewife, though she sometimes helped around the shop. Used to play bridge with some of the neighbor ladies, and so on. But her big thing was the church. St Dunstan's, over on Sixth. She helped out with cleaning pews and such. Also sang in the church choir.

"Well, one night, in October 1919, Mrs Clapham went to choir practice, which ran from six thirty to seven thirty every Thursday. The Claphams lived just around the corner and down the street from church—a ten minute walk—and it was a nice evening, so she walked to practice. Everything went along fine. Mrs C seemed her usual self.

"The choirmaster, a Mr," Delancey checked his notes, "Henry Blank, was a stickler for finishing practice on time, give or take a few minutes. Soon as the church clock rang the half-hour, he was done. So it happened that night. Finished before the chime stopped.

"Like usual, the choir gabbled a bit as they were leaving. Most of them were standing outside the church, talking. Mrs C said her goodbyes and left."

"She didn't stay t 'talk?" Eddie asked.

"For a minute or two, then she left," Delancey replied. "Not unusual. She wasn't much for yakking. Not standoffish, just not the sort to stand around and gab. Anyhow, she headed for home. Some of the choir recall seeing her round the corner, and that was the last time anyone saw her alive. Vanished without a trace. Until, of course, she popped up in that woman's—Miss Agnes Hogwood's—study."

"Murdered!" Eddie said breathlessly.

"Clearly. I mean, no one goes to some stranger's house to have a heart attack, do they? Nah. She'd been hit over the head. Pretty damn hard, too. Caved in the skull on one side. No other signs of violence, though."

Delancey took a drink of cold coffee, made a face at the taste, and continued the story. "When Millie Clapham didn't return home, her husband got worried. He telephoned the church, then the choirmaster. The choirmaster, his wife, and Mr Clapham headed out to look for Mrs C. They retraced her steps from church to home, which wasn't tough, because like I said it was only a short ways. They spent some time around the church grounds and inside, looking. Then they went to see Mrs Shirley Tilbury, the missing woman's best friend, and also a choir member." He spelled Tilbury for me. "The husband figured maybe Mrs C had stopped at Shirley's for coffee. But she hadn't seen her friend since Mrs Clapham left the church.

"The police were called. They hunted everywhere. Church grounds, streets. Nothing. There seemed three options." Delancey held up a finger at each. "One: Mrs Clapham had taken off on her own. Went away with another man. The husband claims there was no hint of such a thing. And the fact that everyone says she was her usual self that night, seemed to put the kibosh on that idea. A woman running off would have been nervous, you'd think. Besides, why go to choir practice? Why not just take off, to give yourself an hour's head start? And finally, all her things were still at home. No missing clothes, jewelry, nothing.

"Two: that Mrs Clapham had been assaulted on her way home. This didn't gibe either, because in a case like that, the victim is generally left for dead where the assault took place. There was no sign of her on the street or in the nearby yards.

"Finally, there was the possibility that Mrs Clapham had been killed by someone she knew. Either someone met her on the street and she went with them to their home... or Mr Clapham himself murdered her."

"I knew it!" Eddie cried. "It's always the husband."

"It's *not* always the husband," Delancey snapped, and Eddie looked a little hurt. "But in this case, it's what the police suspected. It seemed the most logical: Mrs Clapham comes home, her husband murders her, hides the body, then pretends to be all upset that his wife hasn't arrived. A husband wouldn't panic if his wife were a little late coming home. He'd wait. Maybe half an hour or so— which is what Clapham did. That gave him plenty of time to kill her and hide the body."

"How far is it from his house to where Mrs Clapham was found?" I asked.

Delancey grinned. "Now you're thinking like a detective, Iggy." I ignored Eddie's envious glare. "It's only about ten minutes, less if you're running, more if you're moving a body. Clapham would've had just enough time to do it. Of course, at the time we're talking about, no body had been found.

"There were other suspects besides Mr Clapham. There were a few who didn't like Mrs C so much. Said she was a little full of herself because she was well off, and the best singer in the choir, but that hardly seems motive for murder."

"Hang on," Eddie said. "Didn't the cops search everywhere when this happened? Did they grill Miss—what's her name—Hogwood? And her staff?"

"Sure. But they weren't about to go searching every house in the area. Especially since Miss Hogwood and her servants swore up and down nobody knew the missing woman. It's very possible, the police think now, that the body was put in her study after the initial search. Makes sense. Except that rules out Mr C as a suspect because the police certainly did search the Clapham house— thoroughly. So either Clapham did it and parked his wife's body in Hogwood's study right off, or he didn't do it, and the body was elsewhere for a time."

There was a long pause after that. Delancey leaned back in his chair and looked at us both. Eddie contemplated his dirty fingernails. I looked down, then at Delancey.

"So," I said finally, "what you're saying is that the body in Miss Hogwood's study was Mrs Clapham."

"Right. The police files had a detailed list of what she was wearing the night she disappeared. The body was mummified because the room was sealed up tight, and had been for a few years. It still sort of bore a resemblance to the missing Mrs Clapham."

"And she was murdered."

Delancey's face darkened. "Like I said, hit over the head, hard. That put the husband back in the picture, for the killing."

I knew that Clapham Jewelers was still open for business, and that Mr Clapham ran the place. I didn't know much more about it. A jewelry store isn't exactly top on the list of an eleven-year-old boy, even if his father owns one.

"Did they bring him in for questioning?" Eddie wanted to know.

"I suppose so. Look, boys, Beulah talked me into sticking my neck out for you. I was okay with that—to an extent. But the cops couldn't solve the case in '21, and that means no one will. Despite what you read in your detective stories, they're pretty good at catching bad guys. So I'm telling you, let it go. Write your report. Put in whatever you want from what I just told you—most of it was in the newspapers anyway. Let me know what grade you get on it."

We were being dismissed. Eddie started to protest, but the look on Delancey's face told us that he wanted no more argument. So we thanked him and left.

Out on the street again. We went over to an alley and sat on the ground. For a bit, we just looked out at the street, at the Christmas decorations in shop windows and hanging from the lampposts. Eddie picked at an old wad of chewing gum that was now one with the pavement. It was getting dark.

"What do we do now?" I finally asked, glancing dejectedly at my notes.

"I dunno. I don't wanna let this go."

"Me neither," I agreed. "I just don't know what we can do next. Maybe go to the cops?"

Eddie looked horrified. "The *cops!*" he cried. Now, Eddie's never been in trouble with the Law in his life. Once, Mr Peck, the grocer, thought Eddie was snitching apples, but Eddie's not much for apples, so why would he do it? Turns out, what Mr Peck thought was an apple in Eddie's jacket pocket was an old baseball with hardly any cover on it. So he had nothing to fear from the police, but always seemed wary of them.

I tried another idea. "What would Sherlock Holmes do?"

"I think… I *think* he'd go to the scene of the crime."

"We don't know where that is," I reminded my partner.

"Maybe not where she was killed, but we know where she wound up."

We got up, dusted off our pants, and headed for the home of Miss Agnes Hogwood.

Three

Well, we put off going that night. By the time we'd left Delancey's, it was getting pretty late, so we decided to go first thing Saturday.

North Fifth Street is in an old section of town. Lots of very big houses and very big yards supported by very big incomes.

At least that's how it was originally, back about fifty years ago. Nowadays, they're mostly occupied by families of regular means; folks about the same as my own family, only not Jewish. Not most of them, anyhow.

Eddie and I headed over to 1711, where the article said the body had been found. It was a huge house, really—bigger than most in the area—big, fenced-in yard, lots of old trees, maples. The house was three stories, and sprawled like a cat on a sunny porch. The yard and house were nothing fancy, but pretty well taken care of.

A big black iron gate barred our way, five feet high. Eddie shoved at it. "It ain't locked," he said, "but it'll take some doing."

He shoved again, harder. This time, not only did it swing open, it took Eddie along for the ride. He hung on as the gate swung free, around, and then *splanged* against the stone wall on the inside. It vibrated a good twenty seconds. Eddie was pretty shook up. I busted out laughing.

"You shoulda seen your face!" I said. "Like the first time on a merry-go-round!" More laughter.

Eddie glared at me, and I thought he'd give me an arm punch, but instead he just growled, "Come on," and after I shut the gate, we walked to the front door.

There was a fancy knocker—a lion's head. Eddie stepped ahead of me and rapped the knocker a few times. We waited.

"Probably some old geezer of a butler," Eddie said," has to hobble over to—
"

The door was opened, not by a geezer butler, but by a short, dumpy woman around fifty. Her gray hair was all tangled, her eyes watery.

"I don't buy magazines," she growled in a gravelly voice.

"We ain't selling," Eddie countered. "We come about the dead body."

The woman hadn't budged from the doorway. She looked like she could keep even Eddie from pushing past. Her eyes narrowed. It would be only a matter of time before she slammed the door in our faces. Instead, she stepped aside.

"Come in," she said.

We entered the dark front hall. Our eyes adjusted as she led the way to a small front room which was warm and friendly. No sign of anything sinister. Still, I started to wonder if this was a good idea. Maybe she was the type to lure unsuspecting visitors in, stab or poison them, then bury them in the cellar.

"Sit," she demanded, and we did, together, on a sofa. She took her chair where a book lay open, face down, stuck a strip of newspaper where she'd left off and shut the book. "I am Miss Agnes Hogwood." She grimaced at her own name. "Who are you?"

Eddie didn't answer, so I did the honors. "I'm Iggy Silver. He's Eddie McDonald."

"I see. And you've come about the corpse found in my study?"

She said it so calmly, it was like we were discussing a price to shovel her sidewalk. Eddie stayed quiet. I don't think he was scared; more like he was in another world, so I kept on:

"Yeah. See, we're in Miss Postlethwaite's fifth grade class at Lewis and Clark Elementary, and we were assigned to do a report on a newspaper article. We found the one about finding a body in your study—"

"That was four years ago."

"Three."

"Don't argue!"

"Sorry, ma'am. See, Miss P's assignment had to do with old newspapers."

"I see. Very interesting assignment."

"And we found the story about the body in your study, and found out that it was the body of a lady named Mrs Clapham, who was missing for a couple years, and she was murdered."

I can run off at the mouth, sometimes.

"I see. And now you want to see where the body was, eh?" Miss Hogwood eyed us narrowly. Suddenly, she broke into a grin. "Why not? Come along."

She rose with a grunt and led the way down a dark hall. Miss Hogwood walked with a sort of side to side rocking motion, and I found myself swaying back and forth in time, not intending to make fun, just a habit I have of imitating when I shouldn't. It's gotten me in trouble more than once. Miss Hogwood wasn't paying any attention to me, though.

"What do you do here?" Eddie finally managed to say.

Miss Hogwood stopped and eyed him suspiciously. "What do you mean?"

"Well, do you sit an 'read or something? Or paint or some such?"

"Now why would I paint? I can't even draw a *bath*." She laughed, though neither Eddie nor I knew what was so funny.

Anyhow, she didn't answer Eddie's question. We walked through a real long hallway, and it seemed like we were entering a new dimension. The house where we first came in was clean and warm and quiet. As we walked, the air got colder, and more dust and cobwebs started to show. Just as quiet, though. The place got darker, too; drapes were pulled shut and no lamps were lit. Miss Hogwood stopped at a big oak door and took out a key that looked like a movie prop, it was so big. She unlocked the door and stepped aside so Eddie and I could go inside.

For a second, I thought she was going to lock us in, because she just stayed in the doorway. Finally, she entered.

"This was my father's study," she said, and her voice echoed against the wood bookcases.

The room was pretty nice. Lots of dark wood everywhere; a massive desk at the far corner; bookshelves with musty, dusty books. Across the room, a glass door led to her backyard. Above the huge fireplace was a portrait of a couple, he was standing, she sitting.

"My parents," said our host, without emotion. Miss Hogwood led the way to the corner desk. "This was where the body was found." She chuckled. "Scared the bejesus out of Gladys, my maid."

"Was she just lying on the floor?" I asked.

"Yup."

I went to the outside door. "Must have been brought in through the backyard."

"Of course!" she said, sort of insulted at how obvious it was. "The yard is rimmed by those hedges, but the front sidewalk runs along both sides of the house to the back. And there's also a—" Eddie had pointed at something and stuck his finger on the window glass. She slapped his hand. "Don't go getting fingerprints all over my windows!"

"Sorry," Eddie muttered.

"Well, no harm done. I suppose. What was I saying? Oh, yes. There's a gate off to the side there, though you can't really see it from here. That gate goes out into the street."

"Is it locked?" I asked.

"It is now. Wasn't when the body was dumped here. This is a quiet neighborhood. There's nothing for folks to steal in my yard, unless they want to help themselves to dandelions."

"So did the police figure the body was brought in through that gate?"

"Probably."

"Lots of folks knew about the gate?"

"Yes. I had... well, a little garden party that summer."

"You!" Eddie cried before he could help himself. I thought he would sink into the floor. He actually looked scared. But Miss Hogwood sighed.

"Yes, me. A bright idea from my magazine publisher."

"You have a magazine publisher?" I asked.

"I do. I'm one of their top writers," she said with pride. "But let's talk about it somewhere warmer, eh? If you're done nosing around the room, that is."

We left the study and returned to the front room. Along the way, Miss Hogwood took a magazine from a table in the hallway, like she planned to read to us. When we were settled, and Eddie and I were wishing she'd bring out some cookies or something, she sat forward and handed us the magazine.

It was an issue of *Strange and Amazing*, a magazine with some great cover art and lots of stories about flesh-eating aliens and intergalactic pirates. Not that I'd ever read such things, you understand. Anyhow, as Eddie held the magazine and we both looked at the cover, she tapped on one of the blurbs:

In this issue! Blood Sacrifice! by Marco Dare

We looked up at her. Miss Hogwood had poured herself whiskey or brandy from a handy decanter and took a sip.

"I," she said, "am Marco Dare."

Eddie and I held it in long as we could. We looked at each other and busted out laughing. Like I said, I don't read those stories, but even I had heard of Marco Dare, author of such timeless tales as *The Alien with Two Heads!* and *Traffic Jam in Outer Space!* Not that I ever read those stories.

Miss Hogwood got angry. She stood up suddenly and tromped out of the room.

"You think we shouldn't've laughed?" Eddie asked quietly.

"Couldn't be helped," I said.

Our angry hostess was back soon. She had a stack of typewritten pages and handed them to us. They were the original copies of *Martian Thrill-Seekers!* and *War Between the Planets!*—two more Dare stories I'd only heard about. There was only one answer: she really did write those stories. She was Marco Dare! Eddie reached the same conclusion and handed back the pages slowly. I think he hoped to keep them.

"So you are Marco Dare," I said.

"Right." She poured more whiskey or brandy and took a sip.

"Gosh," Eddie said, star-struck. "What're you working on now?"

Miss Hogwood looked sad. "I've got a title: *Death-Stalker Sails the Stars!*"

"Sounds great!" Eddie said.

"Sometimes," she sighed, "the title brings out the whole story. But sometimes not. I've even got a picture of the Death-Stalker in my head. Can't decide if he's a hero who blasts enemy aliens to atoms or a villain who consumes whole planets with a Death Ray."

"Both good ideas," Eddie had to admit.

When Miss Hogwood took another sip of her drink, she saw me eying the glass. Prohibition made liquor illegal, though plenty of folks still had it.

"I suppose you're wondering how I get this stuff when the law says you can't. My publisher has contacts. It's the only thing I like about him, really."

"What got you started writing?" I asked.

She warmed to the question and sat back. "Oh, I was always making up stories as a child. Quite a fertile imagination. I even had my own little world—Agnes Land, I called it. Don't laugh!" she snapped, though neither of us did. "I made up all sorts of adventures. When I got older, I decided to write for a living. Easier said than done, boys, I can tell you. I had visions of writing a great novel, one people would talk about for ages after I was gone."

"Did you?"

"Nah. I started—I don't know how many times—laid out my plot on little card; wrote detailed accounts of my characters 'lives, as background. I never got beyond a few dozen pages. I finally decided to write whatever would bring in money. Thus, my stories for those magazines. Dreadful stuff, I thought at first. But it kind of grows on you."

"Did you ever get married?"

27

For a moment, her eyes got dreamy. Then she snapped to attention. "No. And don't ask again."

"Then," I followed up logically, "why do you have such a big house?"

"It was inherited. My folks always had plans for a large family, and my old man was big in the banking field, so they could afford it. But the only child to pop out was me. It was great for Agnes Land, because I had the run of the house. My mother was… well, that's neither here nor there. I wanted to sell the place, but my publisher thought it would be a great idea if I kept it, held seances, and had people interview me in mysterious surroundings… all that sort of crap. I don't know why I listen to him; the man couldn't find his backside with a flashlight. He did talk me into having a party on the back lawn one summer. Dreadful business. It was supposed to be for newspapers and such, to drum up publicity. People standing around, exchanging bon mots."

"Is that like jam on toast?" Eddie asked.

"Might as well have been. The only people who came were neighbors, for the free food. What the numbskull who is my publisher didn't realize is, truly witty people only give out bon mots if you pay them. Oh, I also had my publisher and his wife over for dinner once. But she laughed like a banshee's wail and he got drunk and morose. So I'm here in this big house, where everyone and his cousin think they can just deposit the odd corpse." Having had her say, she sat back, exhausted.

"But tell me more about your assignment," she said after a while.

Eddie was more talkative now, and he described what we were supposed to do. But Eddie can ramble sometimes, and I could see Miss Hogwood get impatient, so I cut in and finished the story.

"So," she said," now that you know as much as you do, what's your plan?"

Eddie and I looked at each other, then shrugged.

"Come, come," she said impatiently. "You have to have some sort of plan!"

"We weren't sure," I said, "if we'd investigate it any farther."

This was a lie. Eddie and I wanted like anything to be detectives—like Delancey, only successful and famous. Sherlock Holmes without the violin. But we hadn't a clue how to go about it.

Miss Hogwood sat back and drummed her fingers on the arm of her chair. Didn't even take a swig of whiskey, she was thinking so hard. Finally, she sat up straight – so suddenly, Eddie and I gave a little jump.

"I'll help you," she said.

"But what about the Death-Stalker?" Eddie asked.

She looked blank, then remembered her story and waved it off. "I'll get around to it. This is more interesting. Now then. Here's what I think we should do…"

Four

After a quick lunch at my house, Eddie and I headed back to Miss Hogwood's in the afternoon. My folks looked at me funny as I headed out, because it was the Sabbath, after all, but it wasn't as though they went to synagogue. They took God at His word, that the Sabbath should be a day of rest, and mainly sat around, reading the newspaper or some such.

Miss Hogwood greeted us dressed in tartan tweed, a nod, she said, to her mother's Scottish roots. All that passed over our heads; we just wanted to get on with it. We stayed in the hallway as she prepared to go out. She had a scarlet cape that she tried four times to swing over her shoulders. Refused Eddie's offer to help. The cape wound up on the floor, draped over her head, everywhere but where it belonged. "Damn short arms," she muttered.

Finally the cape was on. Her plan was to visit the neighborhood where Mrs Clapham was last seen. We'd try to talk to people connected with the case. And we'd start at the church. Before we set out, though, she had something to say.

"I want," she said as she put on her tam, "you to call me Marco Dare."

"Marco Dare!" I said. "People will think we're crackers. A lady called Marco?"

"Very well. Make it Marion Dare, then. *Miss Dare* to you."

"But why?" Eddie wanted to know.

I kind of suspected why: Hogwood is a terrible name. I'd have changed it, too. But she actually had another reason.

"Because my name was in the papers at the time. I don't want the people we speak with to make the connection."

"What if they remember you from that party you had?" I asked. "You said neighbors came around."

She surveyed herself in the hall mirror, made a face, and took off the tam.

"To tell the truth, I spent most of that day in my front room, reading a book. Can't stand parties."

Eddie was really thinking this over. We watched him frown and strain, and finally, he said:

"But maybe it's better if they *do* know who you are. You want to know why someone dumped a body in your study."

"It was three years ago," she reminded him. "If I suddenly say I'm investigating, without telling them about you, they'll think I have the reaction time of a glacier."

We sighed. Miss Marion Dare, it was.

We headed for the church. The weather had turned real Christmassy, with cold and a touch of snow. All around, houses had lights on. It was only a little past noon, but the sky was so overcast, rooms were too dark without some artificial light. On our way, nobody spoke. To tell the truth, Eddie had been pretty quiet through this whole thing. I could see it when we were around Beulah, 'cause Eddie was smitten with her, and everyone knows a guy what's smitten acts pretty stupid... and with Eddie that isn't much of an act. Now, he was real quiet and I didn't know why.

Anyhow, we got to the church and were surprised to see lights on there, too. No services on a Saturday, after all. 'Miss Dare' kept heading forward, so we followed. Our aim had just been to look inside, get an idea of where things were, but she didn't seem to mind if folks were around. She marched right up to the heavy oak front doors and with a hard yank, opened one.

Eddie and I followed her inside.

It wasn't much warmer, but the place sure was cheery- looking. A few lights here and there looked sickly yellow, but the big Christmas tree in front glowed with those new-fangled electric bulbs. Clearly, then, a liberal-minded congregation.

The reason lights were on was that the church was getting ready for Christmas. A group of women were busy polishing pews, and a couple of men were hanging green swags from the stained glass windows. And in front, a man in clerical collar was talking to another man in a suit. Miss Dare made for them. We followed, and the men looked up as we got close.

"May I help you?" clerical collar man asked.

"You're the minister. What's your name?" Miss Dare asked.

"I am Reverend James Willoughby."

"Been working here long?"

He was patient, I'll give him that. "Seventeen years."

31

"Fine." She turned to the other man. "And you? What's your excuse for being here?"

It was pretty clear the other guy wasn't as patient as the minister. He turned red and started to blurt out something that would've made the cross tumble from the wall, but Reverend Willoughby cut in front.

"This is our esteemed choirmaster. Henry Blank."

"Good," said our leader. "Just the fellows we want to see. This is Eddie, that's Iggy, and I'm Miss Dare. And before you say something we'll both regret, no, they're not mine. Just friends. But we want to talk to you."

"I don't mean to be rude," said Mr Blank in a tone that said he sure did want to be rude, "but we are very busy with Christmas preparations, as you can see."

"Yeah, well, Jesus comes no matter how bad the choir sounds."

Blank blustered; I thought I caught a smirk from the reverend. Anyhow, Miss Dare played the trump card right off.

"Actually," she said, "I go by another name besides Dare. Hogwood. Maybe you remember it?"

There was a pause. Both men looked puzzled. Then lights dawned, first in the choirmaster, then the minister.

"Your home was where they found the unfortunate Mrs Clapham," the minister said.

"Got it in one," Miss Dare replied.

"What is it you want with us, then?" Blank asked. He wasn't as cocky now.

"The police may have given up on who murdered Mrs Clapham, but not me. I want to know who plonked her body in my study."

"It's been some time since they found the body," Blank went on. "Why are you going on about it now?"

Here it was. Would Miss Dare really tell them this was about a school assignment? I was ready to run, but Miss Dare was cool as you please. She'd obviously thought this through.

"These two lads have come to me," she said, "saying that they saw something the night Mrs Clapham disappeared."

Now, if you do the math, Eddie and I were barely alert in 1919, when Mrs C left church for the last time. Eddie looks older than he is, maybe by a couple of years. I, however, have always looked like a little kid. Whether the minister and choirmaster calculated ages and got it wrong, or whether they just took Miss

Dare's word for it, I can't say. The fact is, neither batted an eye. Instead, Blank said:

"What did they see?"

"Never you mind. The fact is, for years neither knew exactly what to make of what they'd seen. Now, they're older, and they want answers."

"Perhaps," said the reverend, "they should go to the police." All this, like we weren't in the room.

"The police," Miss Dare sniffed, "won't give them the time of day. They figure the lads are just up to some youthful hijinks. I disagree. I think they did indeed see something and, as this involves me and my domicile, I intend to pursue the matter."

There was a pause. Finally, the minister spoke.

"Very well. But can't this wait? It's been years, after all. And Christmas… the church… we have so very much to do." He waved a hand around at the church, like it was falling apart.

"I'll only take up a little of your time. And I can speak to you singly," Miss Dare added. "Perhaps you first, Mr Blank?"

The two looked at each other, then the reverend shrugged. He put a hand on Blank's elbow to tell him to stay, and went off to supervise something. Blank sat down in a pew. Now, church pews aren't the easiest to speak to someone in. I mean, either you're in the same line, or someone has to lean over the back of the pew to face the other. Miss Dare kind of slid sideways and propped an arm on the pew back. We sat next to her.

"What do want me to tell you?" Blank asked. "That night is etched in my memory, because of the tragedy, and how many times I spoke to the police about it. We had a choir practice like any other. Reformation Sunday was approaching, and I had a nice rendition of *Onward Christian Soldiers* planned for the choir. We always make a big deal about that day," he said with pride.

"Right. Go on," Miss Dare prompted.

"Well, we broke up after practice. The choir stood in the front hall as they often do, talking, then slowly moved outside, still talking. My wife and I remained in the church, tidying. It's amazing, the mess a few dozen Christians can produce in an hour. One of the ladies came back for her purse; otherwise, we were alone."

"So you didn't see Mrs Clapham leave for home?"

"No. She was gone by the time I got out of church. In fact, everyone had gone by then. It generally takes me fifteen minutes or so to clean, and most of the choir don't stay around that long."

"What was Mrs Clapham like?"

"Oh... I actually didn't know her very well. A talented soprano. I knew both her and her husband, but not closely. We weren't what I would call friends."

"And you helped in the search that night?"

"Of course. Mr Clapham came to me, and we went to the church door, retraced the poor woman's steps. Then we went to see her best friend, Mrs Tilbury—"

"Is she a church member?"

"Yes. Not a choir member, though she was at one time," he added with a smile.

Just then, one of the cleaning women came over. She was built like a German tank and had spit in her eye.

"What the devil is this, Henry?"

"Gilda! These people are just here to talk about the Clapham case."

"*Gott in Himmel!* That old thing? Why are you bothering with it for? The police have talked until they are blue and still do not know who did it. Why are you bothering?"

Blank looked embarrassed. "This is my aunt. Gilda Blank."

Miss Dare ignored this revelation and said, "We have reason to believe someone connected with this church is involved with Mrs Clapham's disappearance and murder."

Now, we hadn't talked about anything of the sort. Eddie and I were just as stunned as Blank and Gilda were. So I don't know what she was thinking by saying such a thing, but it sure got a reaction, after they had gotten over their shock.

"What the devil are talking about?" Miss Blank demanded. "Do you accuse us of doing something to that woman?"

"The idea!" was all Mr Blank could get in.

Miss Dare held up a hand. "I didn't accuse you personally. I'm simply saying that the killer was most obviously from the church."

"What about her husband?" Gilda Blank demanded.

"He is also a member of this church, I believe," Miss Dare said calmly. "And we will speak with him. But the choir members were the last to see the poor woman alive, and that is highly indicative."

Miss Dare started to her feet, had some trouble, sliding on the polished wooden pew, and Eddie grabbed her arm to help. She was about to tell him to lay off, but realized she needed the assistance, and let him.

"I thank you for your time. I see," she said to us, "the reverend is free. Come, boys." We followed along. I have to admit, Miss Dare knew her way around an investigation.

She was no Delancey, but she was pretty good.

The reverend had heard Gilda Blank's cry of outrage and looked uncomfortable. He's one of those clergy who don't want any waves. I had a rabbi like that. My father didn't like him.

"I heard a bit of trouble with Gilda," he said with a quiet smile. "She can be... demonstrative."

"I'm not afraid of Teutonic ire," Miss Dare said firmly. "Now if I could just have a few minutes, Reverend?"

He sat on the steps up to the transept; we took seats in the front pew, about ten feet away, which wasn't the easiest for talking, but we could see each other pretty well. The reverend waited for Miss Dare to begin.

"What can you tell us about Mrs Clapham?" she finally asked.

He sighed. "She was a good woman. Quiet, except when singing. She could belt out *Amazing Grace* pretty well. Was very popular to sing solo at weddings and funerals."

"And her husband?"

"Mr Clapham has served as church treasurer and been an usher. Very dedicated to the church. Also rather quiet."

"Was Mrs Clapham attractive?"

The question embarrassed him. He seemed to not want to answer, thought better of it, then smiled again.

"I believe most men would say she was attractive, yes. But not in the movie starlet sort of way."

"Not given to flashy things, then."

"Not at all. You'd think that the wife of a jeweler would wear lots of it, but really, she was very understated. A necklace or bracelet, perhaps. Certainly nothing you would notice."

"I'm surprised you did notice, then."

He looked embarrassed again. "I have found that you can tell a lot by how a person dresses—if they're full of themselves or not; if they are putting on airs; if they are coming to church to worship God or to draw attention to themselves. And I would say that, except for her singing, Mrs Clapham was very averse to calling attention to herself. She sang because she was good at it and believed it was her way to praise God. Not because it got her noticed."

"And that night? You weren't at choir practice?"

Another smile. "I'm afraid my singing is shaky at best. I like to sing praises to God, but I don't think He's particularly fond of my efforts. So I sing when I'm presiding, but would never do so in a choir. In fact," he said confidentially, "I often just mouth the words during hymns. No sense annoying the congregation."

Miss Dare got up with Eddie's help again, and shook the minister's hand. We walked out.

"Where to now?" Eddie asked.

"Now, I think we should go to my house again, to reconnoiter. See where we're at in our investigation."

"I think," Eddie said, "we should visit Mrs Tilbury first – Mrs Clapham's best friend. She lives just down the block. I looked it up in the city directory," he added with pride at his ingenuity.

Miss Dare pondered this for a moment, then agreed. With her leading the way under Eddie's direction, we headed for Mrs Tilbury's house.

The door was answered by a short, muscular guy of about fifty. He wore an undershirt and faded green work pants with suspenders. No slippers; socks that were so loose his feet looked about fifteen inches long with floppy ends. His hair, thick and dark with streaks of gray, was a jumble of snags. He had a newspaper under his arm, turned to the funny pages. I caught *Gasoline Alley* facing us.

"Yeah?"

Miss Dare didn't bat an eye at the gruff tone. "Is Mrs Tilbury at home?"

Without another word to us, he tipped his head to one side and called, "Shirley!" Then he left us on the doorstep and headed for another room. I thought I heard him say something like, "Damned church people, here to collect."

There was a pause, and pretty soon Shirley Tilbury came to the door, purse in hand.

You couldn't find two different-looking people. She wore a house dress, very neat, and a pretty necklace with a heart locket. Her hair was done up nicely, too. She smiled, and started to open her handbag, but Miss Dare held up a hand.

"I think your husband has the wrong idea. We're not here on charity. We're here about the murder of Mrs Clapham. Your best friend, I believe?"

Mrs Tilbury's face sure did go gray. I thought she'd faint. But no, all she did was shut her purse and invite us in. She motioned for us to sit in chairs around the kitchen table. Miss Dare turned down the offer of coffee. Eddie and I weren't asked, though Eddie sometimes drinks coffee so strong you could tap dance on it. Miss Dare made introductions. She used her real name, Hogwood, so it would ring a bell with Mrs Tilbury. It didn't. Miss Dare explained.

"So," Shirley Tilbury asked, "what do want, then? Why have you come?"

"I won't fib to you," Miss Dare said. "The whole thing started because these two boys had an assignment to read old newspaper articles, and they came across one about finding your best friend's body in my study. To their credit, they've decided to pursue it, and I've agreed to help."

Mrs Tilbury was no dumb bunny, but she did have to concentrate to follow our companion's explanation. Even my head spun, and I already knew what she was saying. So after a moment to think, Mrs Tilbury managed a weak smile.

"I have to admit, Millie's disappearance bothered me no end. Then when they found her... and in a total stranger's house! No offense, I'm sure." Seeing Miss Dare nod, she went on. "So whatever you'd like to ask, please do."

"Who is it?" came a call from the next room. It was our doorman, Mr Tilbury. "Folks collecting?"

"No, dear," Shirley called back. "Just someone... from church." She paused, waiting for follow-up questions. When none came, she spoke to us again, quieter this time. "I'm sorry. My husband works hard all week and likes to spend his weekends quietly; read his newspaper, put his feet up. He does go to church, but it isn't something he cherishes."

"Speaking of church," Eddie surprisingly cut in, "we been there just before this. Your minister's not bad but that choir guy is a sliver in the thumb."

Shirley Tilbury paused, then laughed. "Very well put, young man! Mr Blank is all right, I assure you. But he's very proper. You interrupted his Christmas preparations, I'm sure. Oh, don't worry about it," she added quickly, as if any of us looked sorry. "He just gets in a tizzy about these things. Christmas and Easter are the big choir days, after all."

"I'm surprised he doesn't have the choir there, rehearsing," Miss Dare said.

"He thought about it, I believe. But Henry—Mr Blank—doesn't like to overdo. Too much rehearsal can sometimes be detrimental. Come Christmas Eve, though...!" She shuddered.

"So you're not in the choir?" I put in.

"No. I do love to sing, and I was a member for a time. Then, after what happened to Millie…" She got wistful. "She had a *beautiful* voice. Just wonderful."

"Let's get down to brass tacks," Eddie said. "Anyone want your friend dead?"

It was like he'd clocked her between the eyes. Mrs Tilbury sat back, drained of life. I started to apologize, but she waved it off.

"I shouldn't be stunned by the question," she said. "It's been something I've asked myself since Millie first vanished, and again when they found her. And of course the *police* asked the same thing." I could tell she wasn't pleased by the police, and said so. She smiled weakly again.

"Oh, I suppose they do their job well enough. But to be honest, how hard would it be to find out who did this? I don't believe it was some tramp who killed her, and neither do they. No tramp would bother to move the body. Clearly it was someone who knew her. So how hard can it be to find out who did it?"

"What about Mr Clapham?" Miss Dare asked.

She hesitated. "James Clapham is a fine man. He is… not overly friendly, but I wouldn't call him a bad man. Just quiet. And of course, once his wife disappeared, he kept even more to himself."

"Still goes to church?"

"Oh, yes. But when he was offered condolences by the congregation—after Millie was found—he simply thanked us, without any trace of emotion."

"Think he killed her?" Eddie piped up.

"No, I do not," Mrs Tilbury said, real cold. "Maybe the Claphams weren't lovey-dovey in public, but I never heard Millie say a word against James. That's why, when Millie disappeared, and many thought he had done her in, I spoke against it. I could never believe he would harm a hair on her head."

"Then who did?" I asked.

"I've no idea." Still cold. "That's a job for the police. And they don't seem to be doing much about it." She turned to Miss Dare, and thawed a bit. "If you can find out who killed my dear friend, I'd be very grateful."

Miss Dare stood and we followed suit. "We'll do everything we can," our leader said.

We stood on the sidewalk outside for a bit. Eddie prompted Miss Dare, asked if we were going to Clapham's next. For a bit, it seemed like she was going to say no. Then, she sighed and said, "Okay" and off we went.

Clapham's Jewelers is competition for my parents 'place, but that's okay. Lots of folks buy watches or jewelry or such, so there's plenty of business to go around, my dad always says. I don't know if Mr Clapham felt the same way, so I was a little trepidatious about going to see him. Hopefully, he wouldn't recognize the name. He did.

Clapham doesn't live above his shop, like most small shopkeepers do. Instead, he's got a fancy place, not far away. Miss Dare knocked. It took a long time, and two more knocks before the door was opened.

James Clapham was around fifty, balding. He had thick round glasses and stubby little fingers. How he could work with fine jewelry was a mystery. He wore baggy pants, a white shirt opened at the collar, and a vest, unbuttoned. He didn't look happy to see anyone at his door.

"I was taking a nap," he said, curt but quiet. "What do you want?"

"I am Miss Hogwood. These are Eddie McDonald and Iggy Silver. We are—
"

The little man was quick, I'll give him that. He recognized the Hogwood and the Silver names.

"I have nothing to say to any of you," he said, and started to close the door. Eddie, quick, stuck a foot in the way.

"Hang on," he said. "We just want t 'find out who bumped off your missus. Anything wrong with that?"

"The police haven't found anything yet. What makes you think you can?"

He was pressing against the door, but Eddie's strong, like I said, and Clapham couldn't get it closed.

"Just let us in and we can talk," Eddie said.

Finally, Clapham either got tired of pushing against the door, or decided to hear us out. Either way, he suddenly let go of the door and Eddie flew in and nearly stumbled to the floor. I laughed and Eddie glared my way.

Unlike at Mrs Tilbury's, we weren't invited to sit, though there were plenty of chairs around the living room. Miss Dare sat anyway; the rest of us stayed standing.

"Now that you've barged in," said Clapham, "why are you bothering? I've already told you, the police couldn't find out anything about my wife's death, and it's been three years since she was found. So what hope do you have? A woman and a couple of kids?"

Eddie and I had only known Miss Dare a short time, but we knew enough to tell she wouldn't sit still for the way he talked about 'a woman 'as if she couldn't tie her shoes without a guy to help. Sure enough Miss Dare turned red as a beet, and I thought, *here comes the blow-up* but she kept her cool and managed a smile.

"Of course we are not professionals, like the police. But, as the police failed to find who killed your dear wife, perhaps a few outsiders might."

There was logic in this. It was just a question of if Clapham could see it. He did, at least enough to listen.

"Fine. What do you want to ask?"

Before Miss Dare could start, Eddie near ruined it. "Did you kill her?" he blurted out.

I swear, the room temperature dropped ten degrees. Miss Dare gave Eddie a good scowl. I think my mouth hung open. Clapham, though… he just cleared his throat.

"No. Now if that was what you came for—"

"Then who did?" Eddie demanded, figuring, I guess, he'd already tied the noose, he might as well stick his neck through it.

"What my impetuous friend means," Miss Dare cut in, "is, do you have any suspicions?"

"Yes. Your 'friend 'needs to watch his mouth," Clapham replied. "My wife was a fine woman. A good wife, a good friend, a good churchgoer. I'm sure she rubbed some the wrong way, and *maybe* someone could've taken offense enough to kill her. But as I told the police, I don't know who it would have been."

"Would she have confided in you if someone or something was bothering her?"

"Of course. Especially if it were serious."

There was a long pause. Finally, he sighed and said, "I told all this to the police, and they believe that Millicent was murdered by some stranger. Perhaps a thief who wanted her purse. I don't know! Don't you think I've been going over this in my head until I can't see straight?"

Miss Dare stood. "We're sorry to have troubled you, Mr Clapham. Please rest assured we do not mean to cause you pain. Rather, we want the same thing you do: to find the person responsible."

He seemed to feel better about that, that we weren't just some ghouls who wanted to hear the gory details of his marriage and his wife's death. He actually thanked Miss Dare and nodded to us as we left his house.

Back on the street, we stood around for a bit. "What do we do now?" Eddie asked.

"Are we sunk?" I wanted to know.

"No," Miss Dare said slowly, "I don't think we're sunk. But I do think we need to ponder this a bit. I suspect Mr Clapham—for all his denials—knows *something*. Let's meet up again tomorrow, after I've had a chance to think."

This seemed like a good idea. It was late afternoon, and the short winter day was ending. It was getting cold and damp, too. Eddie and I thanked Miss Dare for her help, and she nodded in reply, then marched off for home.

Five

Eddie and I stood on that street corner for a few more minutes, after Miss Dare left. I could hear the gears turning in Eddie's brain, and I was puzzling over it all myself. Then I had an idea.

"Let's go back to the church," I said.

Eddie frowned. "Why?"

"'Cause it all starts there, doesn't it? That's where Mrs Clapham was last seen. Maybe if we follow her trail from there, we'll find something."

"Iggy, it's been five years! Do you think there's a knife with fingerprints on it, up in the choir loft?"

That stung.

"I didn't mean that. It's just that, when we were there earlier, I never quite looked at the layout. I was busy with the choirmaster and the pastor. I wanna see how things are in that church."

Eddie considered this. He's always up for an adventure, but wasn't sure whether this was the best thing. Especially since he was getting tired and a little hungry.

"Come on," I prompted. "It won't take long."

That, as it turned out, would be a big mistake on my part.

Eddie agreed, but said we should work our way backwards, from the Clapham house to the church. Since we already were outside the Clapham place, I agreed.

Like a couple of bloodhounds, we slowly walked along toward the church. It was a simple walk, really, just down one street, a right-hand turn, then to the church. After a few dozen yards, we got to the cemetery wall, which ran along one street, turned, and along the other until you got to the church entrance. But our initial clue came on that stretch.

"What's this?" Eddie said, when it was clearly a door.

The door was a heavy old oak one, on ancient hinges, and it was set in the stone wall that ran along the church grounds. Eddie tried the door, and it opened.

I expected the hinges to squeak real loud, but they didn't. Barely a sound. The door was used, and regularly.

We peeped inside. It led right into the graveyard. There was a path from the door to the front and side entrances of the church. The path was well-worn, not overgrown at all, so I guessed folks used it, like they did the door.

The cemetery, in the setting sun, was a little creepy, with the trees bare of leaves and a light wind moving the branches like fingers. There hadn't been much snow so far that year, but the ground was hard and frost hung on cold surfaces. What little snow we'd had, rimmed headstones like cobwebs. Eddie had had enough of that scene. We backed out, he shut the door and we continued on.

Nothing remarkable the rest of the way. Low-hanging tree limbs hung over the wall, even with no leaves on them. At the corner, Eddie and I tried to picture Mrs Clapham rounding it, and whether anyone could see her. I ran to the head of the church walk and watched as Eddie pretended to be Mrs Clapham (the sashay was a nice touch) walking home. By now, the darkness was getting deeper, but it was still light and I tried to imagine it being completely night. Could the choir members still have seen her? Was that street lamp on the corner there back then?

Eddie joined me at the front gate. "Well?" he asked.

"I think anyone standing here could've seen Mrs Clapham. Whether they would've seen anyone lurking in the shadows, I dunno."

"Right. My deduction, then, is that Mrs Clapham was attacked after she rounded the bend."

"Fair enough," I agreed.

We entered the churchyard. It was a creepy place from this angle, too. But somehow, knowing Eddie was as nervous as I was, made me braver. We walked past the graves to our right, all tilted and mossy, and reached the church door. No lights on inside the church now.

"How do we get in?" I asked.

"My mom says churches ain't locked. I guess t 'let those who want t 'run from the law, get sanitary."

"Ain't that 'sanctuary'?"

"Ain't *what* sanctuary?"

"Folks runnin 'from the law. They want sanctuary, not sanitary."

Eddie was getting peeved, as he always does when I correct him. When he gets peeved, I let it drop. He tried the door, and sure enough, it opened. A breath

43

of cold air came at us, as if the spirits of the dead had just escaped. Eddie shuddered, and I had to admit that got me too.

We went inside, our footsteps clicking loudly on the stone floor. Eddie looked ready to bolt. I shut the door behind us to prevent that.

Inside, the church wasn't anywhere near as scary. There was the Christmas tree, decked out, though dark. The final rays of sun shone through stained glass, dotting floors and pews with specks of blue and red and green. That sun, which had been hide-and-seeking all day, now was coming out in full force, and the church actually brightened a little as we took a few tentative steps forward. There was a mixed smell of furniture polish and evergreen all over. Made my nose tickle, and I held back a sneeze until it passed.

We went on cautiously, like Moses approaching the burning bush. The more we went though, the less there was to make us nervous. By the time we reached the chancel (Eddie told me that's what it's called – the spot between the railing and the altar area. He'd paid more attention in Sunday school than I thought), we were pretty calm.

"So," I said suddenly. My voice echoed in the empty church, and Eddie and I both jumped a little. I started again, quieter. "So, where does the choir sit?"

"Up there," he said, waving a finger to a loft in the back. "Where the organ is. That way the choir director, Mr Blank, and the organist, over there, can look at each other for when t 'start and stop."

"Got it. How do we get up there?"

Eddie didn't know this church any more than I did, but he led the way to the back. There was a staircase, out of the way unless you were looking for it. We went up.

I'm none too fond of heights, but this was pretty amazing. You could see the whole church, except for directly beneath. Eddie and I poked around the loft for a bit, decided there wasn't anything to learn there, and headed down.

"Satisfied?" Eddie wanted to know. He sounded like a car salesman after a test drive.

"I guess," I said. "No. Wait. Let's look around the rest of the church. Offices and such?"

Eddie sighed. He's actually pretty patient most times, but when he's had enough, he'll let you know. Well, he'd clearly had enough, so I reluctantly agreed to call it a day too.

We were standing a little ways up the center aisle.

I don't think I'll ever forget what happened then, if I live to be fifty. As we stood in that center aisle, buttoning our jackets, ready to leave, there was a sound from up around the chancel. There are two doors up there, one on each side, like those doors on clocks where guys in lederhosen come out with mallets to strike the bell.

Anyhow, the sound came from the right side from where we were facing. It was hard to make out what it was, and I thought maybe it was a church mouse, but no, this sounded human. Eddie grabbed my arm, to get me to run, but I couldn't. My arm hurt like Hades from his grip, but I couldn't get my legs to move. Looking back, I must've figured if it was someone like the minister, come to holler at us, there was still plenty of time to light out.

It wasn't the minister. In fact, it wasn't anyone we could recognize, because whoever it was wore a hooded cloak – black. The cloak covered everything except the hands and just above the ankles. The figure seemed to stagger, and it was moaning like some ghoul from the grave. Eddie's grip tightened even more, but I noticed he wasn't going anywhere either.

Okay, I admit it, I was petrified. Eddie was too, though he didn't like to say so, and I'd never make him. We just couldn't move. It was like something out of a motion picture with a creepy guy coming to seek revenge after he was murdered. Only this was no film.

The whole scene took maybe a minute, but it seemed to stretch for hours. The figure staggered around just a little bit, moaning and groaning. And then it did something that made my arms prickle: it raised a hand and reached out to us! Like it was after the two of us.

Eddie let go of my arm and started to run, but this time I grabbed him. Not that I wanted him to die or anything like that, but because the figure had just stopped where it was. Didn't move an inch after reaching out its hand. The creepiest part, I think, was that with the hood over its head and with the church in only half-light, you couldn't see a face. There had to be one—there were hands and feet, after all—we just couldn't see it from where we were.

Anyhow, for about a quarter of a minute, we three just stood there, not budging. Eddie had stopped when I grabbed his arm, and was watching along with me. What would that creature do next? Eddie told me later he had visions of it swooping down, touching us both, and turning us to stone—or worse, dust. Not sure why dust is worse than stone, but there's no arguing with Eddie about things like that. His logic defies logic.

To our horror, the figure *did* start to move towards us. But it only came a half step. Then, it collapsed in a heap.

"Well, that's that, then," Eddie whispered.

"What?"

"The thing's dead. Let's get out of here."

"No! Eddie, I don't think it's really a ghoul or ghost or something. I think it's a person, and I think it's sick or hurt."

Eddie glared at me something fierce when I said that.

"Are you telling me you want to get *closer?*" he demanded, like I was suggesting we go enlist in the French foreign legion.

"I think we should," I said. I was getting bolder the longer that thing didn't move a muscle.

Eddie still looked at me like I'd gone loco, but he didn't object to taking a step or two closer. He was like a guy on first base, ready to steal second, but not wanting to get caught too far off first. He actually looked kind of funny, with one foot always trailing behind, ready to bolt for the door.

We gradually got closer. The figure on the floor was a mass of black robe, the hood still covering its face. One hand, the one it'd reached toward us, lay above the head, the other was somewhere in the folds of the robe. It was partially on its side, facing us, back tilted away. Perfect position to scramble to its feet if we got too near. But as we got within a few yards, it was clear that thing wasn't budging.

Now we were at the chancel steps—three of them, short and shallow, leading up to the altar area where the figure lay. Eddie actually did a slight bow, like he'd been taught to do in church. At those steps, we paused. Should we get closer? We had to. What if that was just some regular Joe, and he'd had a fit or something? He'd need help. It'd already been a couple minutes since he'd staggered out, and if his life was in danger, time was wasting.

I took the first step up, Eddie went along. A second step, eyes on the figure for any movement—nothing. The final step and we were in the chancel. Now it was just a few feet to the figure. Slowly, we crept forward.

Those last few steps seemed to take forever, but eventually, we made it to the fallen person. Only then did we see the reason the thing had moaned. There was a big knife handle sticking out of its back. The black robe was damp with blood, and some of it had seeped onto the stone floor in front of the altar.

I don't know if it was scarier now, when we knew it wasn't a ghoul but only someone who'd been stabbed, or when we thought it was some otherworldly spirit.

Eddie made it clear he was much better now. He knelt down by the figure and felt the wrist for a pulse. I wasn't sure if he knew what he was doing. I stayed quiet, anyway. After a few moments, Eddie looked up at me and shook his head.

Now to get a look who it was. We certainly didn't want to turn him over onto his back, with that knife sticking out, and besides, every good detective knows you shouldn't disturb a body any more than you need to. Carefully then, Eddie took the edge of the hood with thumb and index finger, and pulled back the hood to reveal the ashen face.

It was Henry Blank, the choirmaster.

Six

"What the devil do we do now?" Eddie wanted to know.

We were just standing there, looking down at the body. Times like this, Eddie depended on me to come up with a plan, but to be honest I had no idea. I suggested we go to Miss Dare for help. Eddie brightened as if that was the greatest idea since Aspirin. I just figure he wanted out of there as soon as possible, and who cared where we went.

We hurried to Miss Dare's. There we encountered Beggars, a sturdy woman of I guess about forty, who had spit in her eye and no nonsense in her heart. Miss Hogwood, she said, was taking a snooze. We said it was urgent; she stood her ground. Eddie brushed past and I followed, no idea where Miss Dare might be napping, and I really had no great urge to go to her bedroom. Fortunately, the housekeeper helped us unwittingly by calling into the living room, "Miss Hogwood!" We headed in that direction.

Miss Dare was lying on the couch and roused herself as we entered, not pleased to see us. "What is it now, boys?"

"There's a dead man in the church," Eddie blurted out. "That Blank guy."

"What?"

She looked to me for coherence. I briefly explained what had happened, and she scowled, but slipped on her shoes as she listened. A call to fetch her coat, and soon we were back in the church, surveying the body. Miss Dare had brought a lantern, because by then it was dark.

We stared at the body for a bit, then Miss Dare turned to me.

"Iggy, I want you to run to my house and tell Beggars to telephone the police. Don't take no for an answer."

Easier said than done. I didn't knock this time, just went in, and Beggars looked around a doorway to see me. Figured I was up to no good, and warned me to leave or she'd call the cops.

"That's just what Miss Hogwood wants you t 'do," I said. "There's a man, been murdered in the church, and she wants you to call the cops. Toot, sweetie," I added to show her how learned I was.

The maid looked at me with daggers in her eyes. I sighed in frustration, and finally she said, "On your head be it."

She telephoned the police—which took a good long time, what with getting the number and such. I told her to ask for Inspector Fenrow, which made her maybe think I was being straight with her telling, especially when she was told on the phone there really was such a guy on the force, but that he was home, as it was his day off. The maid, serious now, told whoever answered that the inspector should be sent to the church, and that there was a chance that a murder had been committed. After a long pause, during which time Beggars listened, screwing up her mouth every which way like she wanted to tell the cop to drop dead, finally she hung up.

"They're sending an officer to the church. He will determine if it's worth sending for the inspector."

That was about as close to accomplishing my mission as I was likely to get. I thanked her and ran back to the church.

Nothing had changed since I'd left. Eddie and Miss Dare were sitting in a front pew, chatting about Christmas. They had found the light switch, so there was a faint glow where they sat. I told them what had happened, and they went back to talking yuletide. I sat down to join them, though I didn't add much to the conversation.

Around ten minutes later, two policemen came in, huffing and puffing. Both were out of shape, but acted like they were Red Grange.

Eddie said, "The body's over here, boys," like they couldn't see the mass lying in front of the altar, especially since the lights were on now. The two just nodded.

"It appears to be murder all right," declared one, pointing to the knife. To us they asked," Have you moved the body?"

"Just to see who it was," Eddie said defensively.

"Oh? And who is it?"

"Gentlemen," Miss Dare cut in. "Maybe you should send for Inspector Fenrow? He should be asking these questions."

The two looked at each other, one nodded, the other nodded, and finally one of them left to telephone headquarters. Meantime, the one who stayed behind stood guard, as if we planned to pick the poor victim's pocket, folded his arms and looked stern.

It took a good twenty minutes for the inspector to show. Miss Dare had lost all interest in the Christmas conversation, and was strolling around the church, hands behind her back, looking here and there like she planned to buy the place. Eddie joined her. The officer wasn't sure this was cricket, that maybe they'd mess up the crime scene, but they didn't go anywhere near the body, so he sat on the chancel steps to wait.

Inspector Fenrow was disheveled and grouchy, frowned when he saw Eddie and me, but ignored us for the time being. He crouched next to the body, lifted the hood to look at the face.

"You say you know who he is?" he asked no one in particular.

"Yes," said Miss Dare. "He is Mr Henry Blank, the church choir director."

"You attend this church, then?" Fenrow stood and dusted his hands as if he'd been handling a mummy.

"No, sir. I am a woman of no discernible church. I believe in God, but do not believe in the patriarchal teachings of the church."

"Fine. Your name is…?"

"Miss Agnes Hogwood."

"And I know who these two are," said the inspector. He had his fists on his hips, eying us like we'd stuck the knife into Blank. "Now perhaps you might explain what the devil the two of you were doing in an empty church?"

What followed, did not go well.

I knew it wouldn't. After a little humming and hawing, and hoping the inspector would lose interest, I resorted to a final, desperate ploy: the truth.

"We're tryin 'to find out who killed Mrs Clapham, who was found in Miss Hogwood's place. An 'we thought the best way was t 'follow the route she took home from choir practice the night she disappeared, only we took it backwards, and naturally we wound up here in the church. We looked around here—not hurting anything—and then *he* came out of the side door there and staggered and moaned like a spook, and then he suddenly fell down an 'Eddie and I checked him out—just to see who it was, you *unnerstand*—and there he was, all dead, an 'it was the choir director."

Doggone if Inspector Fenrow didn't follow that whole explanation! Delancey always said the inspector was sharper than he looked, only I never believed it until then. Now, he rolled his tongue around in his mouth, made a face like he'd eaten a sour apple and wanted to clear out the taste. Then his eyes narrowed, just like Sam Sharpe in the funny papers, before he's ready to put the kibosh on the bad guys. It was pretty effective, I've got to say.

"Now look here, boys. It's all very well for you to go playing cops and robbers in the back alleys. But this is real life. Mrs Clapham was murdered. Clearly this man has been too. You could be in trouble. So why don't you skedaddle and leave the detecting for the real police?"

That sounded like a good idea, but Miss Dare had other ideas. She glared at the inspector and said, "Now you look here, Inspector. I respect the police and the work you do, but it seems to me that these boys have done you a service. They've shown a lot of gumption, coming here in the dead of night—" (that was an exaggeration; it was quarter past five)" and they did everything right, checking to see if the poor man was still alive, and reporting to you. Seems to me, you wouldn't have known about this murder until tomorrow morning, if not for them. And who knows how much tromping around the crime scene others would have done? Instead, these two lads, because of their interest in detective stories, knew exactly what to do. You owe them thanks, not a dressing down."

Inspector Fenrow went back to rolling his tongue around. Miss Dare was only getting her second wind:

"Now, you asked why the boys were here at such a time, and that was a logical question. They answered truthfully, and you know how difficult *that* is for boys their age. Now that you know why they were here, and—assuming *they* are not suspected of running the poor man through—I think it best if you go and attend to your duty, and leave these two alone."

You'd figure Fenrow would have had enough, thrown up his hands in surrender, and gone about his business. Not him.

"Don't you go around telling me my business, Miss. I'll conduct my investigation the way I see fit, without any interference from *amateurs!*" He jabbed a finger in her direction, but was talking to all three of us.

The next person to speak was Eddie. A real bolt from the blue, it was.

"Inspector, sir, we don't mean t 'be tellin 'you your business. But we did what any good citizen should do, an 'called the cops. An 'besides which, don't it make sense that our pokin 'around in the killin 'of Mrs Clapham was why Mr Blank was killed? Maybe Mr Blank knew somethin'. We spoke to him just earlier today, an'—"

Up until that time, Inspector Fenrow seemed willing to listen to Eddie. But we hadn't told him about our earlier visit, and the inspector didn't take kindly to that. His face got kind of red, and he balled his fists like he wanted to belt us one. Finally, he stormed off, calling," Just get out of here!" over his shoulder.

We didn't have to be told twice. Eddie and I beat it out of the church, through the cemetery, and out to the street. Only when we were clear, did we realize Miss Dare wasn't with us.

"Maybe she's reading the riot act to Fenrow," I suggested.

Eddie blanched. "He'll *kill* her!"

"Nah. Maybe rough her up some. So what do we do now?"

Eddie and I sat with our backs to the stone church wall. The sidewalk was cold, but we'd been running so much it was good to sit. And the cement was only a little harder than the church pews.

"I dunno," Eddie said. "Maybe we should just write our report. Heck, we got a lot more information than I *usually* stick in a report. Miss P will be impressed… She'll probably say it was 'cause of you."

I got embarrassed. There was talk that Miss P liked me, that I was teacher's pet. I disagreed, but the more I protested, the more kids said it was true. Eddie didn't razz me much, I think because he saw I could help him on stuff like this, where we shared the grade. If Miss P favored me, which she most certainly *did not*, but if she did, then he stood to benefit.

"We both get the grade, no matter how good or bad it is," I pointed out.

"Right," Eddie grinned. "So should we call it quits an 'just write our report?"

I pondered the whole thing, yanking at a tuft of stubborn dead grass in the sidewalk crack. I was just about to agree, when a pair of feet in sensible shoes clacked up to us and stopped. We looked up to see Miss Dare, still holding her lantern.

"Up, boys! I am completely fed up with that inspector." We scrambled to our feet.

"Did he belt you?" Eddie asked, looking her over for signs of violence.

"He wouldn't dare! But I gave him a piece of my mind, and he gave it right back to me! The insolent chowderhead!"

We giggled.

"Tell us," Eddie prompted.

"Well, I simply repeated that you were showing initiative, and that is something we should encourage in young lads such as yourselves. I asked the inspector if he hadn't shown that same initiative when he was a boy, and he simply said it was none of my beeswax! Can you imagine? He actually used the term, beeswax! The clod."

"So then what happened?" Eddie asked.

"Why, I grew angry! I said that you boys might be in danger, because if the killer of Mrs Clapham also killed that choir person, he or she might not stop there. When I told him that, he grew calm. I thought I'd carried the day with my unassailable logic. Instead, he turned to a police officer and said—and I quote— 'Ames, please escort this woman out of here. If she doesn't leave, put her in handcuffs and drag her out by the ankles'. Imagine! I wasn't going to stand for that, I can tell you. I stormed off, but I believe I made my point."

There was a long pause.

"So what do we do now?" I asked.

"Do?" Miss Dare acted like she'd never really thought about it. "I'm… not entirely sure. I meant what I said, boys. You could be in danger, and I wouldn't want that. I've known you only a short time, but I'm rather fond of the two of you."

That was uncomfortable. Anyhow, Eddie stepped in with one of his out-of-left-field brilliant ideas.

"Let's go talk to Delancey. He'll know what to do."

Seven

We had about a half hour before I was expected home for supper. Delancey didn't live far away; we could be there and back in no time. At Miss Dare's suggestion, we started walking toward Delancey's place as we talked. Now that the sun was down, it was getting blasted cold, and we hurried.

"Who is this Delancey person?" Miss Dare asked.

"Tom Delancey," I said. "Everyone calls him Delancey. He's a private detective. We met him back in... March?" Eddie nodded. "In March. We'd been involved in a murder case and wanted to hire him. Delancey didn't laugh or call us a couple of kids. He took us seriously."

"Sounds like a good man."

"Yeah…"

"But?"

"Well, Delancey can get a little cranky. Not as bad as Inspector Fenrow—we met him back in March, too—but still cranky."

"I can see that. Mr Delancey has to make a living. He might like you, or take you seriously, but at the end of the day, he has to earn money. Sometimes, you might be interfering with that."

"We'd never keep 'im from makin 'money," Eddie said defensively.

"Oh, I know you wouldn't do it on purpose," Miss Dare replied. "But sometimes, we don't know that we're bothering people unless they tell us. They're just being polite."

Eddie blew a raspberry. "Wouldn't call Delancey polite."

"No, but he might call *Beulah* polite," I cut in. Then I regretted it. Eddie gave me a punch to the arm that would go black and blue pretty quick.

"Now who is Beulah?" Miss Dare asked.

"She's Delancey's secretary," I put in, rubbing my arm.

"His *assistant*," Eddie corrected.

"And why would she provoke a sock to the arm?" Miss Dare asked.

"It's nothin'," Eddie said sullenly. He didn't want Miss Dare to know how much he fancied Beulah.

"Is she Delancey's girl?"

Eddie panicked. "No! I mean t 'say, Delancey goes with other dolls, and Beulah—she's a widow, y 'see. Been a widow for a year. That's how she and Delancey met. He investigated the murder of her *husband*." He said the last word like it was poison.

The subject was dropped.

We walked the final hundred yards in silence, then stopped. There was a light on in Delancey's upstairs apartment, so we went through the side door and up the dark stairs, lit only by one feeble yellow bulb at the top and one at the bottom. On the landing, Miss Dare knocked. After a moment the door opened.

Delancey was unshaven, but dressed in open-collar white shirt and clean pants with suspenders. He wore socks but no shoes. His thick dark hair, never neat, was a tangle. He squinted at us, then spoke.

"What in the hell are you two doing here? And who are you?"

Now, Delancey might have guessed we were bringing him a potential client, but he didn't much care. He likes to take off between Christmas and New Year's, and it might not be Christmas just yet, but close enough. He was not thrilled to see us, especially if we were bringing him work.

"I am Miss Agnes Hogwood, otherwise known as Marco Dare. May we come in?"

There was a pause, a faint glimmer. Delancey likes his adventure magazines, though he's more a reader of *Jake Sharpe: Detective*. He does buy others, though, so maybe he knew the name. Whatever the reason, he let us in.

The place was neat. Eddie and I had been to his apartment once before and were amazed at how tidy he kept it. We always figured a bachelor was also a slob, but none of that with Delancey. Anyhow, he told us to sit, then took a chair opposite.

"Now, what's all this about?"

Miss Dare looked around. Besides the neatness, there wasn't much to see. Sparse furnishings, a small Christmas tree on a corner table with about three ornaments on it, and a set of fire-hazard lights lit. There were also around ten Christmas cards on another small table. Otherwise, it would've been hard to tell what time of year it was.

"We've come," Miss Dare began, "because of a murder."

"Is this about the Clapham murder?" Delancey shot us a withering look.

"I suppose you could say *two* murders. Just this afternoon, Mr Blank, the choirmaster for St Dunstan's, was stabbed to death. Inspector *Fenrow*," she said it sourly," is even now at the church, though he may very well be home again with his feet up."

"Jacob Fenrow is a damned fine policeman," Delancey snapped. We should've told Miss Dare that Delancey and Fenrow were childhood buddies, and though they sometimes get on each other's nerves, they're still good friends.

"My apologies," Miss Dare said quickly, holding up palms in surrender. "He was very truculent with me, and I allowed it to cloud my judgement of the man."

"Fine. Now you say two murders. I've already gone over with these two, the death of Mrs Clapham. I don't intend to do anything about it, or anything that might be connected."

"But surely today's murder—"

"Is a matter for the police. Damn it, Miss Hogwood, I've got Christmas stuff to do! I'm not going to investigate a case that's fresh to the police, and I'm not going to investigate a stale case either."

"You assume I've come to hire you."

"Well, why else would you have come here?"

Miss Dare kept her cool. "I was under the impression that, while these two rascals might be annoying at times, deep down you like them as much as they like and respect you."

That made him shift uncomfortably.

"The fact is, Mr Delancey, these two have poked their noses into an old murder case, and now someone closely associated with that case has been fatally stabbed—in their presence, no less. To me, that suggests they themselves might be in danger. What if the dead Mr Blank knew something about the Clapham murder and was killed to silence him? Would that not suggest the killer might come after them as well?"

Delancey had looked surprised when he heard we had witnessed Blank's murder, but now he calmed down again.

"They're amateur detectives. You hire me, the killer *might* come after me, but I don't think Eddie and Iggy have anything to worry about."

"Maybe they don't, but I *am* concerned about them. Perhaps if you investigated, the killer would be less likely to go after them, and focus on you, a man whose very occupation is fraught with danger. Someone who is used to it."

Delancey chewed that over. Miss Dare was good, I'll give her that.

"Still can't do it," he said at last.

"Can't? Or won't?"

"Makes no difference. Look, a killer is not going to go after a couple of kids, no matter how clever he thinks they are. He or she will be content that no one will believe two boys over an adult."

"And if those two boys find some evidence? Something that puts the killer in peril?"

Delancey shrugged. "Then they bring the evidence to the cops. Or me. And we deal with it. Until then…"

"So you won't allow me to hire you?"

"Sorry, Miss. I just don't see the point. The police are sharp. I'd be going over stuff they've already covered, and probably annoying them in the process. I'd prefer to stay on their good side, thank you very much."

We sat in silence for a bit. Then Eddie said," I like your tree."

Delancey grinned. "Thanks. Needs a bit more, but maybe not. I kinda like the way it is." Seeing there was nothing more to say, we headed out.

"I'd better head home," I announced. There's a big clock outside a shop door, not far from Delancey's place, and one look showed I could just make it home in time for supper if I left now.

"If you must," Miss Dare said. "Eddie? You have to be going home too?"

He shrugged. Eddie has a pretty quiet home to go to. His dad had long since cut out, leaving his mom to work as a waitress to support them. She'd be home, because it was late Saturday, but was always too tired to do much about supper. It's a sad thing, and I wasn't about to tell Miss Dare if Eddie didn't.

"Yeah, I guess I'd better," he said.

"Well, boys, if you're not doing anything tomorrow, perhaps we could meet again?"

"You wanna keep going?" Eddie asked, hopeful.

"Of course! Just because the police and your friend, Delancey, don't believe there's danger, doesn't mean I agree. We have to see this through."

"Gonna be tough tomorrow," Eddie said, suddenly remembering. "Church in the morning, and then we have Sunday school Christmas rehearsal in the afternoon."

I suggested Miss Dare and I go it alone, but she said:

"Perhaps an extra day's contemplation will do us good. Come back to my place Monday, fresh. Say, around ten?"

"Not earlier?" I asked.

She made a wrinkly-nosed face. "Too much earlier and you won't want to deal with me… Very well. Perhaps nine thirty."

With that, we headed home. I made it for supper with two minutes to spare.

So Sunday was quiet. I sat home, itching to go to Miss Dare's, but staying in, sure the killer was halfway to Mexico by now.

Next day, Monday 22nd, I caught up with Eddie just past nine and we headed to Miss Dare's place. The housekeeper, Beggars, looked amused to see us, and we soon found out why. Miss Dare was in no mood for early arrivals. We were early by only fifteen minutes, but that was too much. Beggars showed us into the dining room where Miss Dare was mulling over breakfast like a general over a battle plan.

The dining room was enormous, with dark wood everywhere. On the walls were ancient landscape paintings. Over the massive stone fireplace were two crossed swords. There were eighteen chairs around a long narrow table. Miss Dare sat at one end, a half-eaten breakfast of bacon and eggs in front of her, a pot of coffee at the ready.

"You're early," she said flatly.

"Sorry," Eddie said. He was so seldom early to anything, I just knew he was excited about this. He took a chair next to her. "Did you come up with anything?"

That seemed to perk her up, though not in a good way.

"*Anything?* I came up with *everything!* Any possibility you'd care to name, ran through my head last night. Damn this fertile imagination of mine! I should be hard at work at my desk, writing *Death-Stalker Sails the Stars!* and instead I'm running around with you two."

Eddie was hurt. I tried to smooth things over. "I'm sorry, Miss Dare. If you want us to leave—"

She waved me into a chair. "No, no. I do *not* want to have spent a night in hell with nothing to show for it."

"Then what do you think we should do?"

"As I see it," she said, warming to her subject, "we have one more possibility, and it's really a long shot. On Saturday, you mentioned a woman named Beulah. Delancey's assistant, you said? I think we should speak with her. Is she intelligent? Would she help you? Do you know where she lives?"

"Yes, to all three," I said. It was a brilliant idea.

"But she visits her sister at Christmas," Eddie cut in.

My optimism faded. "That's true. I don't know where the sister lives, but it's out of town, and I don't know how we'd get a hold of Beulah there."

"Well, then," said Miss Dare, "let us be off. Perhaps we can catch Beulah before she leaves for her sister's."

Along the way, she asked what Beulah's last name was. I couldn't remember—she'd always said we should call her Beulah. Eddie, of course, knew it.

"Mrs Willows," he said. "She's a widder."

"A *widow*," Miss Dare corrected. It's pretty pointless, trying to correct Eddie's awful English, but Miss Dare wasn't to know.

Luck was with us. When we knocked on Beulah's apartment door, sounds came from inside, and soon Beulah was standing in front of us, looking surprised. She wore a simple house dress, and no make-up, and was in stocking feet. All of which made my buddy swoon—naturally.

"Eddie! Iggy! What are you doing here? And who's this?"

"My name is Miss Agnes Hogwood. May we come in?"

Beulah was puzzled, but stood aside to let us in.

This was like night and day compared with Delancey's place. His was neat, hers was messy. His was dark and sparse with decorations, hers was bright and cheery and there was tinsel and holly everywhere. Of course, it was daytime, and we'd gone to Delancey's Saturday evening, but there was no getting around the contrast. The mess was mainly due to wrapping presents and such, so I couldn't fault her for that. Beulah took some paper and ribbon off the couch, told us to sit, then sat opposite.

"Now," she said. "What's up?"

"Right to the point," said Miss Dare. "I like that."

Beulah waited, somewhat impatiently. Miss Dare went on.

"The boys and I are investigating the murder of Mrs Clapham. The body of that unfortunate woman was found in my study, three years back."

"Yes, they told me."

"One of the principals in that case, a Mr Blank, choirmaster, was murdered Saturday, before their very eyes!"

"Good heavens! I saw the headline in the paper this morning, but didn't have time to read the article. You two were there?"

Eddie and I nodded.

"They have informed me," Miss Dare went on, "that you visit your sister at Christmas, and we don't mean to delay your preparations, but we wondered if you might persuade your employer to look into the case for us. He seems reluctant to do so."

Beulah laughed. "That's putting it mildly. I was there when Delancey turned them down for investigating Mrs Clapham's murder. I talked him into at least asking Inspector Fenrow's help, but that's as far as it went. The inspector wasn't much help."

"He was useless," Eddie groused.

"Now, Eddie," Beulah admonished, and Eddie blushed. "The inspector is a busy man. Delancey, though, has no excuse."

"Would you speak to him?" Miss Dare asked. "Convince him the case is serious?"

Beulah hesitated. "Delancey gets real lazy this time of year. He says it's to celebrate Christmas, though he doesn't do much for the holiday. I think he likes to be lazy, mainly."

"Has he no family?"

"He comes from Iowa, and his parents still live there. He has a sister, who lives not too far away, but for some reason Delancey prefers his own company." She shrugged. "He's never explained, and I've never asked. I think he calls his family on Christmas Day."

"Well, be that as it may, we need him now. Will you ask him to investigate the murders of Mr Blank and Mrs Clapham?"

"I can try."

"I know you visit your sister—" Miss Dare started again.

Beulah waved it off. "I love my sister dearly, but ever since my husband was murdered a few years back, my sister has been after me to find another man and settle down. I don't think she quite approves of my working for a private detective. She's seen too many films about seedy detectives chain smoking and drinking too much. Delancey's not like that. It's a clean, above-board establishment, and I've never been in any danger."

This wasn't quite true; Delancey once was hired by a local mob boss, and even though no one's taken a pot shot at her, it wasn't the nicest case.

"I know what you mean about so-called well-meaning relations," Miss Dare said. "I have two male cousins who were always overprotective of me. We were close as children. When I entered the field of writing, they thought I would starve. Suggested I find a wealthy man and settle down. Bah. Why tie myself to a man just for financial security?"

Beulah went on, "I certainly can talk to Delancey, ask him to look into it."

"But your sister—your travel plans…"

Another wave. "I can always get a later train. I'll blame Delancey for being late. It'll be another reason for my sister to grouse about my job. Now, where do we start?"

"We were hoping you might have an idea," Miss Dare said doubtfully. "I'm good at making up stories where I control the characters and what happens to them. This is rather out of my league."

Beulah smiled. "I think the best way would be to tell me what's happened so far. Miss Hogwood, would you like some coffee? I have soda pop, boys, if you'd like."

This was agreeable, and after the coffee was made and Eddie and I each had a bottle of Coca-Cola (with *straws!*) we settled back in to discuss the case. Miss Dare retold the whole story, from the murder of Mrs Clapham to our encounter with Mr Blank's death. Beulah listened thoughtfully. When she had finished, Beulah tugged at her lower lip in thought. Finally, she said:

"I'm sorry. I'm just flummoxed. No idea where to begin with this. Delancey would know."

"Precisely," Miss Dare said. "That's why we wondered if you had enough influence with your boss to get him off his derriere to do some work."

"Won't be easy. Like I said, Delancey is a slug this time of year. I can try. But you know what? Maybe we can grease the wheels a little. Something just dawned on me, and if it works, we might just convince Delancey to do something about this."

"What's your idea?" Eddie asked. "I bet it's amazing."

Beulah gave him a sly smile. She knows full well that Eddie is in love with her, but of course she also knows he's just a kid, so that's not going anywhere.

"Maybe it is. But for now—"

She was interrupted by the telephone. Beulah answered and after a short conversation we couldn't hear much of, came back.

"That's your mom, Iggy. Your dad's taken ill, and she'd like you home right away."

"But… then I'll miss your idea."

"It sounded pretty urgent. Your mom's been calling everyone to find out where you are. You'd better go now."

Beulah saw I was near to crying, I was so upset. She reached over, patted my hand. "I promise we won't do any more than we have to," she said, and then gave me a hug, which nearly made Eddie scream. His reaction made me feel better than her hug did, and I said goodbye to everyone and headed out.

It was a cold, damp day. The skies were overcast and promised snow. As I started out, dejected that I was leaving the mystery behind, it dawned on me that if Mom had tracked me down to Beulah's, she must have wanted to get hold of me pretty bad. She would've tried all sorts of other places first. I started hurrying then, and made it home in ten minutes.

The shop was closed—unheard of during Christmas season. Dad has an assistant, Mr Collins, who can run the place on his own, and when I knocked on the locked door, he let me in.

Mr Collins is twenty-five, short and thin, like some workhouse boy in a Dickens novel. Pretty energetic, though. And stronger than he looks. Not that you need lots of strength in a jewelry shop, but the year before, when some guy tried to rob the place, Mr Collins jumped the robber and wrestled him down, held them there until the cops came.

Anyhow, Mr Collins is never a cheery-looking sort; now he was positively undertaker-ish. He let me in and motioned me upstairs.

That time of year, there's quite a difference between the shop and our home. The shop is all decked out for Christmas, with a small tree in the window and Santa reminding folks how many days are left till the Big Day. A cardboard cutout that Dad always liked, sits in one corner of the window. It's a picture of a guy in suit and tie, one hand to the side of his face, eyes wide, mouth in an O and the caption, *Oh no! I forgot HER present!* It's one of the dopiest things I've ever seen, but the first year he put it in the window, Dad saw his sales go up, so he puts it up every year, and every year he credits that cutout with helping Christmas sales among forgetful husbands.

When you leave the shop and go upstairs, you're in a Jewish home. Hanukkah had started the evening before, and we were in full dreidel mode. The menorah took pride of place on the mantel, the house smelled of latke and other tasty treats and, showing some things are beyond religious boundaries, colorful paperchains were strung in all the windows. There was the little Christmas tree in one corner, like a goy relative at a bar mitzvah.

Mom was seated on the sofa with Rabbi Horowitz. This was serious, then. She stood and hugged me tightly.

"Oh, Ignatz! Your father is very ill."

Up to now, I'd just figured he had a belly ache—he gets them with stress—but this was more than a belly ache.

"What's wrong?" I asked. "How sick is Dad?"

The rabbi, a kindly soul who speaks with the Old Country accent, stood. He is barely taller than I am, and like I said earlier, I've always been a bit of a shrimp. But Rabbi is round in the belly, and in another life could have played Santa pretty well. He's also very plain-spoken. No mincing words with him.

"Your father has had a bad turn," he said. "The doctor is optimistic, but these next few days will be difficult for him."

"Where is he?"

"He's in the bedroom. The doctor and nurse are tending him now."

There was a knock and, told to enter, Brad Collins stepped inside. "Begging your pardon. Should I close for the day, or reopen the shop?"

Suddenly, like a voice from the burning bush, there came a shout from down the hall." Do not close!"

My father would be all right, then. I couldn't help a grin. The adults looked uncomfortable, but Mom managed to say, "You heard my husband," and Mr Collins bowed slightly before heading down to reopen.

Without asking, I went to my parents 'room. Dr Green was standing by the bedside, looking appropriately grim. He was vexed that my dad had expended the energy to call out. Doc Green is tall and skinny, with bushy eyebrows and a tangle of white hair. Dad was lying in bed, still in his dress clothes, though his vest and suit coat were off, his necktie loosened. He looked ashen, and my earlier fears returned. A slightly chubby, earnest nurse stood near the window.

Dad waved me over and I came, took the chair by his side. He reached up a hand and patted my cheek.

"You're a good boy, Ignatz. A smart boy. You will take over the shop someday."

"But not for many years." Truth was, I wasn't sure I wanted to take over the shop, but now was not the time to discuss it.

"Sooner than later," he replied. "But no, not now. I will get well again, the doctor says, and he is sometimes right."

The doctor coughed a bit to show he was listening. Dad ignored him.

"The main thing, Ignatz," my father went on, "is that you are ready when the time comes. Maybe while I'm lying here, having nurses and doctors fuss, you might help out in the shop? We will be busy these days, and Collins is good but he doesn't have six hands. Now is also a time for the thieves to sneak about and steal. So even another pair of eyes would do good."

I was devastated. I wanted to help solve the murders of Mrs Clapham and Mr Blank, not stand around the shop and watch for thieves.

"Couldn't you hire someone else?"

"Please, Ignatz. Do not argue with me on this. After the 24th, you will be free again. Just for these few days?"

I truly didn't want to, but what could I do? Dad was right, Mr Collins couldn't do it all himself. The shop gets very busy this time of year, especially with last-minute husbands—lured in, no doubt, by the window sign *Oh no! I forgot HER present!*

So I agreed. Eddie and the murders would have to wait.

After leaving the bedroom, I went to the telephone, rang Eddie's mom and told her what had happened with my dad.

Mrs McDonald, Eddie's mom, always sounds and looks harried.

"Oh, Iggy! Of course you have to stay and help out at the shop. You're a good boy."

"Yeah," I said, embarrassed. "Could you have Eddie come by the shop when you see him? We've… got this school project."

"Oh, yes, of course. I have to get to work soon, but I'll leave a note. He always reads them if I have them on the kitchen table, beneath the cookie jar."

"Thanks, Mrs McDonald."

"You're welcome. And you give my best to your dad, you hear?"

All I could do then was head down to the shop, where hardly any customers were about. I told Mr Collins why I was there. He seemed a little annoyed but when I pulled up a stool and pretended to be an angel, he relaxed and went on serving his customer.

Eight

At first, it seemed Eddie didn't have much to report, but after a bit of prodding, he finally told me what had gone on after I'd left. We were sitting in the back room of the shop, a small space where Dad does the books. The store was pretty quiet, so we had time.

"We went to Delancey's office," he told me," and Beulah pulled the biggest fast one I've ever seen. She phoned Inspector Fenrow, see, an 'pretended like she was calling for Delancey, that there was something Delancey wanted to talk to Fenrow about. Only he wasn't there!"

"Yeah, I got that."

Eddie started to giggle. "Boy, was Fenrow fried! I thought sure as shootin' he'd haul Beulah in. Miss Dare, too. An 'maybe even *me!* Christmas in the pokey! What a hoot!"

"I take it he didn't haul anyone in?"

"No," said Eddie, disappointed. "See, Beulah calmed him down—she's good at calming folks down—and said why she'd tricked Fenrow: because she and Miss Dare were looking into the murder of Mr Blank. She didn't mention the Clapham case because that's ancient history, as far as the police are concerned."

"What'd he say to that?"

"Well, he wanted t 'know why Delancey wasn't there, an 'Beulah goes and says *she s* investigating this case, an 'she don't need Delancey to hold her hand on every cotton pickin 'case."

Which surely wasn't the way Beulah put it, but I let Eddie tell the story as he wanted.

"I bet that steamed Fenrow," I said.

"Not a bit. He knows when he's licked, I reckon. So he says okay, I'll tell you all we know, not that there's a bit of anything helpful. Blank was stabbed in the back by someone wearing gloves, with a kitchen knife from the church hall. Mrs Blank, his wife, was sittin 'home, wrapping Christmas presents when it happened. She pretty much fell apart when they told her what'd happened."

"Did she faint?"

Eddie shrugged. "Dunno. All Fenrow would say is she was pretty shook up. Anyhow, the cops figure it might've been an intruder, someone tryin 't 'steal the collection money, but I could tell Fenrow wasn't sold on *that* idea. He didn't say anything different, though, so I guess they're stickin 'with that story."

We sat quietly for a bit. "Anything else?" I asked.

"Well, Miss Dare asked the inspector if he thought you and me were in danger. 'Cause we saw the guy stagger out, you know? Fenrow said that all depends. Then he gave me the third degree, which is why I think he settled down after Beulah tricked him—'cause he saw his chance t 'grill me. He says t 'me, 'Did you see anyone else in the church? Hear anyone'? An 'I says I didn't, an 'I didn't think you did, neither."

"No, I didn't."

Eddie nodded. "Right. That's what I figured, an 'that's what I told Fenrow. Then, he says, we should be okay. But Miss Dare won't let it go, an 'now Beulah's on her side. Beulah asks the inspector, 'What if the killer *thinks* the boys saw him'?"

"Good question," I said.

Eddie beamed like a guy does when his best gal is complimented.

"The inspector says, 'Well *then* maybe they're in danger'. That don't sit too well with either of the ladies, I can tell you. I thought sure that Miss Dare would clock 'im one. She looked like she wanted to. Instead, she just asks why the cops aren't protecting us, then. Fenrow says he doesn't think there's any reason to."

"And what was his logic behind that?"

"Well, I guess I can understand it. See, Fenrow figures that the killer knows we talked to him. An 'if we *had* seen something, why, he'd be arrested already. Or at least grilled by the cops to confess. Since that ain't happened, the killer has t ' figure we didn't say or see anything. Of course, we might've seen something an ' just wanna blackmail him. *That* didn't occur t 'any of 'em," he said proudly.

"True enough," I nodded. "So what happened then?"

"Well, Miss Dare asked if they had any leads at all, an 'she says he don't have t 'say who it is they suspect, just if they have *anybody* they suspect, so she might sleep easier about you an 'me. An 'the inspector says no, they can't come up with anyone just now. So then Miss Dare is about t 'shout at him, but Beulah steps in an 'thanks the inspector, an 'he leaves."

"And that was it?" I was disappointed.

"Not exactly. Beulah an 'Miss Dare talked it over for a considerable time after Fenrow left. They acted like I wasn't there. I was miffed, I can tell you."

There are times when Eddie latches onto a word, like "miffed" and tries to use it whenever he can. Sometimes he even uses it correctly.

"What did they come up with?" I asked.

"Why, the same as Fenrow! Or near enough. They said that they'd look into the murders, an 'maybe they could talk Delancey into doing likewise, but that you an 'me should just drop the whole thing. Too dangerous, they said."

I rubbed my chin. "Maybe they're right, Eddie. I mean to say, now that my old man is sick, I'm gonna have to spend more time at the store, at least 'til after Christmas, and that'd be days lost."

"I could report to you, like I did just now," Eddie offered.

"But what if you get in trouble? Who'll think your way out of it?"

"An 'just what are you implying?" he demanded. "That I can't think of a way out of trouble? Are you trying to miff me?"

"Now, Eddie, hang on. In a fair fight, I'd want you on my side every time. But let's face it, when it comes to brains, I win that battle."

His eyes became slits. "You better take that back!"

"Won't. It's true and you know it. Look, I'm not saying you're stupid—"

"You *better* not."

"No. I'm not saying that. All I'm saying is, I'm better at thinking than you. And," I added quick as I could, "you're a lot stronger than me. It's why we make a good team."

There was a pause as Eddie drank that in, and finally he broke into a grin.

"Yeah, I guess so," he admitted. That's Eddie for you. He might get mad at you, but after a bit, like a summer storm, he blows himself out. "Mind you," he added, "you miffed me for a bit."

"Sorry."

"Hey! You got some time now? Beulah gave me ten cents. We could get sodas at Finnegan's."

I looked over at Mr Collins, who was studying his fingernails. It sure was quiet now.

"Be back in half an hour," I called to him. He didn't even look up; just waved me off, and we headed out.

Finnegan's is a local pharmacy with the best soda fountain this side of everywhere. The place is run by Pat Finnegan, a jolly Irishman who's shorter than most, red-faced, and chubby. He's a good pharmacist, my mom says, but truth is, he'd rather serve sodas, and whenever possible he leaves the actual drug dispensing to his assistant, a crabby little man named Queen.

"Well, boys!" Finnegan called when we entered. "What brings you to my place of humble employment?"

"Two chocolate sodas, my good man," Eddie said, playing along as we climbed on stools. He produced the dime Beulah had given him, let it smack on the counter sharply.

"And from whence does yon booty originate?" Finnegan asked.

"A young lady what fancies me."

Finnegan's bushy eyebrows shot up. "Indeed! I have always said, it's a fortunate man who has a lady that will pay for his chocolate sodas."

We nodded solemnly at his sagacity, and soon had twin glasses of frothy heaven in front of us.

"So what have you lads been up to?" Finnegan asked. It was pretty quiet in the pharmacy. The only other person at the counter was a guy mulling over a hot dog and Coca-Cola, deciding if he had really ordered such a thing.

"We've been investigating a murder," Eddie said.

"Indeed! For the police? For Mr Delancey?"

"Nope. In the cause of justice."

"A fine cause it is, Edward. But is it not fraught with danger?"

"Of course. We live for danger."

"So I've heard. A Roman candle in Mrs Higgins's garbage can comes to mind."

"That was never proved."

Finnegan turned to me. "And you, Ignatz? Do you live for danger as well?"

"I prefer to live for chocolate sodas," I replied.

"Ah! A hedonist, then."

We had no clue what a hedonist was, but I nodded.

"Good. Without hedonists, those of us who are not, would not know what we're missing."

"Then," said Eddie, "maybe he deserves a licorice whip. An 'one for his friend."

Finnegan burst out laughing. "Nice try. Unless you've got a penny, the licorice jar stays closed."

It was worth a shot. Eddie winked at me and we went on relishing our sodas.

We were there maybe another twenty minutes. During that time, Finnegan had another chocolate soda customer, a lady who was weighed down by shopping bags and looked like she could use something stronger than phosphate. Her voice boomed clear across the pharmacy as she proclaimed that if her husband ever hinted at another child, she'd take a carving knife and change his mind. Finnegan chuckled; Eddie and I didn't see what was so funny with a gal threatening to stab her husband.

A look at the Hires Root Beer clock behind the counter told me it was high time I headed back to the store. As it got closer to the end of a work day, business would pick up, what with guys coming home from work and buying their wives Christmas gifts on the way.

So Eddie and I climbed off the stools, said goodbye to Finnegan, who waved his towel and went back to drying dishes behind the counter.

We weren't twenty feet along the sidewalk, headed for my dad's store, when a shot rang out, and before I could move, a second blast came. I dove for cover in time to see Eddie drop like a stone to the sidewalk.

Nine

One hour later.

I sat in the police station, worried. Where was Eddie? Had he croaked? If so, there wasn't anything Fenrow or Delancey could say that would've stopped me from getting whoever had done it.

I was in a dark hallway with lots of echoes. You could hear talking and footsteps from far off. And I was getting impatient. Why wasn't someone coming? I had half a mind to go up to the desk sergeant and complain. Holler at him, maybe. If he arrested me for hollering at a policeman, so be it, but I would have answers!

For his part, the desk sergeant ignored me. He was a young man with thin blond hair and glasses. All he basically did was shuffle papers here and there. Behind the little counter where he stood, there was a bunch of pigeon holes, like at a hotel where they keep keys and messages for guests. A few had papers; most of them were empty. There was a lamp on his counter so he could read the papers. I guess all he was doing was sorting mail. What a job!

Like I said, I was ready to go up and complain. I sat up straight and was just getting it in me to walk over when a door to my left opened and a uniformed cop popped his head out.

"Iggy Silver?" He looked around as if the place was jammed. Spotting me as I stood, he said my name again, then curled a finger and told me to come with him.

"Where am I going?" I asked. "Where's Eddie?"

I saw the cop exchange a glance with the desk sergeant, and it got me really mad that they seemed to smile at each other. How dare they! My best buddy could be dying in a hospital somewhere and they found that *amusing?* I was ready to demand to speak to the police commissioner himself.

That's what I was thinking as we walked along the interior hallway, which was brighter than the outer room, but only by a bit. I had to squint to see; I guess the cops all get to be like moles and can see each other in the dark.

Anyhow, we went down about twenty feet, past six or eight closed doors, rounded a corner to the left, and down another ten feet before the cop stopped at another shut door. This one had a name plate: *Inspector Jacob Fenrow.* He knocked, was told to enter, and we stepped inside.

Seated at the desk was the inspector, and across from him, with a sheepish grin, was Eddie! I sat next to him without being invited, and asked how he was doing. In reply, he raised his right arm a bit. I hadn't been able to see the arm from the doorway. It was in a sling. A bandage on his bicep had a small blood stain.

"Did you get *shot?*" I asked with a mixture of worry and envy.

"Nah."

He was about to explain when Fenrow, having dismissed his flunky, spoke.

"Your friend is damned lucky. The first shot hit the brick wall behind him, splintered it, and sent one of the shards into his arm."

"And the sling?" I asked, still talking to Eddie. The inspector answered anyway. "When he fell, he landed hard. Looks like a cracked bone in the forearm."

"But you'll be okay?"

This time Eddie answered. "Sure. Wait'll the guys at school hear about *this!*"

Once I'd seen Eddie okay, I took a look around.

The office was smaller than I expected for a detective in charge of murder investigations. There was a desk, four filing cabinets, five chairs (counting the one behind the desk where Fenrow sat) and not much else. The one thing it had going for it was that it had two windows. They needed a good clean, but let in enough light to tell that it was still daytime. Fenrow's desk was orderly, but there were huge stacks of paper all over. He was either writing a novel or was a very busy man.

"Now," said the inspector. "Maybe you want to tell me what happened?"

"Didn't Eddie—?"

"I've been on the telephone to your mothers."

"Our *moms!*"

"Yes," the inspector snapped. "Don't you think they deserve to know that their sons have been shot at?"

"So you figure the shooter was aiming for us?"

"I'll ask the questions around here— What is it?"

A knock had come, and the same officer who'd brought me, stuck his head in. "Excuse me, Inspector. The two mothers have arrived."

"Well, send 'em in, Simms!"

"Yes, sir."

In a minute, our mothers burst into the office. They reacted as you might figure moms would when they'd heard their only sons were shot at: they hollered at us.

"What in the name of heaven were you *thinking?*" Eddie's mom was saying.

"Your father will have fits," my mom put in. "And with his own health worries!" she added.

Eddie's mom came back with, "It's all I can do to keep body and soul together."

How long this would've gone on is anybody's guess, but Inspector Fenrow cut in. "Ladies, please have a seat." He waved a pencil at the two empty chairs, and they sat. "I was just getting to what happened, when you arrived. It's possible the boys aren't to blame for it."

"You mean it was random?" That was my mom.

There was quite a contrast between mothers, one I had never noticed before because the two were seldom in the same room. My mother looked like a typical housewife. She wore a simple blue and green print dress, hair done up. She had probably been baking something when the call came, or maybe fixing some chicken soup for Dad. Eddie's mom was dressed in her pink waitress uniform, with her name plate, *Edie*, pinned to her chest. She wore sensible work shoes and a frazzled look. That look, at least, the two moms had in common.

Fenrow ignored the question for now. "If you can spare a few minutes, I'd like to hear their story while you're both here. Otherwise, you can go and I'll see to it the boys get home safely."

"I can spare ten minutes," Eddie's mom said, checking her wrist watch.

"I can stay too," my mom said.

"Good. Boys, what happened?"

Eddie and I looked at each other. Since I'm better spoken, Eddie usually lets me talk and if I miss something, or get it wrong, he chimes in.

"We had gone to Finnegan's for chocolate sodas," I started.

"And where did you get the money for that?" Eddie's mom demanded.

"Found a dime," Eddie lied. Whether his mom believed it or not, she let it go.

"And," I went on, "we were heading out. I was coming back to the store to help out," I put in, so maybe Mom wouldn't be so testy. "And Eddie was headed home." Might as well put in a good word for him, too. "And we got only a little ways when two shots came. Bam! Bam! I fell down, to stay out of the way, and I saw Eddie go down and thought he was hurt."

"Which I was," Eddie put in, proudly.

"In a short while, the ambulance and a couple flatfoots—policemen, I mean—came, and next thing I know, Eddie's off in the ambulance and I'm off for the station."

"They didn't really take me away," Eddie admitted. "I just needed some fixin' up, so they did it in the back of the ambulance. Then another cop—police officer—took me here. An 'I been sittin 'here for near an hour!"

"Twenty minutes, tops," Fenrow snapped.

"What does it mean?" my mom asked. "Some sort of gang shooting and the boys were caught in the crossfire?" she asked hopefully.

"I'm afraid not," Fenrow replied, kindly. "Those sorts of things don't happen as often as the movies like to suggest. And anyway, they come from passing cars. These shots were almost certainly done from a building across the street."

"Good heavens!" Eddie's mom cried. "You mean someone shot at our boys on purpose?"

"Again, it's only a possibility. I just got off the phone with a couple of men at the scene, and based on the angle of the bullets, they figure the third floor of a building across the way was where the shooter was. That floor is abandoned, so it would've been easy to slip in."

"What kinda gun?" Eddie wanted to know. "Sawed-off?"

The inspector eyed him suspiciously but answered. "No. A pistol. We took the bullets from the brick wall. Could've been owned by anyone, really."

"Do you think," I began, "that the shooter missed us on purpose, or was he just a lousy shot?"

"It's tough to get a good aim at a distance with a pistol. Not impossible, but tough. So either the shooter was good and missed on purpose, or an average shot and missed wild. Or maybe even a little of both."

"But why?" Mrs McDonald wanted to know. "Why our boys?"

Fenrow arched an eyebrow to us in triumph. This was where our mothers would find out what we'd been up to, and put an end to our investigation. Only it didn't quite come out as bad as I expected.

"The boys have been playing detective," he said in a patronizing tone I sort of resented. "And it might've gotten them in a bit of trouble."

"A bit of *trouble!*" Mrs McDonald cried. "My son and Iggy were shot at!"

"I know, I know," Fenrow said, patting the air. "And it's nothing to sneeze at. But the fact is, the person who took a shot at them doesn't understand that the boys mean no harm. They're no threat to him—or her. My best guess is this was a warning, not a true attempt to injure them. So, if the boys leave this alone, if they go back to playing football or cowboys and Indians, the killer will leave the boys alone. He will have accomplished his purpose of warning them off."

"Do you hear that?" my mother asked me. "The inspector says you should give up all this nonsense. No more playing Sherlock Holmes. It's too dangerous."

Inspector Fenrow gave us a kind smile, but I could tell underneath he was gloating. He hadn't liked us honing in on his business from the beginning, and this was his chance to put a stop to it. He knew that if our mothers told us to knock it off, we'd have no choice.

"We weren't runnin 'around with gats," Eddie said defensively. "All we wanted t 'know was who killed that lady years ago an 'dumped her in Miss Hogwood's place. An 'then someone goes an 'bumps off the choir director! It wasn't *our* fault!"

"No one's saying it is," Fenrow said. "But why not leave the investigations to the professionals? The police are hired to protect you, but we can't do that if you go chasing after trouble."

There was a pause for a few seconds, then Mrs McDonald said, "I have to be at work in forty-five minutes," as she checked her watch. "And I can't tend you all the time, Eddie. You know I can't."

"I know, Mom," he mumbled. She was getting to him, I could tell. Eddie's a good son.

"All I ask is for you to behave, to stay out of trouble."

"I know, Mom."

"Well, then. You know what you need to do."

"Yes, Mom."

"I can see to it the boys get home," my mother offered.

"Thanks," said Mrs McDonald flatly.

Our two mothers didn't know each other all that well. Of course they knew Eddie and I were best buddies, and that provided a connection, but otherwise, they had little in common. I sure wouldn't call them friends. Or enemies. Just… two women who knew each other.

"Is there anything else, Inspector?" Eddie's mom asked.

"Not really. You're all free to go."

Mrs McDonald put a hand on her son's shoulder and looked about to say something, but she didn't. Instead, she just nodded to the inspector and left.

"I understand," said Fenrow to my mom, "your husband is ill."

Mom was about to ask how the hell he knew that, but didn't. She just said yes, he was bedridden.

"And," the inspector added, "you have a shop to run. A nice jewelry store... I should stop by to get something for my wife."

"Could you afford fine jewelry on a policeman's salary?"

Eddie kind of suppressed a snicker. Fenrow shot him a glare.

"You'd be surprised," he said calmly. "I am, after all, an inspector. Anyway, my point is, your son is needed around the shop, isn't he? At least until your husband is better?"

"He is," Mom said. She was starting to resent this.

"Then may I suggest he goes back there and helps you in your hour of need?" This was laying it on thick, and even the inspector knew it. He added, "What I mean to say is—"

"I know what you mean to say, Inspector. I appreciate your concern, but it is our family matter, after all, not yours. Your job is to keep us safe, as you said, and I'm sure you do a fine job of it. So I understand what you said about the boys keeping out of trouble. But how we keep them out of trouble, that is our business, isn't it?"

"It is," Fenrow admitted.

"Then if there is nothing else—"

"Just a moment. I'd like one last word with the boys."

Mom sighed. "I have things to do."

"I know, Mrs Silver. So why don't you head home and we'll see the boys get back safe. I promise, they're not in any real trouble, and I just want a couple minutes with the boys alone."

For two cents, Mom would've stayed. But she didn't. With a warning look for me and Eddie to behave, and a curt nod to the inspector, she left us.

"Now then, boys. I— Yes, Unger?" Fenrow sounded tired of the interruptions.

A policeman, even younger than the previous one who brought in our mothers, popped his head in. "Begging your pardon, sir, but there's a lady—"

"Right. I'm expecting her. Show her in, Unger. Now," the inspector went on. "I want you to think hard about what I told your mothers. This is not a game. You were shot at, and no matter if it was a warning or an actual attempt on your lives, it's still dangerous. Whoever this is, whoever killed Mr Blank, is not fooling around. You have to leave this to the professionals."

"Do you think whoever killed Mr Blank also killed Mrs Clapham?" I asked.

Fenrow hesitated, not sure how much to talk about it, I guess. "It's a possibility," he said at last. "But we may never know for sure. Not until we find out who did this."

Another knock, and Unger was back… with Beulah.

We were floored. Had Beulah turned on us? Was she now on the cops 'side?

"Mrs Willows," Inspector Fenrow said with a smile. "Come in. Take a chair. Thank you, Unger, that's all for now."

The officer left and Beulah sat next to Eddie, which of course got him all nervous.

"Thank you for agreeing to come by," the inspector told her.

"I heard about the shooting, and felt I had to come. Are you all right, boys?"

"They're fine," Fenrow said before we could. "Eddie's got a bit of a boo-boo, but he'll live. Now the reason I asked you to come by, Beulah, is this. I know you like these two reprobates. I have to admit, when they're not interfering in police business, they're okay. Neither of us want anything to happen to them, right?"

"Of course."

"Then I'm asking you, will you try to talk some sense into them?"

Beulah hesitated. She looked sidelong at us, then said, "I can try, Inspector. But as you know, they look up to Delancey—"

"Lord knows why."

That made us all a little hot. And why would he say that, anyway? He and Delancey were good buddies. Had been since they were kids. So why would he run down his best friend? I wouldn't do that to Eddie. Well, not in front of anyone else. So all of us liked Delancey, Beulah most of all. I think she'd do anything to defend him.

Anyhow Beulah glared a little but said nothing.

"But I do understand," Fenrow went on, "about kids looking up to an adult they want to be like. Hell, I get kids who want to be like me—"

Eddie couldn't keep in a laugh. He cut it short when Fenrow shot him a look.

"As I was saying, I understand about hero-worship and so on. And if the boys want to be detectives, or better still, policemen one day, great. But right now, they're in over their heads."

I didn't like that he was talking as if we weren't in the room.

"I'm sure you're right, Inspector." Beulah turned to us. "Well, boys? This started as a school assignment, and I think you've earned top marks for it, but now maybe it's time to let it go. How about it?"

Eddie would follow Beulah to the moon and back, but he also wanted to continue our investigation. So he was really torn. When she gave him her sweetest smile though, I knew we were sunk. There was no way he'd turn her down, at least for now.

"Okay," he said sullenly. "Iggy?"

I wasn't as captivated by her charms, but without Eddie, and given that I had to be at the store and needed him to be my eyes and ears, there was no way I could continue, so I said, "Sure."

Inspector Fenrow sighed with relief. "That's great, boys. Now I wish you both a merry—well, merry Christmas, Eddie. And happy Chanukah, Iggy," he said, pronouncing the *ch* like "church".

We thanked him and said our goodbyes. Fenrow suggested he could have an officer see us both home—I don't think he trusted us—but Beulah said she'd do the honors.

"No sense bothering an officer with such a petty chore," she said, giving Fenrow the same smile she'd given Eddie.

"No, of course not. Many thanks, Beulah."

I don't know if he trusted her completely, but he had no choice. It really made no sense to have an officer babysit us on the way home.

We got out to the street, and for a time it looked like Beulah meant to take us home. Suddenly, though, she stopped.

"Come with me," she said.

Ten

For the first time since I'd known her, I didn't trust Beulah. Even Eddie, who worshiped the ground she walked on, gave me a sidelong glance like he wasn't so sure about this. As we went along, I started to wonder. Where had she been when we got shot at? And while I was at it, she was the one who had given us money for chocolate sodas, and knew where we'd be. Had she actually taken pot shots at the two of us? Maybe it was better if Eddie and I just went home and took the inspector's advice to stay out of it.

My worries were for nothing, though—at least for now. Beulah was clearly headed for Delancey's office. She didn't say a word as we headed inside the building and started up the stone stairs to the second floor.

It's a squat little building, just the two floors. The first floor has attorneys, the second has Delancey and some accountant we've never seen. There's a clanky old elevator that mostly works, but no one but newcomers ever use it. Easier and safer to climb the stairs, a set of low-built marble steps.

The door to Delancey's outer office was open. That made me hesitate. Had the shooter come around to finish the job? I was suspicious of Beulah again.

No—inside the office were Delancey and Miss Dare.

"Well!" Delancey said, not in good humor. "About time you got here."

"Is it my fault Fenrow yakked so long?" Beulah shot back.

"Yeah," Delancey admitted, "he could talk the ears off a brass donkey. Well, sit." There were three chairs all ready for us.

"I can't stay long," I said as I took my chair. "Mom will be expecting me."

"I understand," Delancey said, nicer now. "How's your old man doing?"

"Okay, I guess."

"Yeah. Can't mess with your health. I'll be brief. You have now convinced me to look into this case officially. I am convinced the killings of Mr Blank and Mrs Clapham are connected, and I think the inspector believes it too. That makes two people this killer has bumped off, and that's nothing to mess with. I kinda like you boys, and don't want you in any more danger. So, if you'll allow me, I will take over the investigation." He added with a grin, "I *live* for danger," which was a line from the detective magazines he reads.

Beulah rolled her eyes. Miss Dare, who writes those kinds of stories, nodded intently. "So, to sum up," Delancey said to Eddie and me, "I'll take over the investigation. I'll let you know how things are going, of course, but from here on out, it'll be my baby."

"But your fee," Eddie said. "We can't pay—"

Another grin from Delancey. "No trouble there. Miss Hogwood—Agnes," he nodded to Miss Dare, "has agreed to foot the bill. Just expenses. I won't take a fee."

"I offered," Miss Dare said. "After all, I'm taking him away from Christmas celebrations. And Beulah, too."

There was a pause. I guess Eddie and I didn't realize we were being asked. Only when there were stares our way did a light dawn.

"You want our permission?" I asked.

"Well," Delancey said slowly, "not so much permission as your agreement, that you'll leave this be and I'll investigate."

Before I could reply, Eddie cut in.

"No! I mean, come on! Iggy and I got in on the ground floor of this. We don't deserve t 'get cut out now. You *can t* cut us out!"

Beulah said, "Now, Eddie. Delancey's not cutting you out. He said he would let you know what's happening. I'll make *sure* he keeps you informed."

For once, Beulah didn't have any effect.

"But it ain't the same," Eddie snapped. He started to get up, stopped halfway. "We want t 'be in on the investigation. It's okay if Delancey takes the lead. We don't mind that." Eddie often spoke about us as if we'd already discussed it "but gettin 'cut out, that ain't cricket!"

It was Miss Dare who calmed the waters.

"Eddie," she said calmly, "why don't you tell Delancey everything you've learned so far? Bring him up to speed?"

Now, Delancey already knew most of what we did, and there was really no reason for Eddie to repeat the whole shebang, but the suggestion seemed to work. Eddie calmed down, sat back and, when he looked at Delancey, who nodded encouragingly, he launched into a really long and muddled explanation of everything that we'd found out.

I stuck around just long enough to make sure Eddie told it the way it should be told. Then I stood.

"Sorry, but I really got to get going."

"Of course, Iggy," Beulah said. "Give our best to your father."

I've never known what that meant, "our best". I guess it means "best wishes", but then why not say it? Like when my Uncle Bert died a year ago. All these people I'd never met before came up to me at the funeral and said, "My condolences" or "I'm so sorry for you". Sure, some of them were sad because Uncle Bert died. Though I can't say it could've been many, because my own mom called Uncle Bert a jackass. *And he was her brother!* But anyhow, it seems like folks just say those things because they don't know what else to say. And now, I like Beulah, but it was Uncle Bert's funeral all over again. None of them knows my dad except Eddie, and even he doesn't know him well. Someday, I figure, someone will explain those kinds of expressions to me.

For now, I just nodded and said to Eddie, "Keep me posted," which he solemnly promised to do.

So from here on out, the story of what happened was told to me by Eddie that evening. "I think," said Delancey after I'd left, "that I'd like to look at both scenes. The church, and your house, Agnes."

"Dontcha mean her study?" Eddie asked.

"Nope. The whole house. I want to get an idea of the layout. Of course the study will be the most important part, but—if you're agreeable, Agnes—I'd like to see the whole place."

Miss Dare pondered this. She's a private person in many ways, and I don't think she was terribly thrilled with the idea of a stranger poking his snoot all over. Delancey didn't try to sugar-coat it: he really wanted to look around, though he promised with a grin not to rummage through her unmentionables.

That comment brought a gasp from Beulah, who can be kind of old-fashioned sometimes. Miss Dare patted the air to calm Beulah.

"Quite all right, Beulah. I'm used to men thinking they are being funny when talking about ladies 'undergarments."

"Still," Beulah began.

"I apologize," Delancey broke in. "I was being crude. All I was trying to say was that I won't snoop around closets and what have you. I just want a basic layout. The only place I'll really look at closely is the study."

"The police have already been over the study with a fine tooth comb," Miss Dare said doubtfully.

"I'm sure they have. And, depending who was in charge at the time, it was probably very thorough—"

"It wasn't your Inspector Fenrow. I believe it was an Inspector Klein?"

"Klein," Delancey nodded. "Yeah, I know him. Retired now. Kind of officious, a little snooty, but he knew his oysters. So I'm sure he and his boys did a thorough job of it, but that doesn't mean nothing was missed."

"Let's head for the church now," Beulah suggested, "while it's still daylight."

Eddie could tell that Delancey wanted to say they should let him go alone, that he didn't want three people hanging around. Beulah, he might've allowed, because she's helped him in various cases since she started working for him, but Miss Dare and Eddie were amateurs. And Eddie was still a kid, one who'd just been told to leave the investigation alone. All that, Delancey was thinking about, sure as shooting. But he didn't say a word.

Hard to say what they expected. I mean, it was still a murder scene, and Christmas was only a few days off. So there might've been cops prowling around, there might've been all sorts of church folk about. As it turned out, there was one cop and one church person. They encountered the cop first, a uniformed officer, standing outside the front door.

"Not sure you should go in, Delancey," said the patrolman. He was a little older than your usual pimply-faced cop, and had run into Delancey before. The cop didn't seem to notice the gang he'd brought along.

"Come on, Officer Schmidt," Delancey said, as if they were two buddies and Delancey wanted to sell the cop a used car. "If I *really* wanted to sneak in past you, there would be a few other doors I could try. But no, I came right up to you and asked to go in. No skullduggery here, Schmitty, my pal."

Officer Schmidt arched an eyebrow. He was seasoned enough to know when he was being snowed. Still, he said it would probably be okay, so long as they didn't muck about too much. Delancey promised, and the foursome went inside.

The church person they encountered was even tougher than the cop to get by. It was the janitor, a guy by the name of Walker This fellow was irascible (a word my father likes to use, for some reason), and was in no mood for intruders. He was short, muscular, and around fifty years old with a grizzled face and short hair.

"Can't come in," he said curtly. "I'm busy."

"We won't get in your way," Delancey promised.

"Makes no never mind," Walker snapped. "Can't come in. I'm busy. All them cops left a damned mess." He didn't flinch at using a curse word in church. "And then there's blood near the altar. Can you figure? What do they think, this is some Jew place?"

I took offense at this when Eddie told me, but he swore he was only repeating what the idiot had said.

Before Delancey could respond, Miss Dare cut in.

"My good man. You *will* let us in. We are investigating the murder of the choir director, and will not be stopped by the likes of you. This gentleman has assured you that we will stay out of your way, and we intend to keep that promise. But if you insist on being obdurate, I shall have no choice but to barge past you, sending you into next week, with no regard to how clean your church is!"

Walker looked like he'd been slapped. He chewed his lower lip for a moment, wide-eyed, and finally said, "Just don't mess up my church, that's all."

Delancey ignored the comment and went straight for the chancel. He crouched at the blood stain that Walker could not remove from the stone, not for lack of trying. Bleach, maybe. No time for it now, not with Christmas coming.

Delancey curled a finger to beckon Eddie. All three of his companions came forward. "Now," he said when they were all gathered around the stain. "How was the victim laying, Eddie? Where were his feet? His arms?"

"I could show you," Eddie offered.

"Not necessary. Besides, you might send the janitor—who is watching with an evil eye—into conniptions. Just point. Where were the feet?"

Eddie pointed to his right, toward the door where Mr Blank had come from.

"And the arms? How were they?"

Eddie lifted his left arm and crooked the elbow. His right, he kept at his side, like he was doing semaphore.

"Good. Now, I assume he was on his chest? Right. Flat on his chest, or tilted a bit?"

"Flat."

"And he came out of that door?" Delancey pointed to the sacristy door.

"Yup."

"Hold on," Beulah said. "He could've been in the chancel but out of sight, couldn't he? I mean, there's a little partition, shielding the door from most of the congregation."

Delancey chewed on this a bit.

"Eddie. You go down and stand where you and Iggy were. Beulah, since this is your idea, you stand in that corner, in the chancel but on this side of the door. Eddie, I want you to tell us if you can see Beulah from where you were standing. If you can't, give me the thumbs-down, otherwise, thumbs up. Don't move until I tell you."

Eddie was puzzled, but obeyed. He went to the place where we'd been standing when Mr Blank staggered out. He nodded that he was ready. Beulah went to the door and stood just outside it. Eddie shook his head, then remembered the signal and gave a thumbs-down.

Walker the janitor, was watching this process with sour fascination. He wasn't sure what to make of it all, but didn't say a word.

"Now," Delancey called. "I want Beulah to *slowly* edge out. Keep your thumb down, Eddie, until you can see her. Then, flip the thumbs up."

Eddie nodded. He understood the experiment now and was excited. He got too excited, actually, and started to lean forward, but Delancey snapped at him and told him to just stand as he was. They were ready to start the experiment when Miss Dare interrupted.

"Hold on, all of you. I understand what you're doing, Delancey, but I want to make sure it's accurate." She went to Eddie. "Were you actually facing the front when Mr Blank came out?" she asked him. "Or was the motion or sound of Mr Blank what drew you to see him?" Eddie thought long and hard about that one.

"I guess I was standin 'sideways," he admitted. "I was ready to go. Iggy wasn't."

"And how was Iggy standing?"

"With his back to the front," Eddie said. "So, stand how you were standing."

Delancey sighed and came down to Eddie too. "That still doesn't answer the question, Eddie. What made you notice Blank? The sight of him or the sound of him?"

"I dunno, do I?" Eddie blurted out. He was frustrated. "I can't remember."

"Okay, okay. Cool down. Let's just do it visually for now. Stand as you think you were standing. Ready? Okay, Beulah. Slowly, now."

Eddie watched and waited. After what seemed a few minutes but was only ten seconds or so, he turned his thumb up. Delancey called for Beulah to stop, then scooted up to the chancel. The others followed.

Beulah was at least a foot outside the door. They re-joined her in the chancel. "What does that prove?" Miss Dare asked.

"Well," Delancey said, "it proves that Mr Blank was not necessarily in the sacristy when he was stabbed. There was plenty of room for him to get stabbed out here. And getting stabbed in the back means he was surprised by his attacker..." He was thinking out loud. "But why was he dressed in that black cloak? And why was he mucking about in the church then, when no one else was around?"

Eddie said, "We figured it was just that he was doing something to get ready for Christmas. Choir stuff."

"Yeah, probably. But a *black* cloak at Christmas? It makes no sense."

There was a pause, and finally Beulah prompted him by saying his name. Delancey shook his head and said, "Okay. Let's head to your place," he told Miss Dare, and the group headed off for her house. What none of them realized was, if only Delancey had pursued that black cloak further, a whole lot of trouble might have been avoided.

Eleven

They headed down the street like a group of carol singers on the march. A few snowflakes swirled down, landing on their coats and noses, and Eddie looked up at the sky. He claims he figured we were in for a bunch of snow, and maybe he did know it because Eddie can fool you sometimes with his perception, but I think he was just making it up. Whatever it was, the snow started slow but we'd pick up a few inches before nightfall, and more overnight.

For now, they hurried on and were soon at Miss Dare's place. The house is too big to heat properly, though it was a darned sight warmer than being outside in the cold wind, and everyone unbuttoned their coats but left them on. Hats and gloves were jammed into their coat pockets.

Beggars, Miss Dare's formidable housekeeper, came striding into the hall like a soldier on a mission as they removed their galoshes.

"Oh, it's you, miss," she said snappishly. "I thought maybe it was them boys, the ones who like to knock on the door and run."

"The little scamps," Beulah said drily.

Introductions were hastily made and Beggars helped Miss Dare off with her coat. Down the drafty hall, past several doors, and finally to the unused section of the house. At the study door, Miss Dare waved a hand for the others to enter.

The study was the same as when Eddie and I had been there a few days earlier. Nothing much to see. But Delancey was looking, anyway. First he stood just inside, surveying the whole scene. Eddie had started to enter but seeing Delancey wait, he stepped back so as not to get in his way.

"Anything changed to the study since the body was found?" Delancey asked.

"Not really," Miss Dare said.

"What does 'not really 'mean? What's been changed?"

Eddie chirped, "The body's gone," which I found a hoot, but Delancey just looked annoyed and waited for a proper answer.

"The police were all over, as you might expect," Miss Dare said. "They really mucked up the front hall. Beggars wasn't very pleased. But in here, they were careful. I hate to say it, but Eddie's pretty accurate. They took away the body but were very sure to leave the room as it was, especially while they took photographs. That door—the one to outside—had been unlocked but is now locked, I can assure you. I *think* they moved that divan, in order to get the body out on a stretcher, but otherwise I think it's as it was that morning."

"Fine," Delancey said with a smile. He slowly walked into the room, and the others followed, as if nervously watching an inspector examine their work.

The room, like I've said before, was neat. Bookshelves lined the walls, with dusty titles Eddie had never heard of. He figured some of them were worth lots of money if Miss Dare ever decided to sell them. Of course, that was just his opinion; they might've just been old books. The furniture was sort of stiff, not built for friendly gatherings.

There was a thin film of dust—not a lot, and Miss Dare pointed out that, ever since the body had been found, she'd had Beggars come in every few weeks to run a feather duster over stuff. It sounded like Beggars wasn't too thrilled with this new assignment, but did it. As if she could read Delancey's thoughts, Miss Dare followed with, "But I'm sure Beggars leaves the room as it is. The sooner she's out of here, the better she likes it."

"I suppose," Beulah put in, "given the body was here. Some are pretty squeamish about things like that."

"Exactly," Miss Dare said. "The maid who first found the body—Mary—quit soon after. There was no need to hire a replacement: Beggars can do it all."

Delancey didn't seem to be listening. He kept wandering around, not coming near the desk area where the body had been found.

It disappointed Eddie a bit that Delancey didn't get down on his stomach and examine the floor close up with a magnifying glass, like Sherlock Holmes would've done, but Delancey told me once that wasn't how being a detective really worked. He said that, while it's true that bad guys sometimes dropped clues or left behind things that a detective might find useful, mostly all you'd find by crawling around were dust balls.

Delancey went to the doors to outside. For a few moments, he just looked out at the backyard. It was pretty barren. The trees at the far edge had shed their leaves and the ground was a swirling blend of brown grass and white snow.

"So these doors are always locked?" he asked without turning their way.

"They are now," Miss Dare said. "As I said, they used to be unlocked."

"Why would your father do that? Wasn't he worried about thieves?"

"My father was not worried about much of anything. In this case, there is a fence that runs along the sides and back of the house. At that end, there's a copse of trees that drops down severely to a creek. Nothing insurmountable, of course, but a thief could certainly find easier pickings. Of course, my father didn't publicize the fact that the door was unlocked."

"But why keep it unlocked at all?" Beulah cut in. "Why not just lock it?"

"Because," Miss Dare said, rather tired of the conversation, "he liked to step outside now and again, and couldn't be bothered to fumble with the latch in order to do it. You must understand my father. He knew what he wanted, thought he was right, and was not going to be dissuaded from his way. To unlock the door every time he wanted to step outside—which he did at least once most days—was an annoyance he would not put up with."

"And since the body has been found, the doors have been locked?" Delancey asked.

"Since the police finished in the room, yes."

Finally, after looking all around the room, Delancey turned his attention to the desk area.

The desk was set back near a wall, out of sight of the outside door, directly across from the door to the hallway, making a triangle with the walled bookcases. On it were an inkstand with two pens, an electric desk lamp, and a blotter. There was a wire basket for correspondence, and to Delancey's surprise, papers.

There were a few dozen sheets, most with handwriting on them, scattered off to one side, as if someone at the desk wanted the blotter area clear and didn't take the time to stack the papers neatly. That was a clue, though Eddie didn't catch it and Delancey wasn't sure how to interpret it—yet.

"You left the papers on the desk?" he asked. "Weren't some of them important?"

"The police and I looked through them," Miss Dare replied. She smiled—a little sad, Eddie thought. "It was all drivel. My father was a man who fancied himself important, but he really had very little to occupy his time. So he would write letters to people who didn't care what he had to say. He paid bills from here, and those bills he hadn't tended to when he died, I had already looked at long before Mrs Clapham was murdered. So even before the police asked about those papers, I knew they were worthless."

Delancey shook his head. "I still don't know why you didn't clean them up. Throw 'em away."

This drew a snort from Beulah because Delancey's desk is hardly an example of neatness. Delancey ignored her and waited for an answer from Miss Dare.

"One word," she said at last," inertia. After my father died, I didn't have the gumption to clean up his things. Later, I simply forgot about them. It was just easier to leave everything as it was. Of course, the killer didn't."

Delancey perked up. "What? You said things were—"

"I said things were as they were found that day the body was discovered. They are. They are not quite as they were when my father died. And the difference is those papers. My father was not an untidy man, Delancey. He would never have scattered the papers on the desk like that."

"The police—"

"The police looked through the papers, yes, and I cannot say they replaced them exactly as they were, but roughly, they are where they were that dreadful morning."

"Off to the side like this?"

"Yes."

Delancey went around to the desk. The papers were shoved messily to the side farthest from the door to outside. He stood on the side where the papers weren't, then slowly walked around to the desk. The chair was pushed a little away from the desk, not tucked underneath. It was a swivel chair on wheels.

"Did he usually push the chair completely underneath the desk when he was done with his daily work?"

"I don't remember. Probably. He liked things in their place." More silence.

Finally, Beulah said, "What're you thinking, Delancey?"

"I'm thinking there's evidence someone was in here after Agnes's father died but before Mrs Clapham was found. I mean, besides whoever put Clapham's body here."

"Someone else was in here?" Miss Dare cried. She didn't much like the idea.

"Yup. Maybe it was the killer at an earlier date, or maybe it was someone completely different. I don't know. Just… someone else at a previous time. Where was the body found?"

Miss Dare went to the far side of the desk, the one furthest from the outside doors. She pointed down. "Right here," she said.

"And how was it laying?"

"Mrs Clapham's head was propped slightly against the side of the desk, like a pillow. Her arms were at her side."

"Fully clothed?"

The two women looked Eddie's way, but my buddy knows the difference between sex stuff and a dead body. He didn't bat an eye.

"Yes. The police checked their files, and it appeared she was wearing the same clothes she had on at the last choir rehearsal."

"So probably killed the same night."

"That's what they assumed, yes."

"And the cause of death was… a blow to the head." It wasn't a question but Miss Dare treated it that way.

"Yes. At least that was the ruling. The left side of her head had been crushed, probably by a stone. The police believed that if the killer caught her off-guard, she'd have been unable to cry out."

"Takes someone strong."

"Probably, yes."

Delancey arched an eyebrow. He had come to stand next to Miss Dare, and looked down, as if the body were still there. "You seem to know a lot about this. Not that I'm ungrateful; it's a damn sight easier than getting information from the police, even if the case is a few years old."

Miss Dare smiled. "I have to confess, I was persistent in my questions. It helped that, for a time, the police suspected me."

"You!" That was Beulah.

"Yes. Found in my study, after all."

Eddie put in, "You'd have been dumber 'n salt t 'leave the body in your own house." Miss Dare and Beulah laughed. Delancey stayed serious.

"Eddie's right," he said.

"Yes," Miss Dare said. "That's what the police finally figured out. In the meantime, they came at me with all sorts of accusations, and told me of the evidence they had. So I filed all that information away," she added, tapping the side of her head, "and that's how I came to know so much about the manner of death."

"Tell me about the morning the body was found. Leave nothing out."

"Very well. But might we sit? My puppies are barking."

They sat on the dusty musty chairs.

"I could also use a belt," Miss Dare. "Anyone else?"

Eddie started to raise his hand. Beulah gave him a curt shake of the head and he lowered it with a sullen," No thanks."

89

Seeing there were no takers, Miss Dare scowled and stayed sitting.

"That morning, we were doing a bit of cleaning in the house. I say 'we' because I was joining in. Writing for periodicals pays the bills, but not much more. I can't afford a large staff. At any rate, Beggars is the strongest worker of the group and volunteered to take the unused portion of the house. I instructed Mary—a young neighborhood girl who came in sometimes, when there was a lot to do—to give her a hand, though Beggars was not pleased. She likes to do things her way, you understand, and would rather just work by herself than supervise others. Not an easy one to get along with, my housekeeper. Tried the church choir and quit after a month."

"And Mary found the body?" Delancey asked. He could be very patient when people prattled on. I asked him about it once, and he told me that sometimes, if you were paying attention to the prattle, something really important came through.

"Yes. She and Beggars were working in this section of the house. Beggars insisted upon doing this room, however, because it was, after all, my father's study, but Mary convinced her it was such a big room, she would help."

Beulah said, "So Beggars was here when your father was alive?"

"She was. I've known Beggars for some twenty-odd years. She knows the house better than I do, to be honest."

"And she an 'Mary walked in and found the body," Eddie said.

"Yes, but not initially. From the hallway door, you can't really see much of where the body lay. The sofa is in the way. Besides which, the curtains were drawn. It was very dark. Beggars went to the outside door and opened the curtains. Then, she couldn't see the body because she was at the wrong angle. Mary decided it might be better to start at the desk. That was when she spotted the late Mrs Clapham."

"What'd she do?" Delancey asked.

"Did she scream bloody murder?" Eddie wanted to know, which I thought was a reasonable question, but Delancey glared at him.

Miss Dare smiled. "I don't employ people who scream bloody murder, Eddie. Of course, she was startled, and Beggars told me later that she even thought it was some dummy that local kids had put in the room as a prank. Sometimes we have trouble with the little cherubic thugs in the neighborhood."

"And when she realized it was a corpse?" Delancey prompted.

"Well, Mary let out a yelp, and staggered a bit. Beggars gave her a good slap. Brought her to her senses. She told Mary to fetch me, which the girl did. I was stunned too, of course, since Mary could only babble when she came for me, and I had no idea what she was talking about."

"And you telephoned the police?"

"I did. There was no need to get a doctor because the corpse was mummified, though the police sent for a doctor anyway."

Delancey nodded. "Standard procedure. How long were the cops around?"

"They stayed a few hours. I think they saw how shaken I was, so the inspector very kindly held off with a lot of impertinent questions. Those came later."

"But surely," Beulah said, "you were so clearly shaken that they couldn't suspect you?"

"They did. Not for long, mind you. Especially after they discovered whose body it was. Then they understood I didn't know the woman, so why kill her, let alone dump her in my own study. Beggars knew her slightly because she attends the same church."

"Yeah," Delancey said with a grin, "the police catch on eventually."

"I suppose they were simply following procedure," Miss Dare said with a sigh.

"They're big on procedure. And I really can't blame 'em. A smart defense lawyer can get a client off because 'procedure 'wasn't followed. It covers their backsides."

There was silence in the room for a bit. Beulah remarked that it looked like the snow was falling sort of heavy. They looked out the window and saw it was coming down pretty brisk.

"Well," Delancey said, standing, "I guess that's it for now. Time to chew on this for a bit. Thanks for letting me see the room."

"Thank you, Delancey, for taking the case."

They shook hands and were about to leave the room when Delancey spotted something.

Everyone went quiet. It was liking watching a diamond cutter about to strike a precious stone. Delancey looked puzzled, staring at the area directly behind the desk. He slowly walked to that area, careful to avoid furniture. It took him nearly a minute to cover the short distance.

All it was, Eddie told me, was a book. The book was pulled out an inch or two from the others on the shelf. It was too far away for Eddie to see the title. Delancey reached up a hand and cautiously, as if the book were made of glass, placed his index finger on the binding and nudged it into place. With a slight shrug, Delancey rejoined the others.

"Are we done for the day?" Miss Dare asked as they reached the front door.

"Yep, I think we are," Delancey said. "I'll be in touch." He touched his cap brim and he, Beulah, and Eddie headed out to the street. Snow had begun in earnest.

Twelve

Tuesday, December 23rd.

I woke thinking it was broad daylight, but in fact the sun had just come up. It was snow that lit up my bedroom. I hurried to the window and rubbed the frost feathers away as best I could. The floor was cold on my bare feet, but I ignored that while I peered outside.

Snow had ended, but there was a fair amount of it. Outside, a few brave souls scurried about. Across the street, Mr Donegal, a blustery Irish baker, shoveled snow from in front of his shop. It looked to be about six inches. Not enough to cripple the city—we northerners are made of strong stuff—but certainly enough snow for late openings and tough going until the roads and walkways were cleared.

The night before, Eddie had stopped by for a little bit to tell me what had happened after I'd gone. I was envious. Why was I cooped up in the shop while he had all the fun?

"And," Eddie concluded, "Delancey wants to go back to the church, to talk to the minister." He grinned. "Should be fun, seeing him grill a clergyman!"

"So you're goin 'too," I moped.

"Yeah. So's Beulah. I don't know about Miss Dare." Then he noticed I was down because I couldn't go too. "It's okay. We prob'ly won't get anything."

We spent a bit more time chatting, then he'd left because the snow was falling heavier.

Now, half a foot of fresh snow was on the ground, clouds were still dark, but the snow was done.

Meanwhile, at his house, Eddie got himself some breakfast. He let his mom sleep because she'd be back at work that afternoon and night. He tried to be quiet, though dropping his cereal bowl with a clatter didn't help. But his mother didn't wake, what with her door closed, so Eddie breathed a sigh of relief, finished breakfast quietly, and headed out.

He did a little skidding along the sidewalk (on purpose) shooting snow every which way, though Mr Glass, the grouchy janitor of his building snapped at him as he'd just *cleared* that snow! Well, it had drifted, anyway, and wasn't near as clear as he'd had it. That was Eddie's excuse, and he was sticking to it. He decided not to press his luck though, especially since he was still in a sling from the brick shrapnel. He headed for the church, where Delancey had suggested they meet.

Eddie arrived first, and busied himself playing with icicles dangling from the iron gate that entered into the churchyard. He tried to see how strong they were, and kept increasing the pressure with his finger until it broke. 'Pretty strong' was his scientific conclusion.

Delancey and Beulah arrived.

"Agnes won't be joining us," Beulah announced. "She telephoned last night to say she'd caught a cold yesterday. Sounded pretty crabby."

Delancey led the way into the church. A few parishioners were there, doing some last minute preparations as the Reverend James Willoughby supervised. The reverend wasn't very pleased to see them. He gave a very un-Christian sigh when he saw Eddie. Delancey and Beulah, he didn't know, but gave another sigh when they introduced themselves.

"What is it?" he asked. "I have a lot to do. My choirmaster is dead. My secretary has a head cold. Christmas Eve is tomorrow, and we have so much to do."

Actually, the church looked pretty good, and the minister hadn't been doing much of anything when the trio arrived.

"What will you do for a choirmaster ?" Beulah asked. "Direct yourself?"

The minister was aghast. "Oh, heavens no! For one thing, the choir is back there," he pointed to the rear of the church, to the loft, "and I am over there," he needlessly pointed to the front. "And in the second place, I'm no musician." Beulah's plan had worked: the minister was becoming friendly. "No, Mrs Blank— the poor man's widow—has stepped in. I told her it wasn't necessary, that we could find someone else, but she said that having something to do would be helpful. She is a trouper!"

"I'm glad to hear it," Delancey said sincerely. "And I don't mean to bother you or your crew, but I just wanted a few words."

The minister looked ready to sigh again. He inhaled deeply, but let it out slowly this time. "I wanted to look over the choir loft," he said, "to make sure all is in order. If you'll come with me, we can talk as we go."

94

They started for the loft stairs.

"After the police were through with their work," Delancey started, "did you find anything out of place, in the church or in the back?"

"You mean apart from a blood stain in front of the altar?" the minister snapped, then apologized. "I'm sorry. I always get so nervous before these big services. Before Easter two years ago, I nearly vomited in the sacristy! Anyway, the answer is no. Nothing seemed out of place."

"And the knife came from the church kitchen?"

"It appears so. We have several items of cutlery there—all manner of sizes and patterns—though I can't tell you the last time some of it was used."

"So whoever wielded it would have been someone familiar with the church?"

The reverend looked surprised, like it hadn't dawned on him before. "Yes! I suppose that's so. Though I hate to think one of my *parishioners*—"

Delancey waved off his worry as they reached the loft.

"At ease, Reverend. It *could* be a parishioner, or it could simply have been someone who'd been in the kitchen before. You ever serve a hot meal to vagrants?"

The minister made a sour face. "We used to. Then we started noticing pieces of silver used in Holy Communion missing or moved. We tried locking it up, but that was an imposition to those who clean the silver or prepare the Holy Elements. So we stopped serving such meals. Now we contribute to a city-wide effort at the local high school gymnasium. Mind you, we had a quibble about *that* in our council meeting! There were some who said we simply had to continue serving the meals, and hang the bother. Others said no, we had to be smart about such things."

"And which side were you on, if you don't mind my asking?" Delancey smiled to show no offense.

The reverend returned his smile. "I try to be arbiter during such disputes. Smooth troubled waters, and all that. Taking sides is not to anyone's advantage."

Delancey briefly looked put out at the reverend's cowardice.

"Fine." After a quick look around the choir loft, he said, "Now if you don't mind, I'd like to speak to some of your parishioners."

"Be my guest."

Delancey thanked the minister and they went to a couple off to one side who were polishing a pew that already gleamed in the soft daylight coming through the stained glass windows. He introduced Beulah and Eddie, and the couple said they were Marge and John Kepler. They were between sixty and seventy, had heavy

German accents, and seemed anxious to speak to anyone about the murder of Mr Blank.

"That police inspector," said John with distaste. "He don't talk to no one who knew the choir man."

"Did you know the choirmaster then?"

"Man and boy," Kepler said proudly. "We haf been members of this church since our own youth. I vas baptized here, married here, and vill be buried here, yah?" He looked at his wife for confirmation, who nodded.

"So how would you describe Mr Blank? Who'd want him dead?"

"Anyone what had to listen to hiss awful songs!" Kepler broke into a deep belly laugh. His wife frowned and swatted him, then joined in his chuckle.

"To tell the truth," Marge said, "no one would vahnt Mr Blank for to die. He vas a good man. Though he could be strict mit da choir, I hear."

"So neither of you were members of the choir?"

"My Margie vas, ven we were young," John said, "but that was old Mr Oglethorpe, ven he vas director."

"Himmel!" Marge cried. "*He* vas a rotter. Made poor HarrietWest cry, and not just once. But Millie had lost her own husband in that Civil War, and she cried many times, did Millie. A nice lady, though."

Delancey's an expert at waiting people out, like I said. He doesn't interrupt. Now, though, he smiled and said, "So you can't think of anyone who would want to kill Mr Blank?"

The couple looked at each other, then at Delancey, and shook their heads.

"And Mr Blank, you say, was a nice man, though he could be strict with the choir?"

"I vould say," John declared, "dat describes him to a teapot."

"Was he… how can I put this? Was he devoted to his wife? Did he go out much alone?"

The couple were scandalized. "What are you sayink?" Marge demanded.

Delancey held up his hands in surrender. "I didn't mean he was playing around, Marge. But I've known devoted husbands—and wives—who like a little time away. Say, playing cards or bowling."

Marge still looked put out, but John calmed down and said, "Not so far as I know. Oh, he liked his fountain drink now and again, and ice cream—he was very much on the ice cream. Ate tree cones at the church picnic last summer!" He chuckled, holding up three fingers. "But I don't tink he vas the sort to go out mitout his *frau*."

"I see. Did he go *with* his wife, then? Were they social?" Again the couple looked at each other. Marge spoke.

"Not so much as they used to. They used to be laughers, those two. But after Frau Clapham disappeared, why, it shook them to dere socks. Especially Mr Blank. Oh, he was shook, dat vun. His own choir member, gone. And the same night as rehearsal! I tink he wondered what would haf happened dat night if he'd kept the choir just a little later, or let them go a little sooner."

"A crime of opportunity," Delancey suggested. Seeing that puzzled them, he explained, "Not planned, in other words. Just the wrong place at the wrong time."

They nodded and John said, "I can't tink of any other reason vy she would be kilt. No one hated her so much."

Delancey thanked them and started for the door, when Eddie tapped his arm.

"That lady over there," Eddie said, "is Mrs Tilbury, Mrs Clapham's best friend."

Delancey nodded, and they went over to Shirley Tilbury, who was fussing with a piece of garland that would have come untangled sooner if she hadn't been watching them speak to the Keplers. Now, as they approached, she gave up the garland and waited for them to reach her.

"You're investigating Millie's murder," she said flatly.

"Yes, ma'am. I'm Tom Delancey, this is my associate, Beulah Willows, and I understand you've met this young rascal."

Eddie frowned at not being introduced properly.

"Yes, I met him. He was with another lady—"

"Miss Hogwood, yes," Delancey said. "She's hired me to look into your friend's death."

Mrs Tilbury frowned, but it was a sad look. "I don't know how much I can tell you. I've already told the police everything I saw and heard that night—"

"Actually," said Delancey, holding up a hand, "I'm more interested in what your friend was like. Not whether she had any enemies—apparently, she was well-liked."

"She was."

"Yes. So I don't need that. I'm just interested in what she was like as a person. Good and bad. As her best friend, you would know better than anyone, except her husband, of course."

"Oh, but James—Millie's husband—might not have known her as well as I did."

"Really?"

"Don't misunderstand me, Mr Delancey. The Claphams were happy enough, for all I know. But Millie often said that James was not the most... open of husbands. Liked to keep things bottled up and not tell a soul what he was thinking. Typical man. So when Millie had something to get off her chest, she didn't think James would care or understand, so she tended to tell me."

"I see. What else can you tell me about Mrs Clapham? I mean, she sounds a good egg, but surely there was something, some fault? Something that might've griped others?"

"Well..." Mrs Tilbury hesitated. She chewed a bit on a fingernail. Delancey waited patiently. "Well, if I'm to be honest, Millie could be a bit full of herself. Mind you, I didn't find her so, but there were a few who thought her proud."

"Proud of...?"

"Why, *everything*. What I mean is, she had so much going for her. She was pretty, and smart, and funny. She was the best singer in the choir, with the possible exception of Mr Hawes, who's a fair baritone, I must say. And, though she wasn't rich, she certainly didn't want for anything. James would give her a new ring for her birthday, or Christmas, or some such, and she'd show it off. Oh, I don't think she offended consciously. To her, it was sharing her newest ring with others, like a person would share good news with a friend. She didn't see that it rubbed some folks the wrong way."

"Did you ever tell her that?"

"I did, once. She just laughed, said I was mistaken, that everyone would be happy for her good fortune." Mrs Tilbury shook her head. "She just never thought. Oh, but please don't get the wrong idea. She was mostly a gem of a gal."

"I see. Well, thanks, Mrs Tilbury."

As they left she called out that she hoped they'd find who killed her friend.

Next, it was to the shop of Mr Clapham. Trouble was, Clapham was busy. He had a business to run, and it was a few days before Christmas, so he was busy as a pup on fire. Mind you, the shop wasn't quite so busy now as it would be later that day, when all the men coming home from work would stop to buy baubles for their missus. But he was still annoyed at the interruption.

"I have customers to tend to," he snapped, though at the time they arrived there were only two in the store, each being handled by a clerk.

"Yes, sir," said Delancey, though he was just being polite. "It's a busy time for everyone. But I just have a couple of questions and I'll be out of your hair."

Clapham still didn't want to bother. Finally, Beulah cut in.

"May I see that bracelet?" she asked, pointing to an item in the case.

The jeweler caught on. If he pretended to help Beulah, no one could gripe. He didn't really expect her to buy anything.

"Now," said Clapham as he removed the bracelet to show Beulah. "Ask your questions, Mr Delancey. But before you do, maybe I can save some time. No, I don't have any idea who murdered my wife. No, I had no hint she might run off. No, I didn't do it."

Delancey grinned. "You've been through this before."

"Dozens of times. The police, the reporters. Now you."

Beulah didn't take her eyes off the bracelet as she said, "Were you happy?"

This was a bolt from the blue, and Clapham blinked a few times before he answered. "Reasonably."

"That's faint praise," Beulah said flatly.

"And what would you expect me to say?" Clapham didn't raise his voice during this whole thing. Unless you were nearby, you would've thought they were discussing the fine points of the bracelet. "We were no longer newlyweds," he went on. "The time of flowers and candy were long since passed. Did I love my wife? Absolutely. But we had slipped into that comfortable stage, when we simply… lived."

Beulah grew a little sad about that expression. She had been married, her husband murdered a couple of years before, and they'd only had a few years together, so she hadn't experienced that stage Clapham was talking about. She liked to believe, Eddie thinks, that Clapham was wrong, that some couples *did* keep the flowers and candy stage.

"How much?" she asked.

"Eh?"

"For the bracelet."

He quoted a price that Eddie thought was out of line. Beulah considered it, suggested a slightly lower price. Clapham looked insulted, then agreed.

"You didn't have to buy that," Delancey remarked as they left the shop.

"Of course I didn't. I wanted to."

"For yourself?"

"Who else for? I'm not in the habit of buying jewelry for others."

She didn't say anything more. It was a few weeks later, when I was talking with her about this whole business, that she told me why she'd bought it. Her late husband had always bought her something nice and sparkly for Christmas. Buying that bracelet made her feel that maybe he wasn't gone. She didn't say so, but I suspect she even wrapped it up and put it under her tree.

For a bit, they just walked. No one seemed to know where to go next, not even Delancey. Then he stopped.

"Not sure why you two are following me," he said. "I'm just headed back to the office to think."

"We'll go with you," Beulah replied, "and help you ponder."

Now it's a fact that Delancey prefers to do his thinking alone. He thinks long and hard, and anyone might think he was just loafing, but Beulah assures us he really is working, and has come up with the solution to more than one puzzle while sitting at his desk, staring into space. I'll take her word for it.

Anyhow, he told Beulah and Eddie to go home, that he would handle this. Beulah shrugged and started off. Eddie caught up with her and said he was headed to see Miss Dare, to see how she was doing, and then heading to my house to fill me in.

Little did he know how important that second visit would become.

Thirteen

By now, you're wondering what I was getting up to. Maybe you aren't wondering but I'm going to tell you anyway.

The fact is, it was good news. The doctor came around and after a good half hour, he emerged to tell us Dad was improving nicely.

"He isn't ready to return to work," said the doctor, "but I believe he will recover completely. And," he added, "he would like to see you, Mrs Silver."

After the doctor left, Mom went upstairs and I insisted on going along. She made me stand back from the bed, in case Dad wanted to impart some big secret to her, I guess. Anyhow, I stood back like I was told.

Dad *did* look much better. And he had no intention of speaking softly so I couldn't hear. "The doctor said I should be up and about tomorrow," he proclaimed.

"The doctor said," Mom corrected, "that you must rest yet."

"I have a shop to run!" His last words were strained. He still wasn't well.

"And it will still be there when you are better. You have an assistant—"

Dad made a rude noise. "Mr Collins is a good assistant. I have no quarrel with Mr Collins, but," (he said something in Yiddish that does not translate well into English, so I won't repeat it), "if you insist on keeping me cooped up like a chicken, I have another idea. Fred—"

"Not *Fred!*"

Fred is Dad's brother. He is never spoken of by my mother. When Dad brings up the name it's as if he suggested they should visit a leper colony. I was never sure why Mom didn't like Uncle Fred, but I was soon to find out.

"He is a lazybones!" Mom cried. "Never held a job for more than two weeks."

"But he is honest," Dad countered. "And he would be ready to help, I am sure. And he could probably use the money."

Strangely enough, for all his laziness, Uncle Fred never has trouble finding work. Every time he's talked about—and like I said that isn't often—he has a different job. Now, it appeared, he was unemployed. (At Christmas, this was not a good sign, I admit.)

"Bah. If he didn't spend the money he had on women—" she stopped and looked back at me for signs I knew what she was talking about," and gambling, he'd have money."

"Well," said my dad, "I don't know about all that. But I am going to ask Fred to help at the shop. If," he said over her protests, "there is trouble with him, I will handle it."

There was nothing else to say. The telephone call was made, and in an hour or so, Uncle Fred arrived at the shop. He went upstairs to visit Dad.

Uncle Fred is everything my father isn't. Dad is quiet, not easily ruffled. He holds fast to his faith as much as he can, and tries to follow the Law of Moses (except with what he eats: he has a weakness for ham). Uncle Fred couldn't tell you the difference between the Law of Moses and the law of gravity. He is as friendly as Dad, but in a bombastic way. He likes to back-slap and tell jokes. I've always liked him, but looking back I can see why Mom didn't trust him. He spent money like water and liked to play the high-class gent.

Now, when he saw me in the shop before heading upstairs, he greeted me with a bear hug.

"Ignatz! How wonderful to see you again!" he cried with a voice loud enough to rattle the glass cases. "And how you've grown! Egad, I really must be less of a stranger, or I shall miss your childhood altogether." As you can tell, Uncle Fred has also dropped any of the Old Country way of speaking. Fully American, is my Uncle Fred.

He slapped my back, nearly sending me into a customer who glared at us both. Uncle Fred went upstairs and after a half hour of conversation, he returned, ready to assume a place behind the counter.

Later, even Mom had to admit a change came over Uncle Fred. He had dressed nattily, and went immediately from his boisterous attitude to one of quiet grace. He complimented the ladies when they tried on a piece of jewelry; he cajoled the gentlemen who hesitated to spend so much on a wife or sweetheart, and thereby made a sale that otherwise might not have been made. He was, in short, the perfect salesman.

After watching him like a hawk for an hour, Mom turned to me.

"I don't see why you need to stay. Mr Collins and your uncle seem to have things well in hand."

I barely got out my thank you before running into the kitchen to grab my coat and hat and dashing out the door. My first stop: the church.

Meanwhile, Beulah and Eddie were off to visit Miss Dare, to see how she was doing. Beggars the housekeeper met them at the door with a sour look.

"Miss Hogwood is indisposed," she said coldly, and was about to shut the door on them when a call came from inside.

"Who's that, Beggars?"

"Just one of the boys and Mrs Willows, ma'am," Beggars called back. Eddie was startled by the sudden outburst from the normally quiet maid, but it was done so easily that apparently shouting back and forth wasn't unusual for them. "I told 'em you're indisposed!"

"Nonsense! Send 'em in!" came the call back. Miss Dare sounded perfectly healthy.

They entered the sitting room. Miss Dare was dressed in a bathrobe and fuzzy slippers. She had a cup by her side with coffee and probably something else. All around her were papers with scribbling—lying on the floor, in her lap, dangerously close to the fireplace where a fire burned brightly, and in a stack on a small table at her side.

"You find me," she said, "in the throes of my greatest dilemma. I have written—sit! Sit!—I have written the opening pages to *Death-Stalker Sails the Stars!* but have rather painted myself into a literary corner. My hero, Slake Thirsty, is held captive by the nefarious Death-Stalker, and is about to be dumped into a flaming pit of lava on the Planet Darkling. His belt, containing all he would need to escape, is about to be tossed into the pit with him, and he cannot reach it. Now! Do you have a clue as to how he gets out of this?"

She waited for her visitors to respond.

"Maybe," said Eddie, "he kept some stun bombs in his pocket, just in case. He throws one at the Death-Stalker, then leaps to safety."

"Eddie," Beulah warned.

"No, no," Miss Dare cut in, musing. "It *has* possibilities. I'd have to rewrite part of it, hint that Thirsty carries spare stun bombs with him. Otherwise, the whole thing might not be believable. But I think I might pull it off. Thank you, Eddie!" She jotted down a note to the effect. "Now. What brings the two of you here?"

"We wanted to see how you were doing," Beulah said, "and to tell you everything that happened in your absence."

"Good! To answer your question, I am better. Touch of the sniffles, was all. I get chilled easily. I blame my grandmother, on my father's side. All you had to do was turn the calendar to November, and she'd start complaining of a cold. Mind you, I'm no hypochondriac, not like she was, but I do believe I inherited her lack of physical ability to fight off colds. Now! Tell me everything."

Beulah went on to describe what had occurred with Delancey's interviews. Meanwhile, Eddie sidled over to Miss Dare's notes, to see if he could get a glimpse of her story. Without even looking in his direction, Miss Dare flipped the top sheet over so everything was hidden. Eddie slipped back to Beulah's side.

"So what happens next?" Miss Dare asked when Beulah had finished.

"Now, Delancey mulls it over."

"No, no! I want *action!* None of this lollygagging about."

"I know it seems like he's not doing anything, but I assure you, Delancey is working. His brain doesn't necessarily work fast, but it does work, and it works well. You just have to give him a little time."

Miss Dare sighed. "I suppose," she said slowly, "the mystery has remained in place for five years. Another day or so won't hurt." She eyed Beulah suspiciously. "But you're sure Delancey is smart, as you suggest?"

Beulah gave an involuntary laugh. "Not in a bookish way, but he knows a thing or two about human nature. And that helps him solve crimes."

Miss Dare still wasn't sure, but let it drop.

"Maybe," said Eddie, "we should try 'n 'figure out things for ourselves. I mean, Delancey's a sharp tack, for sure, but he don't know everything."

"Out of the mouths of babes," Miss Dare remarked. Eddie took offense at being called a baby, but didn't say anything. (Or so he says. I don't imagine he would've kept quiet at that.)

So they sat and pondered. It's a funny thing, though: Miss Dare and Beulah are sharp cookies too, but they weren't trained to think like a detective. As they sat and thought, then, no brilliant ideas came. They came up with plenty of possibilities, but none of them were good. Every time someone had an idea, someone else would shoot a hole in it. After an hour or so, they gave it up as a bad job. Eddie announced he was going to visit me; Beulah was heading home to finish wrapping presents.

By that time, I was at the church. The place was dark. All the decorations were up, the music in place, the bulletins ready at ushers 'stations. I was about to leave again, but decided to investigate some more. Now don't ask me what I was going to investigate—the scene had been looked over by police and Delancey—but I was sure they had missed something. And, well, maybe I was just a little curious about a church at Christmas. So I walked around.

One thing we'd not done was to explore the rest of the building. I mean, Mr Blank was stabbed in the chancel (sounds painful) or the little room next to it. Not in the back hallway. But what if there was something of interest there, rather than where the murder actually took place? Since no one else was around, now seemed the perfect time to check into that.

I started for the side door that Mr Blank had come out of that day, then changed my mind and exited through another door near the front, this one intended for parishioners, not the minister.

I was in a short hall that bent to the right. Feeble daylight came through windows near the ceiling. At this point, I worried that maybe there was someone in the church after all, that maybe the minister was in his office or something. So I crept very quietly, ready to bolt if I stumbled across anyone. Then my brain came up with an alternative to running: I could just say I wanted to get warm, or some such lie. Is it a sin for a Jewish boy to lie in a Christian church? Anyhow, I wouldn't need the lie because it soon became very clear that no one was around.

Around the corner, I was in a much longer hallway. This ran along the back, parallel with the chancel on the other side of the wall, so there were no doors to my right at first, just a couple to the left, both shut. I tentatively opened the first—an office—the minister's, if the number of books was any indication. Very neat. The next door was a secretarial space, with a typewriter and filing cabinets. Again, very tidy.

The next door, near the far corner, was on the right. This door was open. I peeped inside. It was quite dark, and my eyes had to adjust before I saw it was an area for the minister to prepare to go out to the chancel. There was a door at the other end of the room. So it was through that door that Mr Blank had gone when he was stabbed. That meant I really had to check this place out.

Of course, the cops would've looked at the room closely, for evidence, but that doesn't mean they didn't miss something. It was curious that Delancey hadn't bothered to look at the room at all. I found a light and turned it on.

The light bulb was weak, but in that little room things got bright enough. There wasn't much to see: a tall cabinet that contained ministers' vestments; a few cupboards for various altar things. Nothing exciting. I was about to go when I heard something.

Where had it come from? And what caused it? The sound was nothing like mice or some such. This was more of a thump, but distant. Had it come from outside, like a car accident, or maybe just a door closing? I waited for another sound, but didn't hear anything more. I was pretty sure now that it had come from outside, but I still wanted to be careful, just in case I was wrong.

I turned off the light and peeped into the hallway. This was stupid because anyone in the hall would've seen the light. Anyhow, the hall was deserted. So I started off, to search further.

Next I came to basement steps.

The stairs vanished into darkness only a couple of yards down, and there didn't seem to be a light switch. I did find, though, a pull cord a few feet away, yanked it, and a bulb lit, barely better than it had been without. But like a trail of bread crumbs, I could now see another bulb and pull cord near the bottom.

Unsure whether investigation was worth the bother, I hesitated. Then with a deep breath as if I was diving into a cold lake, I started down. The stairs were wooden and gave a little groan each time I stepped on one, but they held. At the bottom, I pulled the second cord, half hoping the light wouldn't work so I'd have an excuse to turn around. It lit.

The whole thing was a bust. I mean, all that was there was a small table and chair, the coal furnace and the bin and shovel to go with it, and hanging on the wall were a few assorted tools. I frowned. Wasn't the kitchen in the cellar? And this basement was much too small for the rest of the building. I guessed that maybe there was a separate staircase to the kitchen. Relieved, I returned up the stairs, turning off each bulb along the way.

More investigation revealed another staircase down as I'd expected. This was a friendlier area, a kitchen and hall for holding church functions. Just like the other room, though, it yielded no clues. I did see a wide range of sharp knives, from which Mr Blank's killer could have selected. Back upstairs I went.

For a bit, I just stood in the hallway. I was near the end of my exploration, and while it had been interesting, there really was nothing I'd found out; clear enough that there was no hint who had killed Mr Blank or why. There was the choir loft—maybe a clue was up there somewhere—but I'm a little scared of high places, and going up there wasn't something I relished doing. Still, it had to be done, if I wanted to be a detective someday. I'm sure Delancey does plenty of stuff that scares him.

The hallway made sort of a horseshoe shape around the main church area, with the first end shorter than the second. Now, at the longer end of the horseshoe, the quickest way to the loft was through a door nearby. I stepped out and found myself in the back of the church. There was a staircase that led to the choir loft.

With a deep calming breath, I climbed. It wasn't too bad because the stairs were encased on both sides, like the outside entrance to our home. Once at the top, though, the scene changed. Now, you could see everything of the church below except the section directly underneath the loft. It was dizzying. I gripped the nearest chair and sat.

For a few minutes, I just got my breath and tried to calm myself. I looked around, anywhere except down. There were several chairs, music stands, and the organ, with all its stops and pedals. Impressive pipes shone in the dull light, their slitted openings facing the church.

Deciding I'd seen enough, I turned to the stairs, then caught a glimpse of a little door, maybe four or five feet high, set into the wall near the organ. A clue? I figured it was worth a shot, and went to check it out.

I could've saved the time. It was just a small room with sheet music piled on shelves. Didn't take long, but as it turned out, it was a good thing I had spent some time in the room because it was that delay that caused me to see a movement near the chancel door, the one Mr Blank had come from when he was stabbed. It was just a fleeting glimpse as I exited the sheet music room. The chancel door moved, like sometimes happens to Mom's china cabinet doors when a heavy truck drives by.

This was no truck. I was pretty sure someone had nudged the door open slightly, then thought better of it.

If I'd been thinking straight, I would've figured it was a church volunteer, just making sure all was well. Or maybe the janitor, doing some last minute cleaning. But the idea that someone had started out, that maybe they had seen me, and got scared—well, that idea made me bold. Or maybe it was that I'd been shut out of the action recently, and this was my chance to actually do something. Or maybe I was just being stupid.

Doesn't matter. I headed down the loft steps and hurried to the front of the church to see if I could catch whoever it was. I still had my excuse ready, in case it was someone who was *supposed* to be there.

I was soon at the chancel door, and only then did I stop. Cautiously, I opened the door a crack, then wider.

No one was in that little room, but son of a gun if there wasn't something different. I turned on the electric light, first peeping into the hallway to see if I could spot the intruder. The hallway was empty. So after switching on the light I scanned the room.

There it was. In a corner, about level with my waist, the wall was askew, as if someone had taken a sledge hammer to the other side and knocked it off kilter. I was sure that it hadn't been that way before.

I knelt by the wall and examined it. There was a small gap. Reaching to the side of the wall panel, I dug my nails in and pulled. It was a little door, and it was now open. The whole thing slid up and out of grooves on the sides. Behind it was an opening, about three feet square.

Taking a deep breath, I knelt and looked inside. It was dark, not just a little storage cupboard but a good-sized area. How large was impossible to tell because it was too dark and the light from the room didn't go far. So I put out a hand to feel around. I couldn't feel any wall opposite, and to my terror, I couldn't feel a floor either.

Hoping that maybe I just wasn't reaching far enough, I crept closer to the opening and stuck out my arm again.

Next thing I knew, someone shoved me from behind and I was tumbling down into the darkness.

Fourteen

Eddie entered my dad's shop, sort of sheepish. If Mom or Dad had been there, he would've been okay, but seeing as how it was Mr Collins and my Uncle Fred, he was shy. Mr. Collins knows Eddie, of course, and looks down his nose at my buddy. Uncle Fred doesn't know him from Adam, and came up to Eddie.

"Are you lost, m 'lad?" he said jovially.

"No, sir. I was lookin 'for my pal. Iggy."

Uncle Fred's eyes brightened. "Ah! My nephew, Ignatz. Well, he isn't here, m 'lad. Gone out. I assumed to join his little pals."

Now, Eddie fancies himself more grown up than to be referred to as a 'little pal'—like someone from the funny pages—and he frowned. Uncle Fred ignored this.

"Do you know," Eddie asked, warming a little to Uncle Fred despite the insult to his manliness, "where he might've gone?"

"Not a clue. Bradley?" he called to Mr Collins.

Mr Collins, who was helping a man select a diamond bracelet and did not want to be bothered, scowled at my uncle and said, "I am assisting this gentleman." Seeing that gentleman was a little surprised that the friendly clerk had suddenly turned sour, Mr Collins resumed the happy act and added, "Perhaps Mrs Silver has an idea. Why not go up and ask, Master Edward?"

Uncle Fred turned back to Eddie and flourished a hand, like a vaudeville master of ceremonies introducing an act, in the direction of the back room.

Mom was fixing some chicken soup for Dad. She's always liked Eddie, and welcomed him in, all the while stirring the soup so it wouldn't stick. Eddie's stomach growled, kind of loud, but both he and Mom ignored it.

"No," she said to his question, "I don't know where he went. I do know he was going out to look for you. His *uncle*," that word was said rather distastefully, "is here to 'help 'in the shop, so we let Iggy leave."

"No troubles," said Eddie, "I'll find him. Thanks, Mrs Silver." She wished him well and Eddie left.

The first place Eddie decided to check was the right one: the church. By this time I had been sent through that little door. Anyhow, the quiet church spooked my buddy, and after a few calls in the church itself and down some hallways, and getting no reply, Eddie figured I wasn't there, and left. I never heard his calls, but we'll leave that fact for a bit.

Next, Eddie tried Delancey's office. Delancey was seated at his desk. No Beulah. He was a little annoyed at having his thought process interrupted, and didn't seem overly concerned that Eddie couldn't find me. Neither was Eddie, to tell the truth. Both just figured we'd missed each other, and were probably doing a little comic back-and-forth, like some of the movie comedians; in one door, out the other, that sort of thing.

Next it was to Miss Dare's house. Beggars was just taking off her coat, a grocery bag on the hall table. Miss Dare was napping, Beggars said, and was not to be disturbed. No, his friend had not been there.

One last place. Eddie timidly went to Beulah's place. He was embarrassed to be all alone in her apartment, but managed to ask her if she'd seen me, and she shook her head.

"I've tried his place," Eddie said. "The church, Delancey, Agnes. No one's seen him."

For the first time, someone expressed concern.

"That's troubling," Beulah admitted.

"We're probably just missing each other," Eddie said, trying to be casual.

"Have you forgotten so soon about someone taking shots at you and him?"

To tell the truth, Eddie *had* forgotten, even though he still wore the sling from that event. Now he was worried. (Eddie didn't tell me he was worried, later, but I know when he's trying to act like something's not a big deal. He doesn't fool me.)

"Let's get Delancey," Beulah said, "and have him help us look."

"I been there to see him already," Eddie said. "He didn't want to hear about it."

"We'll see about that."

And so saying, they headed for Delancey's office.

What about poor Iggy? I hear you ask. Well, I'll tell you what happened to me.

First thing is, I was stunned. I'd tumbled through the door, down about ten feet, I guess, to a hard dirt floor. Luckily, I hadn't hit my head or anything. Just scraped myself. And my left ankle hurt like a bugger.

I was pretty shaky when I got to my feet. Not just the fall, or that it was unexpected, but that I was sure someone had shoved me. This was made even more certain because that door I'd flown through was now shut. Someone had left me there to die.

Who could it be? I wondered. Then I shook my head. Time to worry about that later. For now, I had to figure a way out of this mess.

I looked up to the door. There was no way I could climb the dirt walls, even if my ankle wasn't hurting me.

What struck me as odd was that there seemed to be a faint light in the area where I was. And fresher air than you'd expect. So there had to be another way out. I just had to find it.

After a few moments to settle down from my brush with death, I looked around. The room was pretty dark, so I couldn't see much of anything where I stood, but it became clear that this wasn't a little room, as I'd first thought, but the start of a passageway that was vaguely lit from somewhere in the distance. In fact, there was a faint glow. I slowly worked my way towards it.

Were there rats or some other nasty creatures down there? If so, I couldn't hear or see any. I was grateful for that. Eddie's the guy who likes snakes and mice; I'd rather they all disappeared from the planet. Anyhow, none of those vile creatures seemed to be in the passageway.

As I crept my way along, the light gradually seemed to get a little stronger. The passageway didn't have any corners, but it curved ever so slightly to my right. And as it curved, the light grew brighter. When the curve ended and I was in a straight line again, the light could be clearly seen. It was strong now, coming from what looked like a little room maybe twenty feet ahead.

I was ready to call out, or at least break into a trot to get to the room, when I stopped cold. What if someone was in that room? I know someone pushed me down here in the first place, but was it possible there was a second person involved in the killing of Mr Blank? A second person who might have taken those pot shots at Eddie and me? So I stopped to think.

I also listened and waited. Either someone was very quiet or there was no one in the room ahead. I moved forward, very slow and cautious. As I did, the tunnel walls became more rustic. Small tree roots poked out here and there, and there was a dampness to the dirt that hadn't been there before. There were even a couple of small puddles that I avoided—not because it would get my shoes wet but because I wanted to keep as quiet as possible.

It wasn't easy to get myself to move on because even though there was no evidence of anyone around, I felt sure there *must* be someone in that lit room. What could I do, though? I mean, if I went back to where I'd started, there was no way to climb up to the little door. And if there was someone in the room ahead, that person would find me eventually. Might as well get it over with, as my favorite aunt used to say when it was time for bed.

All my dithering, and there was no one in there anyway.

The room was actually sort of cozy. Light had come from a large oil lamp. The oil was low, but there was a bottle nearby that contained plenty more. There was also a box of matches. All this was sitting on a small table off to the side. Two chairs were next to the table, well-used but sturdy.

What really dominated the room, though, was an altar. Not large, but bigger than the table, and head on from the entrance. The altar was stone, and must've been a real bear to get into the room from above. It must have been brought down in pieces. Anyhow, on the altar were two unlit candles in silver holders, a very old Bible opened to Psalms on a gilt stand. There was also a silver cross on a stand in the back center of the altar.

That was a little disconcerting, but for the most part, like I said, it was a nice little room. I sat on one of the chairs to catch my breath. Not that I'd been exerting myself, but I'd been so scared of who might be in the room, my heart was pounding and I was shaking a bit. My ankle was starting to really pain me, and I was also a little thirsty, now that I had time to think about it.

During those few minutes, I pondered what to do next. Nice as this room was, I couldn't see that it was going to help much in my quest to get out of this tunnel. I looked all around the room, and then up. There was a trapdoor in the ceiling.

Excited, I tried to reach it—the ceiling was lower there than it was in the place I'd first gone into the tunnel—but it was still too high. So I pulled a chair around and stood on it. I'm not the tallest kid in my class, not by a long shot, and my fingertips just barely reached the door. Certainly not enough to shove it open. I put the chair back and, after moving the lamp and other things onto the floor, I brought the table around to under the trapdoor.

I climbed on the table, which wobbled on the uneven ground, put a hand on the damp wall to stabilize, and shakily stood. Now I could reach the door easily, and figuring my adventure was near an end, I pushed up.

Nothing—the door didn't budge one bit. I pushed again with all my might, but the only thing that paid me back was a little shower of dirt that got in my hair and on my face. I got down from the table. What was I going to do now?

That decision was made for me when the lamp light suddenly grew dim and went out.

Meantime, Beulah and Eddie were at Delancey's place. He didn't seem real happy to see them on his doorstep, but he let them in.

"As you're here," Delancey said, "here you go."

He handed Beulah a small package, wrapped somewhat slapdashedly in Christmas paper. You could tell, Eddie said to me later, that Delancey had tried to make it look good but failed. Beulah had her handbag with her and took out a similarly-sized box for Delancey. Of course, hers was in perfect shape, even though she had carried the thing in her purse.

"Now," Delancey said, waving them to chairs and carefully placing the gift from Beulah under his tabletop tree. "What brings you here?"

"It's Iggy," Eddie blurted out. "He's missing."

Delancey sighed, a little impatient. "Missing?" He looked to Beulah for confirmation.

"We've been to every place he might be," she said. "He no longer has to work at his father's shop because they have help now, so Iggy went off to find us. I take it he hasn't been here?"

"Nope."

Eddie couldn't read Delancey. Was he worried? Annoyed? Angry? If so, at whom? At me, for getting misplaced, at Eddie for worrying, or at Beulah for taking it all too seriously? After a long pause, Delancey spoke again.

"I take it you checked the church?"

Eddie nodded. "Church, Miss Hogwood's, everywhere."

"And you made sure he wasn't back home?"

"Well, no."

Delancey sighed again. The telephone was next to him. He picked up the receiver and dialed. Delancey has an uncanny ability to memorize things like telephone numbers. He probably found Iggy's number for some other reason and never forgot it. He seemed to hesitate now, unsure I guess whether to worry Mom. Anyhow, he put through the call.

"Mrs Silver? Tom Delancey here... Yes, and happy Hanukah to you... Sure... Anyhow, Eddie seems to be of the opinion your son is missing. Is he home? I

113

see... Well, sure, you've got a lot on your plate... No, I'm sure he's just running around, the little scamp... Yes... Well, if I find him... Sure. Sure thing... Well, goodbye, ma'am. I'll be in touch." He hung up. "Iggy hasn't been home, so far as his mom knows."

"Delancey..." Beulah said, worried now.

"Yeah, I know. By this time, he should've checked in with one of us. Okay. Let me get my coat and we'll go out looking." He paused in mid-rise. "I suppose he hasn't been to your house, Eddie?"

Eddie shrugged. "Mom's workin 'extra hours. No one would've been home."

Delancey completed his rise and went for his coat and hat. As he sat to put on his overshoes, Delancey muttered, "That kid better really be in trouble, or I'll..."

He didn't complete the sentence.

Fifteen

For a few seconds, I panicked.

There I was in pitch darkness, in a strange place. "Get a hold of yourself," I muttered. "At least you're not standing on the table. Not likely to fall." The main thing was to get the lamp and the oil and the matches, and relight the flame. Yeah, that was all I had to do.

I waited a little longer, hoping there might be a little help from the door above; that maybe a sliver of daylight would slip through the cracks, but no. The door must have been so crusted shut, or else was so close-fitting, that not a bit of light came through.

Curse my imagination! Just as I was calmed down, it suddenly sprang to mind that if the doors were sealed so tightly, maybe the oxygen would run out. Was that why the lamp went out? Panic started to come over me again. This time, I shook my head to get the thought out of my brain. There was plenty of oxygen in the room. My breath was gasping a bit because I was frightened, not because I was starved of air.

The best thing was to try for the lamp first because that was glass and on the floor. If I accidentally kicked it, I was doomed. I tried hard to remember where I was in relation to the lamp when the light had gone out, and thought I knew, but when I got on my hands and knees, all I did was crawl into a wall.

I stopped crawling around. I remembered now: I'd set the lamp some distance away so I *didn t* accidentally kick it over. Finding it now, when I was all turned around, could be a challenge. So I changed my tactics and searched for the matches instead. If I lit a match, I'd see the lamp.

But now I had no idea in which direction to go. I chose left and decided that, since the table with the matches was against a wall, I'd run into it eventually.

I went the wrong way. I followed the wall around, and then suddenly it wasn't there. Really panicked now, then calmer: I was at the entrance into the tunnel. Sure enough, a grope into the empty space revealed a corner. So I started back the way I'd come on the wall and finally found the glass oil bottle. I fumbled a bit more and nearly knocked over the bottle before finding the matches. Fumbled a bit more, broke one match, then finally lit another.

In all the movies I've ever seen with people lighting matches in dark rooms, the room immediately gets flooded with light and you can see practically everything. Don't you believe it: I could barely see the hand that held the match. Of course, in those films, when someone lights a match, the bad guy is revealed to be standing right behind the hero. That didn't happen to me either. And the feeble light was better than total darkness by a long shot. But the match wouldn't stay lit forever, and I had no time to bask in its glow. I had to find the lamp, refill the oil and relight it quickly before my match went out.

I picked up the lamp, set it on the table. The match went out. I lit another (lucky there were plenty in the box) and undid the lamp chimney. Pouring the oil while holding the match was near impossible, so I pulled out the stopper to the oil bottle and purposely blew out the match—first making sure I knew exactly where everything was.

One hand on the opening of the lamp's oil well, the other on the oil bottle. I poured a goodly amount in, then lit another match and touched it to the wick. Success! I put the chimney back on the lamp, stoppered the oil bottle, and sighed with relief. I was sweating like nobody's business, though the room was chilly.

After I'd calmed down a bit, I returned to the table and climbed up again. Giving it all I had, I shoved hard on the door. Was it my imagination, or did it seem to give a little? The thought got me excited, and I pushed harder. Sweat was really pouring off me now. No... it must've been my imagination after all. The door didn't move.

I had a new source of hope, though: I thought I heard voices from a distance. Forgetting that it could be the one who shoved me down the hole in the first place, I called out. The noise stopped, as if listening. I called again. My throat was really dry now, and it didn't come out as loud as the first call. I tried again. No more noise was heard. I waited. Maybe it was someone who couldn't tell where the call came from, and was getting closer. So I tried a couple more times.

It was useless. Whatever or whoever it was, never made another sound.

Meanwhile, Delancey, Beulah, and Eddie walked to the church. Eddie was convinced that's where I would've gone.

"But," Beulah said, "surely if Iggy saw there was no one there, he would've left?"

"I thought about that," Eddie replied. "An 'I think he would've done some investigatin 'in the church. Might've really gone over the place, with a fine tooth brush."

"Well," Delancey put in, "we'll know soon enough if he's around. Though I don't know. You already looked and Iggy wasn't there."

Eddie didn't have a reply for that. He just looked concerned, and Beulah gave no further objection.

The church was pretty much as it had been. All decked out for Christmas, but quiet, like a parade ready to start. They stood in the church itself and looked around. Delancey called my name. No reply. I think he was ready to call it quits, at least for the church, but he caught Eddie's look, and agreed to look around a bit.

I won't bore you with their search because it was more or less what I had done, only with three people instead of one. They searched high and low. Beulah went into the room where the little door was, but it was so small she didn't need to call out. She did say my name, in case I was hiding in a cabinet (okay, yes, I was small enough to fit in one of the vestment cabinets) got no reply, and left. I heard none of that.

After another ten minutes or so, they agreed I wasn't there, and got ready to go. They would've left too, except for something happening that startled the pants off them all.

But that's getting ahead of things. Let's go back to me, still in the tunnel.

After my failure at trying to get the door open, I sat on one of the chairs, trying to think of my next move. I wished Eddie was there. He's not the sharpest dart on the board, but sometimes he blabbers on and on and actually runs into something that makes perfect sense. He just thinks of all possible solutions, no matter how lame-brained they might be. I could've used that just then.

But since Eddie wasn't there, I had to come up with my own solution. I thought about going back the way I'd come. The door I'd gone through wasn't blocked—I hoped. I mean, what if the guy who shoved me through and shut the door had also moved a heavy piece of furniture in front of it? I'd *never* get out. And I was getting hungry now.

Still, it seemed to be the best possible solution. Maybe the bad guy had figured the door was too high up for me to reach anyway, so where was the harm in leaving it unblocked? I decided to go back and try. Best possible solution, I thought, was to haul the table and a chair through the tunnel, set the chair on the table and then climb up. It'd be precarious, but I'd be able to reach the door then, for sure.

So I took up the lamp and a chair, and slowly started back through the tunnel. My hurt ankle, which I'd mostly ignored so far, began to bother me now. Between my limp, and lugging the chair and lamp, I must've looked like some poor soldier back from the war. How would I get the table all that way? Moving it around just in that little room was one thing. Taking it down a long tunnel was another.

As I think about it now, I might've run into the guy who'd pushed me down there, lurking in the shadows. Back then, it never crossed my mind. I was too determined to get out to think of such things.

Carrying the chair that way was cumbersome, and my limp got worse as I made my way along, using a leg as sort of a nudge to the chair. I stopped only once, for a minute to rest on the chair, my ankle throbbing. Then I went on

At last I could see the end, just ahead. The glow of my oil lamp caught the opposing wall and the trapdoor, so far above. I wondered if I could ever reach it, even with a table and chair. That was, if I could carry the table. Well, I told myself, I'd have to do it. Maybe, if nothing else, I could take one of those candlesticks and rap on the door to draw someone's attention. Whatever it would take, I'd have to do, or die.

Turns out, I didn't have to lug the table or rap with a candlestick because in the glimmer of lamplight, I saw something I'd missed completely when I first fell.

There was a small recess near the tunnel entry, hidden by shadow. The recess was actually a nook, a small opening in the wall that had a space to the right. The space was easy to miss in darkness. Even in lamplight, it was barely visible. I took the lamp to this recess and shone the light inside.

A ladder, propped up against the wall! So that was how people came and went. They could easily reach the ladder through the opening above. It was makeshift, to be sure, but tall enough for me to reach the door. I set down the chair and lamp and took the ladder from its nook. I examined it in full light. It was, as I said, makeshift: thick branches crudely tied together with twine. But the twine was secure, the branches not brittle, and in fact the ladder was in fairly good shape, not used much, from the looks of it.

I propped the ladder against the wall nearest the door and with tentative steps, climbed. As I've said, I'm no Jim Thorpe. Climbing the ladder—especially with a bum ankle, and especially when the ladder was uneven, as was the floor—proved to be a challenge. No matter, I would do it. Now all I could do was pray that the one who'd shoved me down there hadn't blocked the entrance.

That climb felt like it took ten minutes instead of twenty or thirty seconds. Each rung, I tested with my weight before committing myself.

I finally reached the door. I said another short prayer and pushed. The door resisted. Then I remembered the door slid up to open. I put my palms on it and shoved—success. I think I let out a cry of relief. Forgetting that the bad guy might still be around, forgetting my injured ankle, forgetting my fear of heights, I clambered up the final few rungs and hauled myself up and through the door.

For a time, I just lay there, panting. My ankle *really* started to throb now. After a minute or two, I propped myself up, and gradually got to my feet.

That was when I heard voices. At first I was scared, that it was someone come to kill me, after all. Then I recognized them. I exited through the same door that Mr Blank had come through when he was stabbed and, moving fast and silent, caught up with Eddie, Beulah, and Delancey. They nearly fell over when they saw me, dirty, disheveled, on one foot to save my ankle, but alive and kicking.

Sixteen

Beulah gave me a hug, which made Eddie really jealous. Delancey looked stern, like a parent, and Eddie hid his jealousy with a cry of relief that I was safe and sound. After I got let go from Beulah, they noticed the shape I was in.

"We'd better get that ankle looked at," Delancey said. I couldn't tell if he was angry or what. "And you look like something the cat dragged in," he went on. "What the hell happened to you?"

Explaining was harder than I'd expected. I mean, did I have to go through the long rigmarole about my search of the church? Nah, but I did have to mention my trip to the choir loft, and seeing someone near that chancel door—or at least I *thought* I'd seen someone, I put in, showing how open-minded I was. Delancey always says not to jump to conclusions, that detectives get themselves in a world of trouble if they do.

Then I went on about how I went to the little room, and finding the door slightly ajar, and how when I looked inside, someone shoved me in. Beulah let out a gasp. Eddie looked even more jealous of my adventure without him. Delancey kept his head.

"You're sure someone pushed you." He said it as a statement, not giving me the third degree.

"Positive," I nodded. "There's no way I would've fallen inside otherwise."

"And what happened?" Beulah asked. "Where did you fall into?"

This was going to take more explaining. I'm afraid I did a bad job of it. Delancey lost patience midway through and insisted I show them instead. So we traipsed back through the chancel and I showed them the little door. Delancey got down on hands and knees to look through. The lamp still glowed on the floor at the bottom, the ladder was still there too. He sat up and looked at me critically.

"Now hear this. You two," he waggled a finger at Eddie and me," are off this case as of now. This makes twice someone's tried to bump you off, or at least hurt you. I won't have it. Whatever happened to getting all excited over Christmas? Or Hanukkah, or whatever? So, here's what's going to happen: I'm going down there.

Beulah, see if the church office is open and telephone Inspector Fenrow and get him here. Then telephone a doctor to look at Iggy's ankle. You two will stay right here while I'm down there and Beulah's telephoning. You're not to move a muscle. Got it?"

We looked at Beulah for help, but she shook her head. Eddie and I sullenly said we got it.

Maybe seeing we weren't thrilled, Beulah said, "For once I'm with Delancey. It's far too dangerous for you to stay involved."

There wasn't anything more to say. If we'd lost Beulah, there was no chance of swaying Delancey. She went to the church office, Delancey crawled through the door and started down the ladder, and Eddie and I sat on chairs to wait.

"You've done it now," Eddie said quietly.

"*Me!* Just 'cause I was the one who found the door?"

"Yeah, yeah… Was it really creepy down there?"

"You don't know the half of it!"

I told him what had happened. I *might* have embellished a bit when it came to describing what I'd gone through in the tunnel—maybe. Anyhow, it had been pretty traumatic, and I didn't stretch the truth about that. By the time I'd finished with my story, Beulah had returned, and I could hear Delancey below, coughing a little. Pretty soon we were all together again, and not five minutes after that we were joined by three others.

The first to arrive was the minister. Beulah figured she should call him too, since it was his church after all.

"I just cannot understand it," he said, shaking his head after Delancey had told him what was up. "These are dark days for our church!" he rumbled in his best hellfire voice. "*Dark* days!"

"So you never knew there was a tunnel there?"

"No! To be honest, that little table there was always nearer that door." He waggled a finger at the tunnel door Delancey had shown him, as if the door itself was evil." And besides which, you simply can't see it readily, can you?"

Delancey had to admit that was true. After all, the cops had looked around the room after Blank got stabbed, and had missed it.

"Whatever could it be for?" the minister wondered aloud.

"Not sure," Delancey said, "but there are some things down there you really ought to see. Then maybe you can—"

He was interrupted by the doctor's arrival. The doc looked over my ankle and declared it sprained (not before turning it this way and that, nearly making me jump out of my skin). He said I would be perfectly fine, though it would hurt like a son of a gun for a while. "Don't use it any more than you need to," was his sage advice. A quick bandage job to keep my ankle straight (and cut off circulation) and he left.

The doctor had barely gone when Inspector Fenrow himself arrived. He was none too happy. Turns out, he's one of those mugs who waits till the last minute to Christmas shop for his wife, and he'd had to rush with his purchase in order to get to the church. He turned to me.

"I thought," he said, cold as the grave, "that we agreed you would stay out of this. Do you mind telling me what in holy hell you were doing here, alone?"

The minister let out a little gasp at his language, but Fenrow ignored him.

"I was lookin 'for Eddie. And Beulah and Delancey. Thought maybe they'd be here."

"Right. So you just thought maybe they'd gone through a door nobody knew about? Sweet Fanny Adams!" He was thoroughly disgusted.

"I didn't go through on *purpose*," I protested. Mom always told me not to talk back, but doggone it, he was making me mad. "I was lookin 'around for them, and saw someone going through that chancel door, and thought I'd follow them."

Fenrow threw up his hands. "It never dawned on you that it might be the one who killed Mr Blank? That he might just take a shine to killing you too?"

"I'm sorry. I didn't think." I admit it, he not only was making me mad, he was making me feel like a dope, and I had to fight back tears. Delancey came to my rescue.

"He did what he did, Inspector. The fact is, when he came in here, that little door was open, and when he looked, someone shoved him down the chute."

"And there's a tunnel, Beulah said?" The inspector was all civil to Delancey, talking as if they were chatting about who might win the Rose Bowl. That got me madder still.

"Yes. I think you should see it."

"Sure thing. But first," he waved a finger at Eddie and me," you two, out. Go home."

Eddie and I looked at each other. We didn't want to go, but Delancey looked ready to burst a blood vessel if we refused, so we grudgingly agreed.

What happened next at the church, we were told later by Delancey and Beulah. "I think," said the inspector to Beulah, "you should go too. For safety's sake." Delancey looked amused because he knew what sort of reaction that would get.

"Not on your tintype, buster," she replied—though I think maybe they cleaned it up when they told us later. "I'm staying."

Inspector Fenrow sighed. The reverend excused himself and headed for home. Delancey led the way through the little door and down the ladder. He took up the lantern and the three slowly walked through the tunnel.

"What is this place?" Fenrow said.

"Dunno," Delancey replied.

"I read once," Beulah said, "that in England there are priest holes, places where Roman Catholic priests hid from Protestants when there was persecution. But that never happened in this country, as far as I know."

"And this is pretty elaborate," Fenrow noted.

They finished their trip through the tunnel without another word. In the little room, Delancey set the lamp on the table as they looked around. No one spoke: they were too puzzled by what they saw.

"Maybe," Delancey said slowly, "this explains the black robe Blank was wearing when he was killed. The altar, the Bible—some sort of ritual?"

Fenrow made a sour face. "I don't like the sound of that. When I was coming up through the ranks, we had some cockamamie group who believed the world was coming to an end. Didn't help that we had the Great War and Spanish Flu, one right after the other. They used to do all sorts of sacrificing. Pigs and chickens and so forth. The 'high priest', as they called him, was a shyster by the name of Church, a guy who really just wanted to bilk his followers out of their cash. We arrested him—and his followers *still* believed what he was peddling! We had proof he was a cheat, but oh no, they couldn't believe the *facts*." He shook his head.

"I think," Beulah said quietly, "people just want to believe in *something*. No matter how strange it may be, or even if it's proven false. To them, it will always be true."

They were silent for a bit, then Delancey said, "Well, this is getting us nowhere. Iggy said he tried that door," he pointed to the door in the ceiling, "and couldn't get it open. Let's give it a shot."

Delancey is taller than I am, of course, but he could only touch the door with fingertips. So he pulled a chair over, tested his weight on the seat and then climbed onto it. Now his head nearly grazed the ceiling. He adjusted a bit, and put his hands on the door. It didn't give.

"Sealed?" Fenrow asked.

"Something on top?" Beulah asked.

"I don't think so. I think it's just crusted shut from disuse."

But the more he tried, the more he failed. I thought I had managed to move it a little, but given Delancey's struggles, I must've imagined it. After a few more tries, Delancey felt it give, but he was sweating and red-faced.

"Let me try," Fenrow said. "You take a rest."

The inspector wasn't trying to be cocky. Like I said, they're buddies like Eddie and me. Delancey climbed down, Fenrow went up, and gave it a shot.

I should tell you the difference between the two men. Both are strong, but Delancey is wirier; Fenrow is bulkier, more like a football player. So Fenrow pushed, and the door seemed to give a bit more. After a few more tries, and a little success, Delancey took it back. To make a long story short, they finally got the door open.

Delancey popped his head through the opening. Snow and trees all around.

"I think," he announced to the other two below, "the snow had piled on top of it." When he had climbed out completely though, he adjusted that assessment. "And possibly someone chucked a big rock on top of the door."

Fenrow was just then climbing through. "Sounds suspicious to me," he grunted.

Delancey lent a hand to Beulah—actually sort of yanked her up by the wrists. For a few moments, they looked around to get their bearings.

It was Beulah who spotted it.

"Isn't that Miss Hogwood's house?"

Sure enough. They were essentially in her backyard.

Seventeen

"Now I'm getting it," Inspector Fenrow said. "The killer of Mrs Clapham took her body through that tunnel and put her in Miss Hogwood's house."

They had started to slog through the snow towards Miss Dare's house.

"But why?" Beulah wanted to know. "Why go through all the elaborate gyrations of lugging her through the tunnel? Why not leave her where she was killed? Come to that, why kill her at all? You still haven't answered that question."

Fenrow was a little hurt. He expected those cutting comments from Delancey. Beulah was always a bit nicer—to *everyone*.

"If," Delancey cut in, "Mrs Clapham's body was taken through the tunnel, then it points to someone in the church."

"Mr Blank?"

"Possibly. But then who killed Blank?" Delancey wanted to know. "I don't buy it. I think the same person killed 'em both. If nothing else, it makes our job a lot easier."

"And don't forget," Beulah said, "that same someone is after Iggy and Eddie."

"Right."

The trio had reached Miss Dare's house and walked around to the front, where they just stood for a bit. Finally, Inspector Fenrow knocked. Beggars, the housekeeper, answered, saw who it was, sighed, and let them in. They found the author immersed in pages of scribbled notes, muttering, "Damn it! How do I get Slake Thirsty out of *this?*" Seeing the visitors, she looked relieved and set pen and paper onto a nearby table. As there was already a big stack of papers on that little table, the whole shebang slipped to the floor. Miss Dare ignored it.

"What can I do for you?"

Somehow, Delancey was appointed spokesman. He rubbed his nose with two fingers and began the long explanation of how they came to be there. Miss Dare didn't show a bit of surprise.

Yet she said, "You amaze me, Delancey. A *tunnel*, you say? Ending in the woods? To answer your question, those trees are indeed on my property. My father always intended to chop them down for cheap fire wood, but I talked him out of it. No one wants to look out the back window at a bunch of stumps. Now, it seems, we might've been better off if he had cut down the trees. We would've found the tunnel door then. And you suspect the body was transported to my study via the tunnel?"

"It makes the most sense," Delancey said. "Otherwise, Mrs Clapham's body would have been lugged along a city sidewalk. Even at night, there was a chance the killer would be seen."

"Yes. That would make sense," she mused. "Of course, that means the killer knew about the tunnel, which would seem to cast light on someone connected with the church."

"That's what we thought," the inspector cut in. He'd clearly been thinking about it as Delancey had spoken. "In the original investigation, nearly every suspect was connected with the church. Even the husband attends regularly."

"So," Beulah said, "you had no knowledge of the tunnel, or what it might be used for?"

"Not a bit," Miss Dare replied with a head shake. "I don't go into those woods much. But may I ask you to show it to me? The entrance, I mean. I have no inclination to go into the tunnel itself."

"Delancey can do that," Inspector Fenrow said. "I have to be going." Which he did.

Miss Dare put on a coat and boots and joined Delancey and Beulah outside. They tromped through the yard and were soon at the tunnel door. Delancey opened it, just to show her inside, then shut it again.

"Any footprints leading to or from the door?" Miss Dare asked.

Delancey shook his head. "The ground is too scuffled by furry woodland creatures. Then, too, we had that snow…"

"Yes, I understand. Well, thank you for showing it to me. Now I have to ponder what to do with the thing. It's clearly a danger. What if a child discovered it and fell inside?"

"You forget," Beulah put in," a child was already down there, and nearly didn't make it out."

"Iggy. Yes." She said it matter-of-factly, not with emotion.

Delancey said, "Maybe if you got a strong padlock, until you figured out what to do next? I noticed a loop on the outside, door and frame. Must've been locked sometime before." He brushed snow away with his toe and revealed the loop.

"Good idea. Actually, I think there's one in my father's study. I shall find the key and lock, and do it forthwith."

Delancey was amused. He'd never heard anyone use "forthwith" in a conversation.

Meantime, Eddie and I were commiserating. We trudged along, headed for Eddie's place, hands in our pockets, figuring the world was at an end. Our buddy, Delancey, had kicked us out of an investigation! And Beulah was on his side! And they meant it! It was like someone had told us Babe Ruth was on the take, or that there was no Santa Claus. We just couldn't fathom it. When Eddie suggested we go to his place, to talk it over, there wasn't much zip in the idea, but we had nothing better to do, so I agreed.

Eddie's mom worked long hours during the holidays. Seems Christmas shoppers like to take a break at the lunch counter to refresh themselves. Mind you, Eddie's mom didn't mind the long hours. She looked forward to the fatter pay check and more tips, so maybe they could have a little more for Christmas.

Going to Eddie's place always made me a little sad. I mean, my folks aren't rich, but they do okay, and we have a nice place. The apartment where Eddie and his mom live isn't so nice. Oh, it's clean and neat—Eddie's mom is a great housekeeper—but they just don't have as much, and it shows. And that makes me sad. Times like that, I make up my mind to take over the shop after Dad retires (though I don't really want to) if only to give Eddie a good-paying job. Don't know if he'd take it, working for me, and maybe he'd see it as charity, but I'd offer.

We went to Eddie's room, which is real small but has a bed and a dresser, and I took along a chair to sit on, while Eddie sat cross-legged on the bed.

"So what do we do now?" he asked.

"I dunno. Delancey seemed pretty serious about our staying out of it."

"I know. But doggone it, this is *our* investigation! We brought it to Delancey's attention, what with Mrs Clapham gettin 'herself killed and found in Miss Dare's study, and all. If not for us, there never would've been anything done about that."

"True. Of course, maybe Mr Blank would still be breathing."

"Okay, so that's bad. I admit it. But I still don't wanna give up."

"But if we keep investigating, Delancey or the inspector is bound to bump into us, and then we'll really be up a creek. Especially with the inspector. He could have us *arrested*, for getting in the way, or some such."

"Which means," Eddie said with a crafty look, "we'll have to be careful."

I like that look in Eddie, except when he's got something planned against me. Anyhow, I sat forward. "Got an idea?"

The crafty look evaporated. "No. I was hopin 'you had something."

"Well, lemme think."

So for a good twenty minutes, we sat in his room, pondering our next move. Going to the church again was out. Next day would be Christmas Eve, and there was bound to be folks milling around then. And it was getting late, so there was no time to do it just then. Besides, I'd already searched the place and nearly got killed for my efforts.

"What if," Eddie said slowly, "we went to Miss Dare? I mean, *she* didn't tell us to buzz off, did she? She might lend us a hand."

"She might, though I don't know what good she could do."

"Well, it beats sittin 'around."

This logic, I could not argue with, so we headed for Miss Dare's house.

On the way, who did we meet but Reverend Willoughby from the church. He smiled angelically at us, and started to walk by, when he recognized our mugs and stopped, called us back.

"Ah! You are Eddie? And this is your little Jewish pal, Iggy?"

"That's right, sir," Eddie said. He isn't much for church, but he knows enough to be awed by a minister.

"Well," the minister said to me, "you had quite the adventure! I trust you're hale now?"

I had no idea what "hale" was, but he wanted me to be it, so I said I was.

He beamed. "Good! We are all God's creatures, after all, and I would no sooner wish you harm than I would any member of my congregation."

"Any idea who done it?" Eddie asked.

"Not a bit. The inspector seems to think it's one of my flock, but I cannot abide such a notion. They are all peace-loving, kind—well, even the ones who aren't, wouldn't endanger the life of a child."

"Even if he's Jewish?" I asked, sarcastically.

"Even if he's Jewish," the reverend replied, completely missing my tone. "Well, I can only hope this will not sully the celebration of our Lord's birth. Good day to you both!"

With that, he toddled off. Eddie regarded him with a sour look. "Makes me feel like I'm two years old," he muttered, and we started off again.

The door to Miss Dare's place was opened by Beggars, made me wonder if she ever got a break—who didn't want to let us in to see her boss.

"Miss Hogwood is resting," said the sourpuss, "and cannot be disturbed."

"But we got to talk to her!" Eddie insisted, louder than he had to (I think to try to rouse Miss Dare, in case she was within earshot). It didn't work.

"No," said Beggars coldly. "Now begone!" She shut the door in our faces.

"Now what?" Eddie asked.

"Let's go around to the side. Maybe she's sitting near a window."

We traipsed all around the house, saw no one inside, and were about to give up. Eddie is determined, though, and before I could stop him, he found a window that wasn't locked, opened it and crawled inside. I was frozen to the spot, 'til Eddie reached out his hands to yank me in after him.

We were in the kitchen. Eddie led the way out the door into the hallway. No one was around. Not surprising, since the staff was so small.

"You think she's upstairs?" Eddie whispered.

"Probably. We didn't see her through any of the windows."

Eddie nodded and we slowly crept up the stairs. I glanced back a few times, in case Beggars saw us. Don't know where we would've gone if she had. Anyhow, we made it to the top without being seen and, brazen as can be, Eddie started opening doors. A sudden thought flashed through my brain: what if Miss Dare was taking a bath? That would be all we'd need. When Eddie opened one door to reveal an empty bathroom, I was relieved.

We didn't find Miss Dare upstairs. Eddie stood in the middle of the hallway, fists on hips, his best Sherlock Holmes stance.

"Guess we need to check downstairs," he whispered.

I nodded, and off we went down the steps. Now we had to be more cautious. Beggars had to be somewhere. And we finally found out where.

From a room to one side was the sound of the housekeeper and Miss Dare. They seemed to be arguing but with those two, it could be hard to tell.

"And you turned them out?" Miss Dare asked, accusing.

"You wanted time to rest, miss." Calm as you please.

"I know that's what I said, Beggars. Damn it! How can I rest? My head is spinning with all this! The murders, my story…"

"Maybe a sleeping powder—"

"No! What I *could* use is a stiff drink of something flammable. Fetch me the decanter, Beggars. And if I catch you putting water in it again, we'll part ways."

"Yes, miss."

There was an edge to Beggars's voice—cold, but polite. Made me shudder. Eddie and I ducked into the shadows in case Beggars had to go past us. She didn't; apparently the brandy was in the same room. Before I could think of what to do, Eddie came out of the shadows and headed for the room. Calling out was pointless. I shrugged and followed along.

"Eddie! Iggy!" Miss Dare cried as we entered. I looked for signs of displeasure. There were none, at least not from *her*.

Miss Dare was seated in a wingback chair so large she nearly disappeared in it. She had a blanket over her lap. In her hands were a pen and notebook, though not the mess we had grown used to seeing her with when she wrote. At her side was a small glass of brandy, untouched so far. Clearly, this was serious work she was doing. There was also a neat stack of papers, old from the look of them, on another table at her other side.

Beggars came in, looked ready to boot us out, but Miss Dare waved us over.

"Come!" she said. "Sit. Thank you, Beggars. That will be all. Now sit. What can you tell me?"

"Actually," said Eddie, "we was hoping you could tell us what's up. Any news?"

"There is," she said. "Not over an hour ago, I received a most unexpected visit from Delancey, Beulah, and that inspector. They informed me that the tunnel exit—the one you tried to pry open, Iggy—comes out in my own backyard!"

You already know that, but it was big news to Eddie and me. She told us about the location, in the clump of trees she called her woods, and of course we wanted to see it for ourselves. Miss Dare shook her head.

"For one thing, I've put a padlock on the door, as the inspector suggested, so all you'd be seeing is the wooden door. But that's not the half of it." She placed a palm on the stack of old papers. "I've found something. At least, I *think* I've found something.

"You see, when my father purchased this house many years ago, he did so from a family that was well known in town. The Hagers. You might recall the name."

She looked from one of us to the other. Seeing our blank faces, she shrugged.

"No matter. The Hagers were only one of the founding families of this city, that's all." Her sarcasm was lost on Eddie; it wasn't on me, but I didn't respond. "There were four families who first settled in this area, back when Indians were in charge. Mind you, these weren't those appalling stereotypical natives we see in films or in *some* magazine stories I could name. They were friendly people who simply wanted to live in peace. Mr Hager set up a general store—"

"Hager's!" I cried suddenly. Hager's was a department store in town. It wasn't one of the largest, and to tell the truth, the building was pretty dilapidated. Mom never shopped there.

"Precisely," Miss Dare said. "So Mr Hager set up his store, Mr Delavan, the mill, Mr Peterson, the hotel, and Mr Wesley, the church. At first, they struggled financially, as you might expect. All but the mill. That place was successful almost from the get-go. Pretty soon because we are so close to the lake, and because it was a peaceable settlement, and because the mill required a large workforce, the place attracted more people. The town incorporated. They wanted to name the place after one of the men, but couldn't agree who should get the honors, so they settled for our current name."

Eddie was getting restless. History always bores him. Miss Dare noticed his fidgets. "Do you need a bathroom?" she asked.

Eddie, embarrassed, said no.

"Well, if you do, by all means go. I don't want to reupholster that sofa. Now where was I? Oh, yes. For a time—this was about a hundred years ago—the Hagers prospered as the rest of the founders did. But over the years, as the city grew, competition sprung up, especially for the hotel and the store. Within my own lifetime," (which we thought was a pretty long time)," Hager's became a lesser player in the field of retail."

Miss Dare looked quite pleased with that analogy, and jotted it down on a scrap of paper before she went on.

"By this time, the original Mr Hager was dead, of course. In fact, it was his grandson who now owned the store and this house. The Hagers could no longer afford such a large property. My father made money… through various endeavors and, while we did not need such an immense house, he bought it on the cheap from the Hager family. I sometimes think he took advantage of the situation, but honestly, no one else seemed to want the place. So Father bought it."

"I think it's a great house," I put in.

"Thank you, Iggy. It's really much too large for me, and was too large for my father and me when he was alive."

"Your mother?" Eddie asked. He was concerned about such things as absent parents.

"Died when I was a tot. My father would never talk about it, but I believe it was smallpox or some such. At any rate, it was really just me and the servants here most of the time. Father was busy working. When he died and I took control of the place, I wanted to sell, but as I've said, my publisher thought it might be a good place for entertaining. I despise entertaining. Nevertheless, inertia has kept me here, and probably will keep me here for the foreseeable future."

Miss Dare seemed to drift off into the ether, so I prompted:

"And what about those papers?"

She snapped back into focus. "Oh, yes. No one was more surprised than I to learn about the tunnel. So I did some *digging*." She chuckled at her quip and wrote that down too. "When my father bought the place, Mr Hager informed him he could have virtually all the contents, including the paperwork pertaining to the house and grounds. I don't know that Father ever actually looked at the papers. I knew they existed, and paid no attention to them, either. Came across them after my father died, and still didn't look at them. Nearly burned them, as I recall.

"Good thing I didn't. Because when I was told about the tunnel coming out on my property, I found all the papers, out of the archive that I call an attic. I was just starting to sift through them when you arrived. I'd told Beggars I was not to be disturbed, but I'm glad you boys came. I could use a little help. So, Eddie, Iggy, take part of this stack and see if you can find any reference at all to the tunnel. Anything!"

Despite not liking history, this was part of being a detective for Eddie, and he was just as eager as I was to sort through the musty-smelling papers. We each took a stack and sat cross-legged on the floor to go through them.

During the next hour, that's all we did. I found one reference to the tunnel, and Miss Dare, rather than taking it up eagerly as I'd hoped, told me to set it aside, that we would start a small pile of those relevant papers. By the time we'd finished, we had a stack of six pages. Miss Dare took it up while Eddie and I gathered the remaining papers and tried our best to reassemble them into something neat. When we'd finished, Miss Dare was frowning.

"There doesn't seem to be anything we can use, I'm afraid. It's all so vague."

Just then, the big break came from, of all people, Beggars. The housekeeper entered with a book, and Miss Dare was about to tell her to go peddle her papers, when Beggars spoke.

"Miss, I've found this among your father's things."

"What? Where?"

"Among your father's things," she repeated, as if her mistress were a little dim. "In the study."

"I saw that book," Eddie chimed in. "It was in one of the bookcases behind his desk. Looked out of place, no title, kinda shabby."

I was proud of Eddie. He really pays attention to detail when we're on a case.

Miss Dare looked at him funny, like she didn't believe him, but Eddie was dead certain, so she put out a hand.

"Let me have the book, Beggars."

The book was handed over, and Miss Dare started to flip through it.

"Looks like a diary," Beggars pointed out. "In fancy hand."

"It does, indeed. From… let me see… the first entry is December 3rd 1854. My goodness, this is from when the house was new. I think the house had been built just a few years before."

"In 1852," I proudly said. "Saw it in your papers."

"Well spotted, Iggy. This, boys, may be just what we've been searching for. Thank you, Beggars! Oh, and perhaps some hot chocolate for the boys wouldn't be amiss."

Beggars looked rather miffed, despite her mistress 'gratitude. I think she figured she should be in on the discovery, since she'd found the book. It was a point, but since I wasn't over fond of Beggars, I couldn't feel too sorry for her. She just gave a small dip that was supposed to be a curtsey, and left to make the chocolate. Meanwhile, Miss Dare poured a hefty glass of brandy for herself. She sat down to study the book.

Eddie and I sat quietly for a minute or two, then Eddie spoke up. "Hey, miss. Mind if we hear what that book has t 'say?"

"What? Oh, yes, of course!"

Just then, Beggars came in with the hot chocolate, and Miss Dare made a supreme gesture.

"Beggars, since you found the book, I suppose you should be privy to this too. Take a chair."

Now this tells you how long the two women had known each other: Beggars helped herself to a little brandy too, then pulled up a chair to listen.

What came out during that next hour, would start to make things crystal clear.

Eighteen

About a year after all this, Miss Dare published the diary and gave Eddie and me copies. I have it front of me as I'm writing all this down.

The diary belonged to Mrs Hager, wife of the guy who'd helped found the village. She was high society from the sound of it, and maybe a little snooty, but with a big heart. You could tell that by how she spoke about the servants and the poorer folk of the village. Lots of talk about Christian charity and such, especially in the early pages.

The first important bit came in early 1855. Mrs Hager was all het up because her husband Charles told her about the plight of the Negro. Those folks were still slaves in the South back then, picking cotton and such. Charles went on about how they were human beings, not animals, and Mrs Hager agreed.

I should point out that our town is as lily-white as they come. I've never seen any prejudice here against Negroes because there's no one to get prejudiced about. Far as I'm concerned, they're people too, and folks who think otherwise are just stupid and evil.

Anyhow, Mrs Hager asked her husband if there was nothing they could do, and that's where the first hint of the tunnel comes in. It seems there was a band of white people who thought like the Hagers, and who were helping escaped slaves head north to Canada.

"Even in northern states," Miss Dare told us, "where slavery was illegal, a plantation owner could come after escaped slaves and take them back."

"Don't seem right," Eddie muttered.

"It wasn't." This was from Beggars, who surprised me by speaking so plain and frank. She wasn't embarrassed by our looks though, and went on. "Christians should never have tolerated such a thing. The Good Book says to love one another, not whip him to within an inch of his life."

"You have hidden depths, Beggars," Miss Dare said.

After that, there was a gap in the diary, at least when it came to writing about this plan. Miss Dare seemed to have an idea what the plan might be, but she didn't share it with Eddie and me. Instead, she flipped through the pages slowly, looking for the next pertinent entry. It didn't help our impatience, that she would occasionally mutter, "That's interesting," or "I will have to read this whole book later." Finally, she came to the next important entry, a few weeks later.

3rd March 1855

Charles has assembled a group of five to assist him in the plan. I shan t mention their names, for there could be danger if this diary is read by the wrong people. There are also two servants, long in our employ, who are, by necessity, privy to the plan.

One person she had to mention was the minister Reverend Andersen because the church was so important to their scheme. Otherwise, she kept mum about the other four.

The whole thing was neat as oysters. Escaped slaves would go to a stop on what was called the Underground Railroad and get food and shelter, and instructions of where to go next. They'd head to the new spot and get refreshed, and directions to the next place, and so on. Folks only knew where the next stop was, never anything more about it.

Sometimes, the stop for these poor souls will be a solitary farmhouse, but sometimes the stop will be more elaborate. That is where Charles s plan enters in. Runaways will be directed to the church, where Reverend Andersen will give them such succor as he is able. A church, however, would be a natural place of hiding, and therefore a natural place for those awful men to look. So the poor fugitives will enter the tunnel, which will lead them to our own property. Here, they will remain until it is safe to move on. If there is particular danger, they can simply remain in the tunnel for a time.

Then came another entry, a few weeks later.

10th April 1855

Construction has begun on the tunnel. Incredibly exciting! Dangerous too, however, both for the diggers and anyone involved. It isn t illegal to dig a tunnel, of course, but if the plan is found out, the very purpose for it will be rendered moot. I have seen the tunnel plans. They are elaborate and will require a lot of work. My offers to help are refused, save to give the poor fellows refreshments.

"Did you ever see the tunnel plans?" Eddie asked.

Never," Miss Dare replied.

"Too bad. Might've come in handy."

I refuse to be denied access to the meetings, however. It may look strange to some of the household, my being present at Charles s meetings in his study, but I don t care. I simply tell those servants who don t know what we re doing, that it is a friendly gathering. Whether that fools them is beside the point. I won t go into details of our latest meetings, but all goes well so far.

I wish they'd gone into how the thing was dug in the first place. You couldn't blast your way through, so it all had to be done by pick and shovel, and imagine how dirty it would've got those men who were normally so clean. It really must've taken some work.

A little later in the diary, there were two problems reported.

17th July 1855

A terrible setback. A portion of the tunnel has collapsed. Fortunately, no one was badly injured. A few scrapes, dirt in the eyes. It is frustrating, however, as the collapse will set us back a week or more, and some are losing faith. Thank goodness Charles is such a strong man! He rallied their spirits at a meeting in the church, and work was resumed. I was never more proud of my husband.

The second problem was fear of a stool pigeon. I don't know why they suspected it, but they did. Somehow, someone had found out about the tunnel and the plan, and everyone would be at risk. Easy to see how it could happen, what with all the digging and planning. All it took was one blabbermouth or one wrong word. Mind you, Mrs Hager believed that even if her servants had found out, they wouldn't have disapproved; that she didn't hire those kind of people to work in the house.

But even if a servant agreed with their plan, that servant might've still said something—to a brother or sister, to a parent. So work was stopped for a while, as the tunnel was repaired and for the rumors to die down.

7th September 1855

Work has resumed on the tunnel at last. It has taken far longer than expected to clear debris from the collapse and reinforce the tunnel that remains. There has been nothing further about a possible breach in secrecy. Charles has refused to tell me who was suspected. However, last month Mr and Mrs Trevylan moved away without telling us. As they were friends of mine, this is rather distressing. Were they the ones who found out about the tunnel? Mr T could be rather intolerant of those he considered beneath" him. If they did find out, if they were suspected, what became of them? Charles will not say. Perhaps he simply doesn t know.

"Sounds sinister," Eddie said, and Miss Dare nodded.

"There is fodder for a story here," she said. "Not that I would profit from what happened," she added quickly. "I mean to say, such a story of heroism needs to be told."

"Isn't there more?" I asked.

Miss Dare had been flipping through the pages as we spoke, and finally, a few months later, found the next entry.

21st November 1855

The tunnel is finished! All are confident it is safe, and I insisted upon going down myself. Charles relented at last. I felt as I descended the ladder that I was entering a netherworld, a subterranean catacomb. And yet, the former slaves will see it as a haven. It is impressive, I must say, and I cannot wait for the first arrivals.

12th December 1855

Our first heroic runaways. Two men and a woman. They were in tatters, and very nervous, like hunted animals, yet with a true sense of courage, ready to accept any challenge. To have made it this far, yet still be in danger... I cannot imagine it. Of course, I must act to outsiders as if nothing is happening. I shop, prepare for

Christmas, all as if life goes on as normal. The trio arrived at the church last Monday. Reverend Andersen gave them food and water, ushered them into the tunnel, where they spent the night on cots with pillows and blankets donated from our group. The following day, Reverend Andersen, Charles, and two of our members met with them to discuss what would happen next. It was agreed they would come to our house that Monday night and sleep in the study, where no servant goes uninvited. We gave them food and drink and warmer clothes. It was my first time seeing slaves, and I wanted so much to hug them and weep, but remained stolid for Charles s sake. Tuesday evening, a tall gentleman who only called himself Moses, arrived. He met with the trio in Charles s study. No one was allowed in, not even my husband. When Moses emerged, the trio had gone.

"Sounds spooky," Eddie said, and I had to agree.

"Anything more?" I asked Miss Dare.

Miss Dare, as she idly flipped through the diary said," There is nothing for several weeks, except to note 'three more guests 'or 'two visitors arrived'. Vague things like that."

For a few minutes, she went on through the pages, and finally found another entry. This was important because it answered a question that had been bugging me.

As bad a hand as those folks had been dealt, they still praised God. Only now, it was because they saw freedom in sight. So some of them asked if they might have a small place to worship at the end of the tunnel; somewhere to thank God for how far He'd led them and pray for safety the rest of the way.

The reverend was all gung-ho about that, as you might expect, and some of the group who'd been involved in digging the tunnel put together an altar that they brought down in pieces and assembled there. Also some chairs, a table, and a lantern. The Bible must've been added later.

"That seems to be all," Miss Dare said. She was at the end of the diary, and shut the book.

"So," I said slowly, "that tunnel probably got abandoned after the slaves were freed. What's happened to it since?"

"An excellent question, Iggy, and one I cannot answer. But now we know when and why it was constructed, and why there is an altar there."

"What do we do next?" Eddie wondered.

"Next," said Miss Dare, "we report this to Delancey."

Eddie's face fell. Like I said, we like Delancey. We like him a lot. He's always treated us pretty well. But he's still a grown-up, and still worries about Eddie and me getting in trouble. The case where we met him, which happened about six months before this, well, it was a nasty thing. Then, we had no choice but to be involved because one of our pals had been killed, and the killer was maybe after us too, for reasons we didn't know. So Delancey had to keep us in the loop. But this case didn't really involve us. We hadn't known Mrs Clapham, and barely knew Mr Blank, so he'd want us to stay out of it for sure.

Seeing our reaction, Miss Dare said, "I suppose I could go and speak to Delancey alone. Show him the diary."

"No!" we both shouted at once.

"I mean," I said, quieter, "we know Delancey better 'n you. We'll talk to him. Should we take him the diary?" I held out my hand and she brought the diary closer to her chest.

"No. I'd like to read the whole thing. I may have missed an important clue."

There was no denying that, so we agreed she would keep it. If Delancey wanted to see it, he'd know where to go.

Eddie looked at the mantel clock. "Is that the time? I gotta get home, or Ma will skin me. Come on, Iggy."

It was high time I went home too. The day was getting dark. We said goodbye to Miss Dare and hoofed it out to the street. It was blessed cold, and a biting wind had struck up. So, with no chit-chat, we agreed to meet at Eddie's house bright and early the next day, to go see Delancey. I ran all the way home.

The shop looked warm and cheery when I entered. Mr Collins looked up expectantly, then went back to studying his fingernails when he saw it was me. The shop was quiet, but it often is, even at that time of year, before five, before the mad rush of men who'd forgotten to get their wives 'presents begins. I noticed Uncle Fred wasn't there. Also not unusual. This time of year, one of the clerks will take an early supper so he's ready for the after-work rush. No doubt Uncle Fred would be at the diner across the street, having pigs 'knuckles and sauerkraut. He isn't much for observing Jewish law, like I said.

I said a quick hello, then bounded up the back stairs to our place. When I entered, I was surprised to see Dad at the kitchen table. He looked a little pale, but was in good spirits. Mom was stirring a pot of something that smelled delicious (she's a great cook, and since Dad and I like mostly the same foods, I usually can't complain about the menu). Dad looked pleased to see me when I entered. Mom was just a little impatient. For some reason, Mom always acts a little that way when I'm around.

"Ah, Iggy!" Dad said. "It is high time you got home. We would eat supper without you. And of course, you would miss lighting the candles and opening your present…"

Dad liked to tease. I played along and grinned, and helped Mom finish setting the table. "You're all better?" I asked Dad.

Before he could respond, Mom said, "He is better, but not so much. The doctor said he may help out a bit in the shop tonight and tomorrow, but must not overdo it."

"I'm strong as an ox!" my dad cried, then wheezed a little.

"Yes, dear," was Mom's patient reply.

Nineteen

Well, it's the day before Christmas. I've noticed that a lot of people call the whole day of the 24th Christmas Eve. However, they need to understand that the day begins at sundown. So Christmas Eve is when the sun goes down. That's about four thirty in the afternoon this time of year.

Anyhow, the day was cold and damp and cloudy. Though the thermometer read thirty, it felt much colder. I ate a quick breakfast, then headed over to Eddie's house. He was grumpy, like he usually is first thing, and I sat at his kitchen table while he finished his oatmeal. Eddie's mom was doing the dishes and wished he'd hurry up so that she could finish.

"I've got a lot to do today before I go to work," she told him, and Eddie reacted as though he'd heard it before, which he probably had. After Eddie handed her his oatmeal bowl and spoon, and his mom had washed and dried them, she kissed him on the top of his head.

"Now," she said. "I get off work at three today, so we can have a few hours together before church tonight. I have to press your suit. And," she added with a look of warning, "you can polish your good shoes. I don't want to have to do that too."

"Yes, Mom," Eddie said. He was embarrassed about being told what to do in my presence, but there was no need to be. We'd been buddies long enough so each of us had been subjected to parenting in the other's presence plenty of times.

With that, his mom put on her coat and galoshes, tied a scarf over her hair, and headed out with a final goodbye to both of us.

"Let's go, then," Eddie said.

"Maybe you'd better polish your shoes now," I suggested. "So you don't forget. Anyhow, Delancey won't be in his office yet."

This was true, though Eddie didn't much feel like polishing his shoes. Still, he hauled out the black shoes that he wore for good, took the polish and rag from under the kitchen sink, and set to work as we talked.

"How long's your dad's shop open today?" Eddie asked.

Until four. But we gotta be done by three, when your mom comes home."

"Yeah." Eddie attacked his shoes with a vengeance, seeing them as an unnecessary delay to our adventure. "So we go t 'Delancey first?"

"Right. Tell him about the tunnel, and the runaway slaves, and such. And we pump him for information, anything he's found out about the killer."

"Or killers," Eddie reminded me. He still thought that Blank had killed Mrs Clapham years back, and someone else had killed him. I had to admit, there was nothing wrong with the theory.

"Right. Got another rag?"

Eddie tossed a second rag to me, and I polished his other shoe. (I did a better job on mine, but don't tell him.) Between us, we finished his shoes pretty quick, and were off to Delancey's office.

We thought he might not be there yet, or that he would just be arriving, but we were wrong. The office was lit, though the door was locked. Eddie knocked, and in a few moments, Delancey opened.

"What the devil? Go away! I got things to do."

"Yeah, yeah," said Eddie, barging past. "We're all busy."

To my surprise, Delancey looked embarrassed. He ran past us both to his own office and hastily covered a long box that had a glimmer of red in it.

"You really got to learn to make an appointment," Delancey said as he set the box on top of his filing cabinets.

"No time for that now," Eddie said as he plunked himself down in a chair. Delancey and I sat too. "We got news." And he went on to explain what Miss Dare had found in the diary. Delancey went from being annoyed to getting interested.

"Well," Delancey said when Eddie had finished, "that's pretty good, though I don't know if it brings us any closer to figuring out who killed Blank and Mrs Clapham."

Eddie looked ready to say something he shouldn't so close to Christmas, and I cut in. "Maybe not, but it explains that the tunnel's not new, that it wasn't put there by the killer or someone associated with him."

Delancey gave me the funny look he always does whenever I say something that he expects should come from someone much older, like he wants to ask if I'm really forty. Anyhow, he dropped it and started to say something when a knock came on his office door. He'd relocked it while Eddie was talking.

"What is this?" he demanded of nobody as he went to answer. To our surprise, it was Shirley Tilbury, best friend of Mrs Clapham.

She apologized up, down, and sideways for disturbing Mr Delancey on such a day, but she *had* to come see him on a matter most urgent, and wouldn't he spare her a few minutes— Then she saw us.

"Oh! I'm sorry. I didn't know—"

"No trouble. Eddie, move your backside."

Eddie vacated his chair so Mrs Tilbury could sit.

"Now, don't worry about these two," Delancey told her as he retook his chair. "I've had their tongues cut out so they can't blab."

Mrs Tilbury looked doubtful, realized Delancey was kidding, and gave a nervous titter. "Oh. Yes. That's like a joke. Well... I understand you're looking into the death of my dear friend, and thought there was something you should know."

"Sure. But if you have evidence, maybe the police—"

"No! What I mean to say is..." She took a handkerchief from her purse and immediately started to wad it and twist it in her hands. "Well, I don't know that this is evidence, and don't want to bother them."

"It wouldn't be a bother. It's their job."

She waved it off. "When my friend disappeared, and later, when her... body was found, I was at the police station nearly every day, asking what they were doing. Progress on the case, and such like. Made myself such a nuisance, some of the officers threatened me with harassment charges, and they were quite rude about it."

"I gotcha. So go ahead then. Tell me what it is you know, and if it's important, I'll bring it to the cops myself. They're used to me bugging them."

She forced a smile. "Well, it's just the story that came about that poor Mr Blank, and how he was found." She gave Eddie and me a pitying smile. "But perhaps I'd better approach this differently. A few weeks before Millie disappeared, I was over to her house, to have coffee and a chat, you know? And Millie said to me, 'Shirley, I've just bought the most divine dress'! Well, Millie was that sort, you know? She liked to show off her purchases. Not that I resented it, but some did. It never bothered me because Millie was a sweet soul who didn't mean anything by it. She just wanted to share good news. And to her, a new dress was good news. So I said I'd like to see it."

"Understandable," Delancey put in.

"Yes. Well, Millie was going to bring the dress down to the kitchen, but then she said, oh why bother? I should just come along upstairs. I'd been in her bedroom a few times, usually after she'd bought new bed linens or some such. So it wasn't unusual for her to suggest we go there. We were best friends, after all."

She waited, so Delancey said, "Understandable," again.

"Well, we went to her room, and she showed me the dress, and it was very nice, of course, though a bit gaudy, and with her complexion, she never could wear yellow without looking like some party favor—"

"Mrs Tilbury," Delancey said, sighing.

"I'm sorry. I'm just a trifle nervous, you understand. Well, as we sat on her bed, chatting, she hadn't quite shut the wardrobe completely, and you know how a door will sometimes open further, by itself—wind or whatever it is—well, that happened, and in her wardrobe was a long black robe!"

Delancey finally perked up. "What did you do?"

"I was very surprised, I can tell you. Now, Millie was not facing the wardrobe as I was, we were sitting opposite each other on the bed, you understand. But she saw my eyes get big, I suppose, because she turned and saw what I was looking at. Well! Millie was usually so even keeled! Not this time. She was quite flustered. She went to the wardrobe right away and shut the door, almost slammed it shut. Then she touched her hair, like you sometimes do to recover yourself, and turned back to me. And she said—and I quote, 'It's nothing. Just an old choir robe'. Well! That was a lie. I'd been a member of that church as long as Millie—since we were born, really. And I remember every choir robe they ever used—they don't just buy new robes willy-nilly, you understand. And black! Never. Even at funerals, it was a deep burgundy."

"What color are the robes now?" Delancey asked. I think he was testing, to see if she really did notice the color of the robes.

"Green," she said firmly. "A nice forest green." Then she added, "Before that, they were navy blue. Never, *ever* black." She sat back proudly. "So you see what this means, don't you? I'd heard that Mr Blank wore a black robe when he was… when he died, and that it was very puzzling, but now, it's clear, isn't it?"

"I'm afraid I don't follow." Delancey *must* have followed. Eddie and I did. I think he just wanted Mrs Tilbury to say it.

"Well! They must have been in some group or other— Millie and Mr Blank— and heaven knows who else. Doesn't it make sense?"

"It does." Delancey stood. "Well, thank you, Mrs Tilbury." She was put out that he was dismissing her, and stayed sitting.

"What do you think I should do? Should I tell the police? Like I said, they are rather tired of my insisting—"

"I would still suggest that I tell them. They listen to me, if grudgingly. I'll make sure they know who told me, so that if they want to ask you about it, they can."

She perked up at that. "Do you think they might? The police at my house?"

Delancey could see she was thrilled by the prospect, so he tried to ease her excitement. "I don't know. It's possible. So you head on home, and I'll talk to the cops."

"Very well," Mrs Tilbury said, standing.

She seemed reluctant to go; I think she wanted to stick around while Delancey phoned, but he was having none of it. They shook hands, and she left. I expected Delancey to pick up the receiver and dial Inspector Fenrow's number. Instead, he told us to skedaddle.

"What're you gonna do?" Eddie asked.

"I'm going to talk to Mr Clapham. He clearly hasn't been square with me. And if his wife was a member of some group, maybe so is he. Now shoo."

Eddie and I left. I was upset at being left out, but my buddy pulled me aside. "Let's head over to Clapham's. His store ain't open yet," he said.

"But Delancey—"

"Oh, hang Delancey! We've got to see this through. You game?"

I've always taken courage from Eddie. So even though I was nervous about going ahead with this, I agreed because Eddie was so certain.

We tore off, out of sight before Delancey could head out, so he wouldn't have a hint what we were doing. Delancey's office is downtown, not far from where we live. Mr Clapham's place was also in the area, though it was still a hike.

Like I said Mr Clapham has a house of his own, not in the downtown. Dad had pointed it out to me once, on a walk. We headed along the main thoroughfare for a bit, then cut across the street, dodging a streetcar and nearly getting run over by a flivver before we made it to the quiet street where Clapham lived. We ducked down an alley nearby, and were just catching our breath when Delancey's car pulled up to the curb.

Delancey used to take the streetcar everywhere, or hoofed it, but he'd solved a case involving some rich guy, and that guy had paid him well. Delancey figured a car would be handy for work, especially at odd hours. Now, it was just handier because the streetcar we'd seen was packed to the gills with last-minute shoppers. He'd never have squeezed on.

He parked his car and got out, Eddie and me watching. Delancey went up to the door and knocked, waited. The door was answered by a fancy maid. Clearly, the Clapham store was doing pretty well. Delancey said something we couldn't hear, and she let him in. When the door was closed, Eddie said, "Come on," and we took off for the house.

I expected Eddie to go up to the door too, or maybe peep in a window; instead, he circled around the back and looked in the windows there. There were three of them, and the second one, he ducked down in a hurry and mouthed the word "maid". I nodded to show I understood. The third window would work, he figured, and motioned for me to come along. I did, keeping low and close to the house so the maid wouldn't see me if she looked out.

When I reached the third window, Eddie was already trying it. Fancy as the house was, Clapham wasn't too keen on locking windows, because when Eddie shoved on the frame, it opened. We were lucky: the window barely made a sound as it slid up halfway.

Eddie whispered, "Give me a boost." I laced my fingers so he could put his boot in them and hefted himself up and through. I thought he made enough noise to wake the dead, but he just grinned and whispered for me to reach up. I did, and my strong buddy yanked me up and in.

Our eyes adjusted to the dim hallway we were in. Eddie and I listened for any hint we'd been heard. Hearing no alarm, he pointed to a nearby staircase. It wasn't the main stairs, but I guessed the maid maybe lived in, and it was what she used. Eddie led the way without hesitating, staying to the sides where the steps were less likely to creak. Again, the house was pretty new, so only one stair along the way made any noise at all. *We've been pretty lucky so far*, I thought.

On the first landing, Eddie stopped. A row of closed doors, three to a side, were before us, and at the other end, fancier stairs leading down. This must be the floor where Clapham had his room, I figured.

Eddie whispered in my ear, "Let's give a listen at the other end. Make sure no one heard us."

I nodded, and we crept along the hallway. As we got closer, maybe about halfway along, we could start to make out two voices, Delancey and Mr Clapham.

"You really have some nerve," Clapham was saying. "It's the day before Christmas, and I have matters to tend to. I have to be at my store in half an hour."

"Got to be busy at the shop," Delancey said. "I won't keep you long."

"I have employees to handle customers," Clapham explained, sounding annoyed and haughty. "I'm not some two-bit operation, you know. Not that it's any of your business, but I shall be on hand to make certain everything goes well, and to tend to some of my… finer clientele."

For not wanting to tell Delancey anything, Mr Clapham sure yapped on long enough. I think he was proud of his store, that he didn't have to be there all hours like my dad did.

"As I was saying," Delancey went on, "I won't take up much of your time. Just wanted to ask about one little thing."

There was a pause, and when they spoke again, it was quieter. I think they headed to a living room or some such, to sit. I could still make out a little of what they said, though: Delancey was asking him about the black robe. Clapham wasn't happy about the insinuation, especially when Delancey reminded him that Blank was murdered while wearing a black robe.

"It's none of your business," Clapham said louder, "but I will say once more, I do not own such a garment. No thank you, Marge. You may return to your housework."

For a second, I thought the maid might head upstairs, but no. We ducked down and peered just a bit over the railing to see the maid toddle off across the hall and head for another room. Eddie gave a light backhand to my arm—a signal that we should get back to work. I nodded.

We started on the same end where we were, which was a good idea. It made sense that the bedrooms used would be near the top of the main stairs. I hadn't thought of that at the time; it just made sense to start at one end and work our way to the other.

Eddie suggested we split up, but I wanted to stay together, and he agreed.

The first room was empty. I mean, there was a bed and night stand and all that, but there were no signs of anyone using it regularly. No hair brush or shaving mug. There was a very large wardrobe, and Eddie opened the door. It creaked loudly, and we both ducked, as if a giant bat would fly out. We waited for any sign someone had heard the creak, and I peeked out the door, but I guess it just sounded louder in the empty room. Anyhow, the wardrobe was empty except for a few wood hangers.

Satisfied there was nothing there, Eddie quietly closed the door and we went across the hall to the next room.

This was clearly Mr Clapham's. It was as neat as the other room had been, but in here there was a basin and pitcher, shaving articles, and a dressing gown behind the door. Eddie and I both started for the wardrobe at the same time and bumped into each other. We knew that if Clapham had a black robe, it would be hanging there.

It wasn't. Later, it would dawn on me that the maid probably hung up his clothes after they were cleaned, and if Clapham didn't want her to know about the robe, he wouldn't go hanging it in his wardrobe. It had to be someplace else. There was a smaller wardrobe, and we checked there too, but no luck.

Eddie sighed, and I felt the same. We were striking out. Maybe Clapham told Delancey the truth, that he had no such robe.

Never mind; we were in the house, so we might as well check out the remaining rooms. We got bolder the farther from the main staircase we got because we couldn't hear Delancey and Clapham, so we figured they couldn't hear us.

We went to the next room, which was a lot like the first. In fact, all except the last room were like the first, with just a few pieces of furniture.

That last room was a revelation, as my dad likes to say. All sorts of clutter. Old furniture, a tall mirror speckled so it made me look like I had the pox, and several boxes that contained old books and bric-a-brac. If we hadn't been on a mission to find the black robe, I would've liked to spend more time there, just to poke around.

"Not much dust," Eddie pointed out, which was pretty smart of him, I'd say. "Someone's been in here."

"Maybe they just moved some stuff around," I suggested.

"Nah. There is some dust over yonder. But here, along the path through the boxes, it looks like someone's been walking not long ago."

I beamed. Whenever my buddy comes up with something I think is smart, it's as if I'd thought of it. I was proud. Now, I just nodded with a grin.

Figuring that the trail of disturbed dust might be a clue, we slowly followed it through the maze of stacked boxes and furniture. It ended at a closet. *That is odd*, I thought; I didn't recall any of the other rooms having an actual closet. Eddie put his hand on the knob. I watched breathlessly, wondering if a rotting corpse would fall out as soon as he opened the door.

No corpse. Just two black robes.

For a bit, we just stared at them. One was smaller than the other. Mr and Mrs Clapham each had one, I figured. Eddie didn't seem to know what to do next, so I took charge. I grabbed the bigger one and draped it over my arm, then said, "Come on."

No longer frightened we might be found, I frogmarched us down the hall to the main staircase. We could still hear Delancey, but it sounded like he was getting ready to go. That, we couldn't allow. I urged Eddie on, and we came down the staircase, bold as brass. At the bottom, the maid spied us from the room across the hall, and called out, but we ignored her.

The maid's cry did raise the attention of Delancey and Clapham, though. They looked up as we entered, and I unhooked the robe from my arm and held it up without a word.

Twenty

For a bit, neither man spoke. Neither did Eddie nor I. "Where did you get that?" Delancey finally said.

"Never mind that!" Clapham cried. "Who the devil do they think they are, coming into my house, stealing my things?"

"So you admit this robe is yours," Delancey said flatly.

Clapham spluttered a bit, then managed to say, "I admit nothing. But what if it is? You are no policeman. These children are just that—children. I do not have to explain myself to you or anyone else."

The maid had come in by this time, and looked puzzled at the scene. Clapham turned to her now.

"Marge, kindly call the police."

"Oh, yes, Marge," said Delancey, sarcastic now. "Please call the cops so Mr Clapham can explain. Explain how that robe, which looks a whole lot like the one Mr Blank was wearing when he was murdered, got to be in his house."

"Upstairs," Eddie helped. "With another smaller robe like it."

Delancey suppressed a grin not too well. He looked at Eddie and me, then back at Clapham. "Well? Either you explain, or I will call the cops."

There was a pause. Marge the maid waited for her employer to say the word. Clapham looked at Delancey, at Marge, and finally at me, holding the robe. His shoulders slowly sagged. He told the maid she should go back to whatever she'd been doing.

"If you recall, sir," said the maid, timidly, "I was going to leave now for the holidays."

The words seemed foreign to Clapham. He frowned, then sighed. "Yes. Of course. I shall see you next week, Marge. Merry Christmas to you and your family." All that was said in a monotone. She returned the merry Christmas, and looked like she might do likewise to us, then changed her mind. She turned to go, but Delancey stopped her.

"One moment, please. Did you know about this?" Delancey asked as he lifted a corner of the robe, still in my hands.

"Marge does not know about any of it," Clapham cut in.

"I'd like to hear it from her," Delancey said. "Sometimes maids and butlers know more about their employers than they think."

Another pause. Marge got a little red in the face. Then she said, very evenly, "I am not in the habit of snooping in my employer's affairs. I have never seen that robe before."

I thought she would clock Delancey if he doubted her word, but there was no danger: Delancey just gave his nicest smile and said fine. He also wished her a merry Christmas, which she did not return. I thought that was a little out of line.

Anyhow, Marge left the room and pretty soon we heard her getting her coat and galoshes, then head out.

Meantime, Clapham poured a brandy for himself without offering a drink to Delancey (or us). It was a little early, anyway. Clapham was clearly stalling for his maid to leave. When the door closed, he sat down. We three sat across from him without being asked.

"So tell me about it," Delancey said, not hard-nosed at all.

"About six or seven years ago, just when the war in Europe was underway and looked like it might take longer than expected, a few of us at church got together. Just to talk. We often did, over coffee."

"Hang on," Delancey cut in. "Who are the others?"

"My wife and I, and Mr Blank. You know about them. There were others, but I'd rather not say who they are."

Delancey looked ready to protest.

"I will only tell the police," Clapham went on, "if they ask. Not you."

Our buddy decided not to pick a fight. He prompted Clapham to go on with his story. "Where was I? Oh, yes. A group of us got together for a social engagement. We are a serious lot, and the conversation turned—without our intending—to the state of our country and the world."

"Sounds like fun."

"Scoff if you will, Mr Delancey, but we were very serious. Our concern is that this country, and the world itself, has lost its way. For too long, we have strayed from the wonders of God, the basic tenets whereby all mankind should live. We need to change! To move back to the Lord, our God!"

This was getting to be a sermon. (Yeah, yeah, I know I don't go to Sunday church, but trust me: Christians don't have a monopoly on long-windedness.) Delancey sensed it too, and held up a hand.

"I understand what you're saying, Mr Clapham. Maybe you could continue with the story?"

Clapham seemed to snap out of a trance. He adjusted his necktie that didn't need straightening, then cleared his throat.

"Yes. Well, it is important you understand what we are about, so you don't think we're a bunch of crackpots."

"Now why would I think that?"

"You needn't be sarcastic," Clapham snapped.

"Truth to tell, I wasn't, sir. I fully understand what you're saying. Many of us feel that way at one time or another. Though I can't say we always agree on the cause of the world's troubles."

Clapham looked ready to argue the point, but smiled instead.

"Yes. Well, I can only speak of *our* opinions. We believe that a solid foundation of following Jesus Christ is the way to save our country from doom."

"What about Iggy, here?" Eddie demanded. "He don't believe in Jesus, but he's a good guy."

No one was more startled than I was. Not that Eddie would stick up for me—I knew he'd do that—but that he knew anything about my religion, that was a revelation.

"Yes," Clapham said. "Well, of course we wouldn't dream of shutting out anyone because they were benighted by others 'wrongheaded approach to salvation."

He was really starting to get on my nerves, even if I didn't understand half of what he was saying. Delancey *did* understand what Clapham was saying, and didn't like it. When he spoke next then, he was holding back anger.

"So what happened with this group?"

"Yes. Well, like most small religious…" He fumbled for a word so Delancey helped.

"Covens?"

"*Groups*, I was about to say. Like most such groups, we began quite informally. Didn't even call ourselves a group, in fact. Just gathered together in homes, chatting about what we saw as the proper way forward for our nation.

Slowly, however, the more assertive of us came to the fore and assumed leadership roles. They set about organizing meetings, and also screening potential additions."

"And did you add to your group?"

Clapham frowned. "Not much. Two others joined, but you must understand, we had to be very careful."

I cut in. "I don't get it. Why all the secrecy? You weren't doing anything illegal, were you?"

Eddie suggested, "Like cutting heads off chickens?"

Clapham had looked like he was taking my question seriously, but Eddie's remark (which was also meant seriously) made him look sour again.

"No, we weren't doing anything illegal. But you're too young to understand. If the Church realized we were forming our own group—one which might someday be a separate congregation—they would not be pleased. We might've even been removed from our church. That's not what we want. We like the reverend, though he can be a bit too progressive in his thinking at times."

"Get back to the meetings," Delancey prompted.

"Yes. Well, the meetings, as I said, took place in our homes. We made out as if we were playing bridge those nights. All that changed one fateful day, when one of our group discovered a tunnel under the church."

"Yeah. I've been inside," Delancey said.

That floored Clapham. "You… you have? What on earth?"

"Take it easy," Delancey said. "It wasn't his idea. Go on about the tunnel."

"No! I insist you tell me what business you had in the tunnel, before I say another word."

"I don't think you have to, Mr Clapham. I think what happened was, your group appropriated the tunnel for your gatherings. The church isn't locked at night, so it was easy enough to sneak inside and through the little door. Was there a meeting the night your wife disappeared?"

Despite his obstinate look, Clapham felt he had to answer that one.

"No. We never meet on nights when the church might be used. Choir practice, setting up for a special service, or some evening service—we never meet then."

"Fair enough. Now I'll tell you how your tunnel was discovered. Or maybe Iggy should."

All eyes turned to me. I'd rehearsed the story with the cops, so doing it for Clapham came out pretty smooth, if I do say so. Clapham listened patiently, and when I was done telling how I'd managed to get out of the tunnel, Delancey spoke:

"So what I want to know is, did you push him through the door?"

"What? No!" Clapham looked a little panicky. "Never! For one thing, I would never harm a child. I am a peaceable man. Not an ounce of violence in my body. I was in the Great War, and it turned me away from violence of all kinds."

"Okay," Delancey said, maybe convinced.

"And another thing: our group wants to maintain secrecy. Had one of us caught this boy snooping about, we would have hollered at him and told him to get out. We certainly would not have shoved him into the very tunnel we wish to keep secret."

He seemed to hesitate, as if he'd just remembered something, then shook his head.

Delancey said, "But then we get back to the question: who's in your group? Who else might've wanted to do dirt to Iggy?"

"And again, I shan't tell you. I will tell the police. I shall tell them because this boy was placed in danger, and the police should know about our group." That didn't sit too well with him, so he added, "At least as far as our involvement with the tunnel is concerned."

"Very good," Delancey said. "Then come with me. I can get you in to see Inspector Fenrow."

"What! Now?"

"Of course. Any policeman worth his salt will tell you that you have to stay on top of things or the killer might get away."

Mr Clapham looked grumbly, but agreed to go. He did balk something fierce though when Eddie and I made to go along.

"Why do those children have to go?" he demanded.

"Because Iggy was put in danger, and the inspector might have some things to ask him once you've told him about your group."

Clapham grumbled some more but gave in. Delancey took the black robe from me and we headed off to the police station.

Twenty-One

The police station is a square-built stone building with a cornerstone that reads 1871. Inside, it's cavernous and drafty and does nothing to improve the mood of those who occupy the offices. Or the cells.

Like I said earlier, the inspector's office is on the third floor—the top floor—and while there's an elevator, Delancey led the way up the shallow marble stairs at a pace that left Clapham puffing. We entered the outer office where a no-nonsense secretary sat at a big desk, typing up notes. Delancey went up to her and turned on the charm.

"Hi, gorgeous."

"Buzz off, Delancey."

"Ah, ah. We're here to see the inspector. Mr Clapham, here, has vital evidence about the murder of Mr Blank."

The secretary was clearly used to Delancey's shenanigans and studied his face for signs of tomfoolery. Then she looked at Clapham, who nodded ever so slightly. She excused herself, went to the inspector's door, knocked. After a few words, some of which children should not hear, Fenrow let us in. He scowled at Eddie and me, but didn't tell us to get out.

For the next twenty minutes, Clapham had the floor. He explained about the group, emphasized that this was secret, and finally ended by saying he had nothing to do with my adventure in the tunnel or the murder of Mr Blank.

"So who else is in this group?" Inspector Fenrow asked.

"I'd rather not say in front of these three. The group is—" Fenrow sighed loudly and massaged his temples.

"Mr Clapham. It's Christmas Eve. In four hours, seventeen minutes, I will be leaving for the day. I need to buy a present for my wife, which I have been putting off for ages."

"Jewelry's always nice," I put in before I could stop myself.

Fenrow arched an amused eyebrow in my direction, then went on to Clapham: "Tomorrow, I hope to spend a joyous Christmas with my wife and her annoying relation. I don't have time for your dithering. Delancey and the boys won't say a word. If they do, I'll have them drawn and quartered. Or worse. So spill it."

"Very well. Aside from my late wife and I, and the Blanks, there are two other couples. The Jacksons and the Meyers. Mr Jackson runs the grocery store not far from my home. Mr Meyer is a carpenter for Dovetail Woodworking. They are good people, Inspector. Please don't harass them." It looked to me like he wanted to add something.

"I will do what I think is right, Mr Clapham. Now what about those black robes?"

"They were imposed by our leader, Mr Blank. We are of diverse financial backgrounds, you see, and Mr Blank thought that having a common garment would place us all on equal footing. I always thought they were silly," he added sourly.

"I wish you'd told us all this sooner. At the very least, we might've prevented Iggy's getting shoved into the tunnel. Now go home. I'll want to speak to your group, singly."

Looking back, I can say honestly that I thought Clapham had withheld something. What it was, I couldn't guess, and didn't have any right to ask. I wish the inspector had pressed him. When Clapham had left, and we were still in Fenrow's office, the inspector sat back and sighed.

"Why is it, Delancey, that you never get involved in some clear-cut case? Would it hurt business for a straightforward murder, with the killer holding a smoking gun and gleefully cackling his confession?"

Delancey grinned. "You've been reading too many of Miss Hogwood's stories."

"You're a fine one to talk. I—" Then the inspector noticed Eddie and I were still there. He clammed up and sat back again. "I suppose I'll have to visit these two couples, the Jacksons and the Meyers. Damn it! I forgot to ask Clapham for their addresses. Well, I wasn't going to tackle it today, anyway. Day after Christmas is good enough. Off you go. I need to tidy up before I leave for the day."

Delancey checked his wristwatch. "Yeah, I gotta get going too. Give you a lift, boys?"

"No thanks," I said before Eddie could cut in. "We'll walk."

Delancey and the inspector looked at us suspiciously. Fenrow said, "Remember what I said about not getting involved." It sounded like a command.

He'd conveniently forgotten that we were the ones who had found the black robes. Never mind; I shrugged it off and told Eddie to come on. My buddy was puzzled, but I just winked to let him know I had an idea.

"We'll check in with Beulah," I told Eddie when we got to the street. "We gotta fill her in on this latest development. And she lives not two blocks off."

Eddie nodded. He's always in the mood to visit Beulah.

So we headed off. I looked around as we walked. After getting shot at, we couldn't take any chances. We got to Beulah's without a problem, but when we arrived, she met us at the door, packed and ready to leave.

"I'm finally leaving for my sister's," she said when we were sitting in her living room. "It's not far—a half hour train ride—and two days is about all I can take."

"You an 'your sister don't get along?" Eddie asked, though he already knew that.

"No. Well, we do, as long she doesn't bring up my being a widow, all alone. Which she will, you can bet on it."

"You ever gonna get married again?"

I rolled my eyes. Beulah has a good dozen years on Eddie in the age department, and he isn't even old enough to shave (though that doesn't stop him from checking the mirror every day for stubble) but he's got it so bad for Beulah, that he still has hopes.

Beulah was good about it. "Someday, maybe, but I have to meet the right man." That was a not-too-subtle hint to Eddie that, since they had met, that ruled him out.

"Anyhow," I said, changing the subject, "we came to tell you what's happened today." And I went on to tell her about the robes and the other two couples in this group. She listened and nodded a few times.

"You did good work, boys," she said at last, starting to put on her coat.

"What we can't figure out," Eddie said, ignoring her hint to leave, "is why Delancey's heading off, not working on the case any more today. I mean, it's only…" he checked the mantel clock "…ten thirty."

Beulah chuckled. "I think I know. And I'll tell you, if you promise to never tell another soul—especially Delancey."

We promised, crossed our hearts and hoped to die; showed her our fingers weren't crossed—whatever we could think of.

"Every Christmas," she said quietly, "Delancey dresses as Santa and has lunch with kids at the local hospital. The hospital pays for gifts and the lunch, but Delancey hands out the presents and ho-ho-ho's and all that."

"Delancey don't look much like Santa," Eddie said dubiously.

"He wears padding and a fake beard, of course. Anyhow, the kids don't seem to mind. I never would've found out, except my sister's youngest kid was in the hospital last Christmas, and when Sis asked a nurse about Santa, the nurse told her everything, and Sis told me. So Delancey doesn't know that I know. I think it's very kind of him, and you know how Delancey is when he's caught doing a good deed."

This is true. I once saw him give a panhandler a quarter, and when I smiled at Delancey for his kindness, he just shrugged it off and claimed the panhandler looked like his Uncle Bob. Delancey doesn't have an Uncle Bob.

"Well," said Beulah, "I need to go. I promise to think about what you've told me, on the train."

We stood and exchanged merry Christmases, and headed out. "Now where to?" Eddie asked when we were on the street.

"Not sure. Home, I guess. I just don't know what else we can do."

"We could head to Miss Dare's house. See what she thinks of this black robe stuff."

Since I didn't really feel like going home just yet, I agreed. We started off down the street towards Miss Dare's.

"What you getting for Christmas?" I asked Eddie. Normally, I avoid such questions. Eddie's mom doesn't have a whole lot of cash to spare, and their Christmas is pretty lean. But she does buy him something each year.

"Dunno. A sled, maybe. My old one is pretty shot."

"Sounds keen. There's plenty of snow on Dibley's Hill."

"Yeah."

I could tell Eddie wasn't comfortable talking about it, so I dropped it. We kept on for a bit in silence. The walk wasn't long, maybe half a mile, but there were lots of shoppers around that we had to duck past, so it took us a while. Finally, we reached the quiet street where the church was, the one that led to Mr Clapham's house and also to Miss Dare's. We had just turned the corner, the one that Mrs Clapham was seen going around that night she disappeared, when a big black limousine came up from behind, going slow.

You understand, big black cars aren't all that unusual. We've got some rich guys in town, and we also have some gangsters around, and that means you see flashy cars every so often. And I guess even that quiet neighborhood, with its family homes and well-kept lawns, has them sometimes.

So neither of us thought too much about a fancy black car driving past. What caught our attention was that the car pulled slightly ahead, and came to a stop at the curb. Even then, I figured they just wanted to ask directions. So we kept on walking toward it.

A burly guy got out of the back seat. He kept the door open, and that made me still think a passenger wanted directions. It was a big surprise, then, when the goon grabbed us both roughly by the arms and shoved us into the car. He climbed in after us and the car sped off.

Twenty-Two

There were three of them: two in the front, and the gorilla in the back with Eddie and me.

For a bit, we drove in silence, then the guy on the passenger side up front turned to us. He was square-jawed and squint-eyed.

"Now lookee here," he said. "We ain't gonna hurt you, so long as you keep your mouths shut."

"Where are you taking us?" I demanded.

"Just a little place out in the country. You'll see."

Out in the country! That's where gangsters took their victims to torture and kill them, so no one could hear screams, no one could hear gunshots. Or had I read too many of Eddie's goofy magazines?

I glanced at my buddy, who looked tight-lipped. Speaking of his magazines, I was afraid he might get it in his head to open the door while we were moving, to dive out and roll, like a detective from one of those stories. Eddie often fashions himself as the hard-boiled private eye. Delancey, I think, is even a little tame for his taste. No, Eddie is the shoot-first-and-ask-questions-later variety. He isn't afraid to challenge anyone, and it sometimes gets him in trouble.

I remember once, when two tough boys, three or four years older and a head taller than my pal, came idling by and one of them made a crack about us, something like, 'How'd you get out of your cribs'? or something equally intelligent and witty. Anyhow, Eddie came back with words to the effect that a long walk off a short pier might be to their liking. And one of them went right up to Eddie and breathed fire at him. Eddie didn't back down. He just eyed the dope right back. Well, that settled their hash. The loudmouth just grinned all of a sudden and said, 'Ya got moxie, kid', and walked off with his pal.

So I was a little scared Eddie might try something equally hare-brained now. I had the feeling these guys wouldn't back down from Eddie's glare. And I really worried when Eddie opened his mouth to speak. I shook my head but he ignored me.

"I should warn you guys," Eddie said. "At four this afternoon, I'm supposed to be in my church Christmas program, and if I ain't there, *questions will be raised!*"

He was so serious in how he said it, I nearly busted out laughing. The three guys *did* laugh, and the spokesman turned in his seat again, looking much friendlier this time.

"Don't worry, kid. Like I said, if you and your pal behave, we'll have you back safe and sound in no time at all. You can play shepherd boy."

"*Wise man.*"

"My mistake."

The spokesman turned to face front again. I should've been calmer, and I was a bit because I knew Eddie wouldn't do anything stupid, at least for a while. So we rode a bit more in silence. We wove our way through back streets, avoiding the busy sections of the city where one of us might call for help or where we might get stuck in traffic and be able to jump out. The driver was pretty good: he avoided stop signs, and when we did encounter one, he rolled on through. I prayed for a cop, but like they say in the movies, there's never one around when you need one.

Eventually, we left the city and headed onto a lonely county road, where no one was around. The fields were brown and gray, the trees barren, crusty snow rimmed the road and filled the furrows. I tried to follow the route we'd taken, but the driver had twisted and turned so often, and what with my looks at Eddie and the guy in the passenger seat, I lost track of the route we'd taken. No signposts to help, either.

Anyhow, after ten or twenty minutes, we arrived at an old farmhouse. We parked near the house, across from a dilapidated old barn that looked like one gust of wind might knock it down. The big lug who'd sat next to Eddie and me got out and curled a finger at us to follow.

The spokesman wasted no time. He told us to come on, and headed for the farmhouse door. The other two followed Eddie and me, to make sure we weren't going anywhere besides where they wanted us to go.

Inside, the house was as scruffy as the exterior. The floors were all tilted and bounced a little when the men walked on them. Faded wallpaper peeled from the walls, and one door had a big piece missing, like the Hound of the Baskervilles had taken a bite out of it.

We were ushered into a big farm kitchen with an old stove and rickety furnishings. The table wobbled, the chairs looked dangerous to sit on, but there was a lot of room, and we were told to sit. Eddie glared at them but did as he was told (much to my relief). The driver ducked out and soon came back with a fourth man.

This guy was way out of place. The others were dressed in black, like gangsters, and looked tough as nails. The newcomer was short and kind of chubby, and had on a simple brown suit. He smiled at us, but we didn't return the greeting.

"I hope you haven't been treated poorly?" he asked, gingerly taking a chair across from us.

"Not unless you count throwin 'us into a car and makin 'sure we don't leave," Eddie growled.

The newcomer grinned at my buddy.

"Yes. I'm sorry about that. But I didn't think you'd come, otherwise. And you were told we won't harm you? Good. That is the truth. I merely wanted to talk to you both."

"So talk."

"I will. For purposes of this conversation, please call me... oh, Mister X will suffice."

I rolled my eyes. Another guy who'd read too many detective stories. Eddie nodded seriously though, so I didn't say anything.

"And you're Eddie, and you're Iggy? Good. The names of these other men are not necessary. Now let's get down to brass tacks. I wanted to speak to you about this entire affair, the business of Mrs Clapham, and Mr Blank, of you getting shoved into the tunnel—"

"Did you do it?" Eddie interrupted. "And shot at us, too?" He lifted his slinged arm in accusation.

"No! I am a peaceable man, Eddie. I would never dream of harming either one of you. I have some idea who might have done it, but no proof. Certainly nothing to take to the police. Now where was I? Oh, yes. The point is, I'd rather you both gave it up. What I mean to say is, you're dealing with matters that are far beyond your reach. So it's better if you simply allowed the police, and your friend Mr Delancey, to do whatever it is they do. Just enjoy your time away from school, and the holidays, and be safe."

"And what if we don't?"

Mister X moved his mouth around a bit, like he wanted to smack Eddie, and I wouldn't have been surprised if he had. But he didn't. He just looked at us both, then sat back with a sigh.

"As I said, I've no wish to harm you. But others might not be so keen. Remember the tunnel, Iggy. Remember, Eddie, you getting injured by the shrapnel from a bullet."

For a little bit, everyone in the room was silent. One of the guys from the car, the driver, sniffed a bit. Then I lit on an idea.

"Will you let Eddie and me talk it over in private?"

Mister X and Eddie were puzzled; the other three guys couldn't have cared less what I was asking. Our host mulled it over a bit, and finally nodded.

"I suppose we could allow that. Gentlemen, let's let our two guests speak in confidence."

They left the room. Quite honestly, I never thought they would. That gave me a few second thoughts about my plan, but I presented it to Eddie, anyway.

"You should escape," I whispered to him. "I don't trust these guys. Mister X seems nice enough, but I just don't trust him."

"He could've bumped us off any time," Eddie pointed out.

"I know. That's the only thing that makes me hesitate. But I still don't trust 'em."

"Tell the truth, neither do I. But you should escape, not me."

I shook my head. "You're more of an athlete. You can run faster and jump and all that. I'm too pokey. Besides, my ankle still hurts a little." Actually, it hurt like the dickens, but I didn't like to say.

"Iggy, listen. These guys mean business. They all look like mobsters. So one of us has to escape, and it has to be you. I mean, an escape calls more for brains than brawn. If they—"

"Almost finished?" Mister X called.

"Couple more minutes, please," I called back and got no reply.

Eddie went on: "If they torture me, I can take it better 'n you. And besides which, you're smaller, and can hide better."

There was no more time to argue. I could hear the men in the next room, shuffling around, and figured it was only a matter of time before Mister X would just come in unannounced. So I nodded.

There was a side door off the kitchen, one that clearly led to outside. I hoped it wasn't locked. Really no reason why it would've been, in such a dilapidated house, but it still might've been. It wasn't. With one final look at my brave buddy, I ducked out the door, easing it shut behind me.

No time to get my bearings: I had to get out of the main yard as fast as possible. So I ran to a nearby field, which was overgrown with snowy weeds. I crept through the field, certain at any moment I would hear shouts from the farmyard, calls of them coming after me. It was vaguely creepy that no one came. Had they already pistol-whipped my buddy?

Off in the distance, there was a stand of trees, not really a woods, just maybe six to ten trees, but they would shield me from anyone looking. I hurried over the uneven ground, turning my ankles a few times, especially the one I'd injured, but I ignored the pain and kept going. The trees never seemed to grow nearer. I was starting to get a stitch in my side. See, that's why I wanted Eddie to escape. He'd have made those trees in no time flat.

But maybe Eddie wouldn t have thought to go in that direction, I told myself. *Or maybe he d have delayed outside the farmhouse too long.* As I reached the trees, I worried about what was happening to my pal. Were they really torturing him? He already had a bum arm because of that gunshot. Would Mister X be merciless?

I thought about all of that while I caught my breath. Then it was time to push on.

From the cluster of trees, it was a short trek to the county road we'd come in on. This road wasn't traveled very much, and given that it was nearly Christmas Eve, there was even less traffic now than usual. I had to get my bearings, make sure I was headed in the right direction. Then I started the long walk back to town. My ankle hurt like the devil, but I kept on for my buddy.

It had grown pretty cold. I was wearing my coat, hat, and boots, of course, but that wind, uninterrupted by any buildings, just cut through me. I was glad Eddie had talked me into going. (Eddie's outer gear isn't as warm as mine. It's a sad state of affairs, but there it is. Eddie's mom just can't afford to give him the best clothes.)

Anyhow, I reached the end of the county road, at a T-shaped intersection. I had to wrack my brains now: had we turned right or left to get on the county road? Damn! Think! Finally, I was pretty sure we'd turned right, so I had to turn left now. *Yeah, that is it*, I told myself. *I go left.*

As I walked on though I was hit by doubt. Was I headed in the wrong direction after all? *Stupid! Stupid!* The whole point of sending me and not Eddie was because I was supposed to be smarter, and here I was, unsure of where to go.

There was also the worry that Mister X might send his goons after me. So even though I hoped for a car to come and give me a lift, I was afraid it might be them if a car ever approached.

So when a car finally did come close, I was worried. All cars look alike to me. They're all black, only some are bigger than others. Eddie can tell a Chrysler from a Ford—not me. But I did see the car was occupied by a man and a woman, so I figured I was safe. I waved my hands, and only when they slowed down, did I wonder what the heck I was going to tell them.

I trotted up to them as the car rolled to a stop. "Are you heading to town?" I asked.

"Yes," the woman said. "Hop in."

They were a young couple. The man was handsome, the woman pretty, and they looked happy. The man, I could tell, wasn't completely thrilled to be giving me a ride, but the woman was content enough, so I knew who had suggested they stop for me. I had to use her pity and the fact that the guy would probably do anything for her, to my advantage.

"We're going to my parents'," the woman said, "for Christmas."

"And we should've been there by now," said the man, not nastily.

"My fault," she explained to me with a sheepish smile. "I'd forget my head if it wasn't screwed on. How about you?"

"Mine's screwed on pretty tight," I said with a grin.

She laughed hard at that, and even the guy chuckled. Good, I was winning them over.

I didn't want to tell them the truth; let them think I was just some stupid kid, out in the middle of nowhere, getting lost. Or worse, running away from home. All the time we spoke, my brain was buzzing with plausible story ideas.

"I'm Hazel, this is Max," she said.

"Iggy."

"Oh, I *love* that! Pleased to meet you, Iggy."

"Likewise."

There was a pause. I was hopeful now that maybe they wouldn't ask what I'd been doing on the road by myself in the middle of nowhere. No such luck. Max:

"So, Iggy. How'd you get stranded out in the boondocks?"

"I... well, it was stupid of me. Some buddies of mine and I were playing around, and they dared me to hop on the back of a truck, to catch a ride, you know? I never expected the truck wouldn't stop, figured I'd just jump off again at the next corner or stop sign. But it didn't stop! Before I knew it, that truck was headed for the hills. Finally, he slowed down for the turn to that county road. I took a chance and hopped off. Just dumb, I guess."

This was the elaborate story I'd cooked up. Now I had to wait, to see if they'd swallow it. There was another pause, and finally Max spoke again.

"Well, it wasn't bright, but at least you didn't get hurt. I hope you've learned your lesson."

"You bet, sir."

Hazel let out a giggle for some reason, and the moment of truth passed. We were all still friends.

We reached town, and I was pleased to see it was the right town and not the city that's ten miles west of my own; that I'd hitched a ride in the right direction. At the first intersection, I thanked the couple as nice as I could, and got out. Hazel wished me merry Christmas, and Max just waved.

So now I'd reached the city. What next? The best option would be the police station. So I hoofed it over there. But Inspector Fenrow wasn't in, and none of the cops on duty were in any mood to listen to the ramblings of a kid.

"Listen, sonny," said a nasty desk sergeant with the breath of a foundry. "We got better things to do than chase after wild geese. Go play your jokes on someone with time on his hands."

I started to protest, saw I was about to get the heave-ho physically, and left under my own power instead.

Next choice: Delancey. Maybe he was back from his lunch at the hospital, playing Santa. I could only hope. When I got to his office though the doors were locked and the place was dark.

I tried Beulah's, though I was pretty sure she wouldn't be home—she wasn't. Then I finally lit on someone I should've gone to right away: Miss Dare.

Twenty-Three

Realizing that I'd wasted a lot of time, I ran to Miss Dare's house, and just about threw up when I got there. Just not used to running, and the pain in my ankle almost made me faint.

Anyhow, I didn't knock, but burst right in, calling her name. The sour housekeeper, Beggars, peeked around the corner and looked ready to toss me out on my ear, but fortunately Miss Dare followed her and said:

"Iggy! What's the matter? Come in!"

She ushered me into her living room. To my surprise, she and the crabby Beggars were decorating a small Christmas tree. I never would've expected Miss Dare to be so... festive. I didn't sit, but blurted out what had happened to Eddie and me. Believe it or not, Beggars looked worried.

"We'd best call the police," she said to Miss Dare when I'd finished.

"I tried to talk to the cops," I said. "They tossed me out."

"They'd believe Miss Hogwood," Beggars asserted.

"That may be," her boss said, "but it sounds as if we don't have time for the police. Come along, Iggy. We shall tend to this matter ourselves."

"But, miss," Beggars cautioned.

"You come along. We shall need all the muscle we can get."

The doughty housekeeper squared her shoulders and said she would not be found wanting. To make sure, she grabbed a baseball bat (apparently she was a nifty little third baseman in her day). After Miss Dare and Beggars dressed for the weather, we headed out back, to her garage.

Miss Dare owned a rattletrap old car. Must've been one of the first automobiles ever sold. It was covered with canvas, and she yanked off the sheet as if she were displaying the find of the century. Instead, it was a decrepit old Ford that looked as tired as I was after running all that way.

We clambered inside and, to my amazement, it started right off.

"I do take it out now and again," Miss Dare said to my bewildered look. "Now. Where to?"

I had to recalibrate my bearings, between the rush to get there, my surprise at the car's starting, and just the twists and turns required to reach Miss Dare's house. So I just told her to head west, out of town.

We were soon on the road, though I still hesitated a bit. You have to understand, except for salesmen, no normal people travel a lot. It just isn't done. All our relations live in the city or so far out of town that we don't bother to visit them often. That road out of town, I'd been on before, but the turn-off, to get on the county road, was another matter. I'd only been on it during this adventure. So I'm afraid I waffled, and Miss Dare, at the wheel, grew exasperated.

"Iggy, we don't have time for you to be uncertain! Now where is the turn-off?"

I racked my brains, trying to remember any landmarks or signs. Finally I recalled a sign for County Road A. That was it. I told Miss Dare that, and she gripped the wheel tighter and said, "Right," with determination.

Now, Miss Dare is not the finest driver ever to take the wheel. She was partially snockered most of the time, and on the open road, with a few patches of snow or ice, her driving was more than a little eye-watering. To show that it wasn't just me, Beggars—who never talked back to her mistress—insisted she slow down, for," I don't want to spend Christmas in the mortuary." Which brought a big laugh from her employer. Still, Miss Dare did slow down—a bit.

We got to the farmhouse safe and sound. There was no sign of anyone around, and for a few moments I figured I'd dreamt the whole thing. Or more likely, had I sent us down the wrong road? Was this some other farm?

No, there were tire tracks in the yard—fresh. And I remembered the peeling green paint on the front screen door and the barn about to fall down. This was definitely the place, but it looked like Mister X and his goons had gone.

Maybe they'd bumped off Eddie and we'd find his body, still sitting in a kitchen chair. Okay, I admit that for a second I was kind of thrilled by that possibility. Not that I wanted my buddy dead, mind you. It was just the idea that the kids at school would envy me, that I'd seen his corpse, riddled with bullets.

There was, of course, the possibility that some of the goons had left in the car to search for me, and the others, including Mister X, were still there. That idea seemed to come to all three of us, so we approached the front door cautiously, and stopped to listen just outside.

Miss Dare put a finger to her lips. Beggars wielded the baseball bat. Since the housekeeper was the only one of us armed, she motioned she would go first, then

Miss Dare, then me. I didn't like going last, but she had the bat, so I wasn't going to argue. At least I would fling open the door so Beggars would have her hands free. That much, I could do.

We burst in, ready for action, and found none. It was very disappointing.

The door entered into a living room, which I'd only seen in passing the first time. It was in ratty shape, a tattered sofa and two decrepit chairs; a small lopsided table in the middle; flowered, peeling wallpaper. There was no sign of any recent habitation.

"In the kitchen," I whispered, gesturing. The others nodded and we crept slowly. Why we bothered to be quiet, I'll never know (we'd made enough noise busting in). Anyhow, the kitchen was abandoned too.

There were signs of recent life, though. A couple of coffee cups still had a little liquid inside. Two chairs were pulled back from the table, and another was knocked over on its back. But there was no sign of Eddie, nor was there any blood. That was good news.

Miss Dare, who had been hunched over as if that made her so much smaller, now stood up straight. She still whispered, but a little louder.

"We should search the rest of the house and the barn, just to be sure."

I wasn't too keen on the idea because the place gave me the creeps, more even than when Eddie and I were held prisoners there. Still, I told myself, we had to make sure Eddie wasn't held captive somewhere on the grounds.

Miss Dare didn't want us to be separated, so we three went upstairs together like a bunch of Keystone Kops, and searched the rooms. Just more of the same: broken furniture, peeling wallpaper, mouse droppings. There seemed to be no sign that anyone had been up there for ages. Back downstairs, we headed out to the barn. All the time, I listened for a car in case Mister X and his gang came back.

To me, it seemed impossible that Mister X used this place as a hideout. He looked a fancy man, even if he associated with thugs. Surely this derelict building would be beneath him, at least on a regular basis.

But what if he owned the place? As we crossed the yard and could speak normally, I brought the subject up to Miss Dare, who nodded.

"It's very possible, Iggy. Of course, that would be asking for trouble on his part. If you went to the police, they would surely find out who owned it. My guess is, they knew the farm to be abandoned, and used it to their advantage."

"Do you think they meant for the boys to die here?" Beggars asked.

"Iggy could answer that better than I. But first, let's check out this barn."

We went inside. Well, to say 'inside' is pushing it. The place was falling apart so badly, you could see out of most of the roof and parts of the walls. I wondered if we might not get caught in a collapse, it was so bad. But Eddie could've been left out here, tied up and gagged, so we searched.

There was a bunch of rusted old farm equipment, a scattering of straw and creaking wood everywhere. There was a rickety ladder leading to a hay mow. Before Beggars or I could stop her, Miss Dare clambered up the ladder (well, she went sort of crab-like and not a bit gracefully, but it got the job done). She didn't actually climb into the mow, which was a good thing because I didn't want to see her backside as she scrambled up. Instead, she just looked around, called to us that there was nothing to see, and climbed down.

"So it's pretty clear Eddie's gone," Miss Dare said, brushing off dust and grit from the barn. We started for the car. "I think we'll head back to town. Is Eddie's mother home from work yet?"

"Not yet. She's working until… three or four I think."

"Well, it's not gone noon. Maybe we should go to Eddie's place anyway, just to make sure."

"Do you think we should visit her at work?" Beggars asked.

I cut in, "Eddie says his mom gets sore as a pup if she's interrupted at work. She's too busy with customers to chat."

"But if her son is kidnapped…"

Miss Dare pondered as she started the car. "Iggy, we were about to ask you if you thought those men might kill you. Now be honest: were you in fear for your life?"

I thought about it as the car eased out of the driveway and back onto the road.

"No," I finally said. "I got the feeling that Mister X and his goons just wanted to scare us. Since it didn't work for Delancey or the inspector to warn us off, or me getting shoved in a tunnel, or someone taking a shot at us—"

"Maybe it was Mister X's group that shot at you," Beggars suggested.

"Could be. The inspector thought that maybe the shooter didn't mean to hit us. Eddie just got injured by flying brick from a building."

This was great. I was being treated as a grown-up, even by the grouchy old housekeeper. I was feeling pretty good as we returned to town.

Without a word, Miss Dare headed for Eddie's house. How she knew where he lived, I don't know and never asked. But she did, and we pulled to a stop. Her car sounded like it was utterly exhausted by the excursion; gave a big wheeze as we stopped. I got out first.

Eddie and his mom live in an apartment, third floor. It's not a bad building, really. Most of the tenants have seen better times, but all of them care about how things look, and they keep up their places pretty well. There are a few eccentrics, like Mr Palmer, a daft old man who says his window box grows pixies, and he treats his pixies like children. Between you and me, those pixies look a fair bit like geraniums, but then I'm no gardener. Anyhow, Mr Palmer's harmless, so long as you humor him and say hello to the pixies in his window box.

So up the flights of stairs, Miss Dare huffing and puffing as we went, and when we reached Eddie's apartment, I knocked. Wasn't expecting an answer, but the door suddenly opened and there was my buddy, safe and sound.

Or at least it turned out that way. At first, I wondered if Mister X and his goons weren't there with him, but he just grinned and told us to come in—though he was a little surprised to see Beggars and Miss Dare with me.

Normally, Eddie's a little self-conscious about his place, given that it's not as fancy as some. But that time, he was proud to let us in, and we walked past the pretty Christmas tree and the cards strung up on the mantel with twine, and into the kitchen, where we sat.

"So," said Miss Dare when she'd plopped herself down to the chair. "Tell me how you escaped."

Eddie grinned again. "No need t 'escape. Oh, those guys were darned angry when you ran off, Iggy. I thought for sure they'd torture me or bump me off, or worse, but all that happened was Mister X just ranted and raved for a few minutes. He said there was no need for you to run off, that he meant what he said about not hurting us. I told him that we couldn't be sure about that, that we'd been shot at and you'd been pushed down into a tunnel, and what were we to make of that, I'd like to know."

"What'd he have to say to that?" I asked.

"Well, just like before, he swore up, down and sideways that he'd had nothing to do with any of those things."

"Did you believe him?" Miss Dare asked.

"You know what? I did. I got the feeling this business of taking hostages and threatening and all that, wasn't his style. He was doing it because he was… frightened, I guess. So yeah, I believe him."

"What did he do then?" I asked.

"Well, after he got through ranting, I asked what he was going to do now. He chewed his lower lip for a bit, then told his goons to put me back in the car. I figured he might have one of them shoot me and dump me by the side of the road."

"They could've killed you in the house," I said. "No one's been there in a long time." And I explained how we'd searched the place for him.

"Well," Eddie said, "whatever it was, all through that ride, I asked what they planned to do with me, and they didn't say a word. I think Mister X was trying to figure it out himself. Finally, he told the driver to take me home, and turned to me and said, 'Don't go poking your nose where it doesn't belong. We'll let you go this time'. And they stopped right outside my door, and let me out. No rough stuff at all."

He sounded disappointed.

Miss Dare said, "After all that, the least I can do is treat you boys—and you too, Beggars—to lunch." She suggested a place, but Eddie turned green and said no, maybe somewhere else. It was because that's where his mom works, and he didn't want to go there. I understood, but Miss Dare just looked puzzled and said okay, and named another place.

It was just a diner, where they serve greasy hamburgers and such, but Eddie and I ate like we hadn't had a bite in weeks, and even Beggars liked it.

After lunch, we went back to Miss Dare's house because she wanted to 'take stock' as she called it. "Whenever I'm at an impasse in my writing," she explained as we climbed into her heap, "I rehash things. Lay everything out. It may sound boring, but trust me, it works."

So off we went to her place. When we were settled in, Miss Dare with her brandy and the rest of us with hot chocolate, we started.

"Let's begin at the beginning," she said. "With your assignment."

It might sound dull, but we went through the whole story. If that bores you, then skip to the next chapter; otherwise, I'll skim through what we talked about. Some of it's important.

"We were supposed to find an article," I began, "in the newspaper. Something that we could report to the class on, after we got back from Christmas break. Eddie wanted Hippo Vaughn."

"Who?" That was Miss Dare.

"*Hippo Vaughn!*" Eddie cried. "Only one of the best baseball players—"

Miss Dare waved him off. "I understand. Go on, Iggy."

"Well, I found an article about them finding that body in your study."

Beggars cut in. "How old were these newspapers?"

"Three years. The library was getting rid of them. I think Miss P—that's our teacher—wanted some pretty old news. Anyhow, that's what got us started on it. We went to Delancey, and asked for his help."

"Thanks to Beulah," Eddie put in, "he agreed. Delancey called Inspector Fenrow and we got the straight story, that the woman was identified as Mrs Clapham, who had disappeared two years before."

I nodded. "We found out that in October 1919, Mrs Clapham left choir practice at her church around eight. The other choir members were standing around near the church entrance. Mr Blank, the director, and his wife, stayed inside to clean up. Mrs Clapham headed for home. Some of the choir members watched her round the corner and no one had seen her since."

"Until she was found," Miss Dare said, taking up the story. "My father's study hadn't been used in several years—since he died, actually. One day, I just decided to have a clean, that maybe parts of the house might prove useful again. To be honest, I wondered if I should sell the house, and of course the whole would have to be cleaned before a prospective buyer would look at it."

"I sent Mary," Beggars said, "a maid who has since left us, to clean the study, then decided to join her. The girl was a hard worker but not the quickest in word or deed. We went inside, the room was dark and cold. I went to open the drapes to the outer doors, the ones which lead to the backyard. Mary turned about and didn't see anything unusual at first. The body was lying on the other side of the desk, so it would not have been noticeable from where she stood at that moment."

"The desk is tucked into a corner," I said.

"Correct. Why Mr Hogwood pushed it so far back so he could barely look out—"

"He said the outdoors distracted him," Miss Dare said. "When he was working, he wanted no distractions. So he had the desk set back, away from a full view of outside. He was an outdoorsman. Liked to fish, mainly. He claimed the outdoors was calling him."

"So," Beggars went on, "Mary walked to the desk, figuring it would be a good place to start cleaning, and that was when she saw the body. The poor woman's corpse was so dehydrated, or mummified, or whatever the coroner called it, that Mary couldn't even be sure it had been human. When she finally decided it was, you could hear her cry from across the house. Not a scream, just a shout." Beggars sounded proud that the maid hadn't done something so melodramatic as scream.

"I came running," Miss Dare said, "and saw the body. Mary was close to fainting. So Beggars fetched the brandy while I called the police."

"Not a doctor?" Eddie asked.

"My dear Edward. If you had seen the body, you would have skipped the medical man, too."

"The police came," Beggars said. "That inspector and his superior. I gathered it was so unusual, the boss came along to see for himself."

"They did a thorough search of the study," Miss Dare said, "and then branched out to the whole house and the grounds."

"It was chaos," Beggars snapped. "I thought that boss was officious to the highest degree."

"Beggars, I'll thank you not to use complex words like 'officious', even if you are using them correctly. Now where was I? Oh, yes. The police searched the whole property, as I said, and found no clue. They took fingerprints in the study, what they could find, but really got no help on that count."

"They made a mess of things, that's for sure."

"But curiously, not in the study, Beggars. They were very careful around the crime scene, as they called it—though the inspector was pretty sure Mrs Clapham was not murdered here. At any rate, the police could see no violence had occurred in the study, so except for dusting for fingerprints, they more or less left it as they found it."

I said, "Delancey found a book that was pulled out a bit farther than the others, and pushed it back in."

"Did he? Well, that was… A *book*, did you say? The police never touched the books."

"Maybe your dad left it sticking out," Eddie said.

"Never. My father was almost psychotic in his orderliness. He never, ever would have allowed a book to be pulled out from the others. Beggars?"

"I took the diary from the case, miss," said the housekeeper, "but took no notice of a book pulled out."

I said, "That's because Delancey pushed it back in."

"Hm. Maybe. Iggy, do you recall which book it was?"

"I didn't see the title, but I might remember it from the way it looked, and where it was on the shelf."

"Then let us go to the study, to see if you can determine which book was out of place."

We marched down the hall, to the study. The place still seemed creepy to me, given what was found there, even though it was actually a pretty nice room. Nothing had changed since I saw it last, though the desk had been tidied. The first time, papers had been pushed to one side, kind of messy, despite what Miss Dare said about her dad being neat. Those papers were gone now.

As the others watched, I went around the back of the desk to look at the books there. Puzzled, I couldn't seem to find it.

"I have an idea," Miss Dare said. "Step back, Iggy, to about where you were when you saw Delancey push the book in. I'll be Delancey."

Like they'd done in the church with Blank coming out of the side door. I stood around where I recalled being when Delancey moved the book. Miss Dare went to the shelf, raised her hand as if to push in a book. I watched.

"Left. A little more," I said, as she moved her hand accordingly. "There! That's the one. With the faded red cover."

"Excellent!" Miss Dare cried. "And the winner is… *The Scarlet Letter?* What the devil would that have to do with anything?"

"I'm sure that's the book," I said, faltering.

"I believe you," Miss Dare said as she rejoined us. We started back to the living room.

"What's the book about?" Eddie wanted to know.

"Well, it's about a woman who is accused of adultery and forced to wear a red A, to show her shame."

"Adultery?"

"Sexual relations with someone not your spouse, though at least one of you is married."

"Can you do that?" Eddie shook his head. The marvels of sex were truly unfathomable.

Miss Dare let out a most unladylike laugh. We had reached the living room and were taking our seats again.

"You can, but it's not right," she told Eddie. "It's one of the commandments. I'm not sure which. I know what the commandments are, but I could never keep track of the numbers."

"So what does it mean?" I asked. "The book pulled out?"

Miss Dare shrugged. "Probably nothing. It's very possible the book was pulled out of place by a policeman who always wanted to read it, or even someone who came into the study during my disastrous lawn party many years ago."

175

"Could they get into the study from the yard during that party?"

"Yes. I purposely left the door unlocked, in case it started to rain. The study doors would've been a faster entry into the house than going around to the front."

I thought hard about this.

"When was the party?" I asked slowly. "Before or after the disappearance of Mrs Clapham?"

Miss Dare brightened at my question; Eddie looked baffled but in awe of my intellect (as I'm often in awe of his physical abilities); Beggars looked a little bored.

"It was before. Late summer, Beggars, was it?"

"Early September, miss."

"Right. So a month and a half or so before Mrs Clapham disappeared. Do you think there's a connection?"

"I dunno. I'm just trying to get it into my brain." After a pause, Miss Dare went on with the story.

"So after the body was found, and the police were finished in my house, they went around the neighborhood, interviewing suspects. The key suspect would, of course, be Mr Clapham, but clearly they had no evidence against him," Miss Dare wondered.

"Right," I said. "Even though we now know about that church group."

"Were they a group at the time?"

"I think so. But not in that tunnel. Hadn't found the entrance then."

"What if," Eddie said slowly, thinking as he spoke, "whoever done it, had found the tunnel? Before the group, I mean? Then the killer could've hauled the body through the tunnel without carryin 'it around the streets."

"By George, Eddie, I think you may have something there!" Miss Dare cried. I clapped my buddy on the back, and he grinned, proud but sheepish.

"So," Beggars cut into the accolades, "where does that leave us?"

"To me," Miss Dare said, "it means that the killer may or may not have been one of the group, but that the murder had nothing to do with them."

"Can we say that, though?" I asked. "No offense, miss, but isn't it possible that the killer was a member of the group, someone who found the tunnel first, and used it like Eddie said? I mean, it still could've had something to do with them. It might just mean it wasn't the whole group that did it, or even knew about it."

Beggars was pretty stunned how sharp Eddie and I were and, without asking, helped herself to a little brandy. When she sat down, she asked again:

"So where does that leave us? We still don't know if it was one of the group, or if it was, which one."

"We're not quite finished, Beggars," said her boss. "We have to speak of the murder of Mr Blank, the choir director. He was wearing one of the group's robes when he was killed. That would point to one of them."

"Does it?" she asked, back to her curt way of talking. "Seems to me, that group is pretty quiet about themselves. Would they kill one of their own so he could be found in their robe?"

"Sure," I said, maybe a little cockier than intended. "For one thing, they may not have known Eddie and I were there. Figured they had plenty of time to take off the robe. Or, they could've figured there was no way anyone could trace that robe."

Beggars sighed. "It's all a muddle. I say we let the police try and figure it out."

"Beggars! Where is your sense of adventure?"

"Gone when I turned forty, miss."

With that, the housekeeper left the room. Miss Dare seemed flabbergasted. "Well, I never! Beggars is usually such a zesty woman!"

Twenty-Four

Mostly, I've tried to tell this story from my own experience. I figure that's only fair because that way you can try and figure out who the killer (or killers) was (were) on your own. Fair's fair, after all.

But now I have to break with that—sorry.

We have to visit Delancey because he's got something I have to tell you about. I learned most of it later, straight from the horse's mouth, though I've had to fill in a few things here and there on my own—sometimes, I made a bunch of stuff up, but it's how I figured Delancey would have thought or felt at the time.

It started right after Delancey finished playing Santa.

He was sitting in the head guy's office at the hospital, slowly removing his Santa gear. The administrator who arranged this whole thing with Delancey, sat behind his desk, smiling.

"I can't tell you how much this is appreciated, Mr Delancey. The children love it!"

He was a short, round fella who would've made a better Santa than Delancey, but figured some kids might get wise if he wasn't there—which is baloney; he just didn't want to do it. Anyhow, when he smiled, the whole room glowed, and he was smiling now.

"Well, that's fine," Delancey grunted as he removed the big, black, cramped boots. He slipped on his own boots and wiggled his toes with a sigh. "I don't mind doing it."

"So we can put you down for next Christmas?"

"Sure," Delancey said, figuring that by then his tootsies would recover from getting crammed into boots a size and a half smaller than his feet.

Whiskers removed, red coat off, Delancey put on his own coat and hat. The administrator shook hands with him, and wished him a merry Christmas. Delancey returned the compliment and headed out.

It really wasn't an imposition, he told himself. Yeah, it was a rigmarole, getting into the suit and whiskers each year (and every year the suit seemed to have shrunk a bit, requiring less padding around the middle). But he really enjoyed being around the kiddies. Sometimes it broke his heart, seeing how sick some of them were, and he remembered when he was a kid, figuring it would've been a disaster to spend Christmas in the hospital. Yet, those kids were cheery and just went through all the treatments and such that doctors and nurses put them through. It made him ashamed, for thinking of the hassle it took to play Santa for a couple of hours.

Now, though, he decided to do a little work. Granted, it was Christmas Eve and some of the folks he wanted to see might not be around, but he'd give it a shot anyway. His plan was to visit the others in that religious group, to see what they had to say for themselves.

His first stop was the Jacksons.

Frank and Clara Jackson were a fifty-ish couple who lived in a modest three-bedroom place on the north side of town. Both were home when Delancey called.

Mrs Jackson answered the door and seemed befuddled when Delancey told her why he was there. She let him in though, and Delancey took off his hat. He was about to get comfortable in an offered chair when Mr Jackson came in.

The fellow was big and broad, and didn't put up with nonsense. He was in a tee-shirt and green work pants, and his feet were bare.

"What the hell is this?"

"Dear," said his wife, who wished he wouldn't curse, but he ignored her.

"Are you some salesman?" Mr Jackson went on. "We don't bother with salesmen. So just get out." He came nearer, standing in front of Delancey with menace.

"I'm not a salesman," Delancey assured him. "I'm here to talk about the murders of Mrs Clapham and Mr Blank."

"Oh? And you think we had something to do with that? Get out!" Jackson took another step forward, ignoring his wife's word of caution.

Just as he was about to grab Delancey by the coat lapels and give him the bum's rush, Delancey called out:

"I know about your secret organization. We found robes at Mr Clapham's house."

Jackson looked like someone had poleaxed him, right between the eyes. His fists were still cocked, but his brain was busy telling them to give it up. After a few seconds, he lowered them and told Delancey to sit, which he did. At first, it looked like Jackson wasn't clear if he would sit, too. He couldn't seem to decide,

179

then slowly lowered himself onto the sofa, across from Delancey. Mrs Jackson, who'd let out a little gasp when Delancey said he knew about the group, timidly shrank to the background, watching and listening, like a whipped dog in the corner.

"What is it you know?" Jackson asked quietly.

"Only what your group believes, and that you've been using the tunnel under the church." Another gasp from Mrs Jackson, ignored by the two men.

"You're right," Jackson allowed. "What does that have to do with the murders?"

"Mr Blank was wearing his black robe when he was stabbed to death."

"So?" He was getting belligerent again. "We didn't have anything to do with it. There was no meeting of our group that day."

"Then why was he in his robe?"

"How do I know? He was our leader, and probably was doing something to get the tunnel room ready for us. But I don't know that for sure."

"Who'd want to kill him?"

"I still can't help you. Blank wasn't the friendliest man around, but he wasn't the type to have deadly enemies. He didn't provoke that sort of reaction."

There was a pause. Delancey lifted his eyes to the kitchen doorway. "Mrs Jackson? Any ideas?"

"None."

She said it quickly, and coldly, and then retreated to the kitchen. Delancey stood and put on his hat.

"Well, thanks anyway. And have a merry Christmas."

Jackson didn't respond, and Delancey noticed for the first time there were no Christmas decorations of any kind in the house. That made him more sad than puzzled. He thanked Mr Jackson again and headed out.

Next up was the other couple, the Meyers. Delancey had a little trouble finding their house. It was on a dead end street, in a ritzy part of town with a few big houses with sprawling lawns and long driveways. Delancey parked at the front door. He expected some fancy footman to come out and greet him. Instead, his knock was answered by the lady of the house.

She was a good-sized woman of about fifty, though looking frowzy (Delancey had clearly caught her in the middle of cleaning house or some such). That surprised him, given how fancy the place was. Surely she had servants to do that kind of thing?

"Pardon my appearance," she said politely. "I'm just doing a little dusting before guests come tonight. The maid does such a terrible job of it. Won't you come in?"

Delancey was surprised by the welcome, though he hadn't explained who he was, just that he was working on the murders of Mr Blank and Mrs Clapham.

"I do hope you are able to have better progress than the police. Fred—that's my husband—adores the police, thinks they do a fine job. Sit, please." They sat in a very nice living room where a huge Christmas tree sparkled in one corner. "Maybe they do, but they certainly haven't had much success discovering who killed our friends."

"The cops aren't infallible," Delancey noted. "Sometimes the crook is just too clever. Or dumb lucky. It happens, sadly."

"Yes, I suppose. So what is it you wished to ask me?"

"Is your husband in? I have questions for both of you, really."

"No, he's out." She leaned in conspiratorially. "I think he's shopping for my present. Poor Fred works so hard, he often leaves such things to the last minute. But he does choose nice gifts."

"A fine house you've got here."

"Thank you. Fred's a banker. Did you know that? Vice president. Someday president, perhaps. We'll see. But very well respected."

"I'm sure he is. Anyhow, I suppose I can just ask you the questions, and come back another time if Mr Jackson is available."

She looked doubtful.

"It would have to be after the new year. There are several social gatherings between now and then."

"I understand. Well, maybe it won't be necessary."

Mrs Meyer sat back, smiling. She looked relaxed.

"Actually," Delancey said, "I really have one, very broad question to begin with. Are you and your husband members of a religious organization that meets in a tunnel under the church?"

The smile didn't fade, but it was as if it was frozen on her face. She didn't move an inch, at first. Then, slowly, she sat up straight and looked at him carefully, still smiling. Only when she spoke did the smile disappear.

"We are."

"And Mr Blank was the leader?"

"He was."

There was a long pause, and finally Mrs Meyer sighed and said, "Look, Mr Delancey. The other members have tried to hide our group's existence. They claim that the Church might be upset if they knew, but I don't see it that way. Why should we hide it? It isn't as though we're worshiping the devil. And if we disagree with some things that the Church teaches, why, who doesn't? I think it's a travesty that some people swallow the entire doctrine without thinking it through, don't you?"

"I'm not real intelligent when it comes to religion. I go to church—"

She smiled and was at ease again. "Of course. Actually, it's refreshing to hear your admission. So many people think they know everything... At any rate," she said, serious again and sitting back, "I'm not sure what the group has to do with the two murders."

"Well, besides the fact that each victim—"

"Five years apart."

"—five years apart, was a member of your group. Mr Blank was wearing one of your group's robes when he was killed."

"Was he? I hadn't heard that. Now why on earth would he be wearing the robe? We had no meeting." She seemed genuinely puzzled, but not at all upset.

"So no idea why he was wearing his robe?"

"None at all."

There was a pause. The mantel clock ticked loudly. In one corner of the room stood a baby grand piano. On the piano were a set of photographs, five in all. Delancey stood to look at them. He picked one up. It was a picture of two smiling young people, arms around each other's waist, standing in front of the entrance to a forest.

"This you and Mr Meyer?"

She joined him. "Yes. On our honeymoon in upstate New York. Beautiful country. A local park ranger took that photograph."

Delancey set the photo down, picked up another. This was the same couple, older and heavier now. A posed picture, done by a professional. He guessed it was taken a few years ago.

"That was our silver wedding anniversary," she said with pride.

"Children?" Delancey asked, not seeing pictures that indicated any.

Mrs Meyer's face fell. "We had one—John He died three years ago, in an accident at work."

"I'm sorry."

She smiled her acceptance of his words. "We don't have photographs of him out here because, well, it's painful still. I have photographs of our son in the bedroom, but not here. I suppose that sounds silly."

"How people deal with grief is never silly. They do what they can."

Another smile. "You're wise beyond your years, Mr Delancey."

"Tell that to my assistant. Anyhow, I won't take up any more of your time. Thanks for seeing me."

"Of course."

"Oh. One thing more. There are two young boys, around ten years old, who have it in their heads to investigate these murders."

"Playing detective." The sad smile came back.

"Yep. And of course, no one can warn them off. You know first-hand what boys are like."

"I do." Delancey was sorry he'd said it.

"The only reason I bring it up, is those boys are in danger, and since no one can warm 'em off, I ask you and the members of your group to make sure they don't end up in trouble. I'm not suggesting one of your group would hurt them—"

"Though you are implying it," she said, not harshly.

Delancey grinned. "You understand, I see. Anyhow, just make sure Eddie and Iggy are safe."

"Eddie and Iggy. Right. I'll make sure that if I hear of anything about them, they are safe."

"I appreciate it."

Delancey said his farewells and wished her and Mr Meyer a merry Christmas, and left. He had one more stop, and was dreading it.

Mrs Blank was a little on the stony side, but she let Delancey in when he told her why he was there.

The house was neat, though a little cramped. There was a small Christmas tree in one corner of the living room, half-heartedly trimmed. Maybe that was how the Blanks always decorated. Taped on the woodwork around the entry from the living room to the kitchen were a number of Christmas cards, and sympathy cards were set up on the mantel.

Mrs Blank was dressed neatly in navy blue, and offered Delancey coffee, which he refused. They sat.

"I have to be at church in an hour," she said.

"I won't keep you anywhere near that long, ma'am. And I thank you for seeing me at all."

"What can I do for you?"

"I know you've been through all this with the cops, but I can sometimes look at things differently than they can, go where they can't. So if you don't mind, I'd like to ask you about your husband. What was he like?"

She smiled sadly. "I suppose you expect me to say he was a saint. Well, he wasn't. He was a bit... cold with me. Sometimes he could be affectionate, but other times, not so much. And he was very conservative in his attitudes towards women. What I mean to say is, he didn't strike me or anything—he just believed that I would be better served staying home, cooking and cleaning."

"You didn't have children?"

Another sad smile. "We did, but he died in the flu epidemic of '18. Poor little thing never stood a chance. I wanted to try again, but not my husband. After that, especially, he was cold to me. As if it was my fault our child died!" She was getting angry.

"Not unusual in grief to blame another, no matter if it makes sense or not."

"I suppose that's what he was doing. He doted on our son. Had high hopes for him."

"What about towards others? Was he well-liked by anyone?"

She smiled, a bit more amused this time. "I don't want you to get the impression no one liked him, Mr Delancey. Henry could be a cold fish, it's true, but he had friends. And many people respected his dedication to the choir. That choir—you should come listen to us! Mind you, we may not be as good now without my husband at the helm, but we are excellent, if I may say so, and it was chalked up to Henry's abilities and devotion to duty."

"So what you're saying is, you can't think of anyone who would want him dead?"

"I can't. Clearly someone did, but I didn't know about it."

"I see. Well, I won't trouble you any longer, Mrs Blank."

"It's no trouble, I assure you." They stood. "And if you have no church to go to this evening, please feel free to stop in at ours."

"Thanks for the invitation," Delancey said sincerely. They shook hands and Delancey left.

It had started to snow lightly. Flurries seemed to lose their way to the ground. A cut to the air frosted his cheeks. Delancey jammed his hands in his coat and headed for home.

He didn't really know what to do. When Mrs Blank had first suggested he visit their church for Christmas Eve, it was tempting, but he decided against it. He needed something livelier. And yet...

It was so tranquil at his apartment, Delancey was sorely tempted to just sit home, put on a Christmas record or listen to the radio, maybe have a cocktail or two. This whole business of the murders, and of Eddie and me in trouble, was weighing on him. He didn't want to see anyone get hurt. Going to the church where Mr Blank had been director might help solve the case. He might hear something that would crack it open.

But he didn't want to think about the case. Couldn't he just have a nice Christmas, and put all this out of his head for thirty-six hours? Delancey decided to do just that, and it wasn't going to happen by going to their church, and it wasn't going to happen sitting home alone.

After a quick shave and a change into better clothes, Delancey headed out.

Twenty-Five

While Delancey was speaking to the suspects, Eddie and I were pondering what else we could do. The answer was simple.

"Nothing." I sighed, and Eddie sighed too. We were walking home under the snowy clouds. "We've taken it as far as we can, at least for now. You gotta get ready for your Christmas program, and I better head home before my folks rent out my room."

"Right," Eddie said, his eyes big, like I was serious.

"They wouldn't really rent out my room," I assured him, and he was relieved.

Along the way, an idea hit me, and after a little worry at what my parents would say, I decided to give it a try. Eddie and I parted with a promise to meet up the next day.

"Mom," I said, getting cleaned up after my day's adventures, "I'd like to go see Eddie at his Christmas program, at his church. You know, lend him a little support. He's devilish worried about how it'll go, playing a Wise Acre or something."

Dad was still down in the shop. Mom was busy scrubbing the kitchen counters. She takes Moses's laws about cleanliness to the hilt. All during my little speech, she didn't even look my way. Mom has that way about her. Until she's ready to pronounce judgment, she tries not to give anything away. In a way, it's good because it means she doesn't fly off the handle; in another way, it's unsettling. Now, she paused in mid-scrub, slowly turned my way.

Here it comes, I thought.

"I think," she started, tentatively, "that if you want to go and support your best friend, you should do it. Just don't get *ideas!*"

"I promise not to listen to the story. I just wanna be there for him."

She went back to scrubbing. "Won't he be embarrassed, having you there?"

"Nah. He knows I'd never tease him if he messed up. Well, not a *lot*, anyway."

I breathed a sigh of relief. Now, you might wonder why she didn't tell me to ask my dad for permission. That never would've entered her head. First of all, he was busy in the shop, and only military invasion would justify interrupting him on the busiest day of the year.

Secondly, it was understood that, in our household, Mom was in charge of me. Dad worked and paid the bills, and led the family in religious observances; Mom did everything else, including my upbringing. If there was trouble at school (which I made sure there never was) or if I needed emergency funds for something important, like licorice, Mom was the one to decide.

The store was just closing when it was time for me to head out. I'd dressed well for the occasion. Mom insisted I take my yarmulke, though I certainly wasn't going to wear it in a Lutheran church. Anyhow, Dad glanced up as I passed through the store to the front door, but he was busy with the day's receipts, and didn't say a word. He'd ask Mom later, if he thought of it.

I'd been in a Christian church a few times—aside from the investigation that brought me to the Blanks 'church—once for a wedding, twice for funerals. Some of my folks 'stricter friends were appalled that they'd let me go, but I couldn't see what the fuss was about. To be honest, except for Jesus statues and crosses, it wasn't that much different from our synagogue.

I did feel a little self-conscious though, and I checked my head more than once, to make sure I'd taken off the yarmulke, even though I could feel it in my coat pocket. I didn't have to worry, actually as there were so many people—mostly parents fussing and kids getting fussed with—that I was mostly ignored.

Still, I wanted to sit as far back as possible and, after taking a program from a nice usher at the door, I slipped inside and sat in a back pew, trying to make myself invisible. No worry—the place was so crowded, nobody paid me any mind. I couldn't see the attraction, myself: a bunch of kids who couldn't sing, trying to belt out a tune; kids dressed up like biblical grown-ups and farm animals, missing cues and tripping over robes too long for them. But the congregation seemed to enjoy it.

I got a shock though, right before the program started. There was still a little space between me and the nearest adult, until some guy came up and squeezed in right next to me, filling the gap. I was about to tell him to buzz off, when the voice rang a bell.

"Delancey!" I said, looking up.

Sure enough, it was everybody's favorite private detective. He grinned and asked what I was doing there.

"Same as you, I guess. T 'see Eddie in action."

So we settled back to watch and listen. I was a lot more comfortable now, with a grown-up I knew, and it made folks around me more at ease too because a solitary kid at a Christmas program seems out of place, I guess.

Anyhow, it was pretty good. Some of the songs were nice, though you couldn't make out most of the words because the kids tended to think they should start singing whenever they felt like it. Sort of like singing a round. On the couple of tunes where the congregation joined in though it was pretty rousing, I have to admit.

As to Eddie and the players in general, they did okay. Eddie was a Wise *Man*, and he came walking in like a guy with a hot date waiting. He pronounced, "Behold! We have seen God's star in the heavens!" and did a pretty fair job of it. I was proud of him.

After the program ended, the hall out front was more jam-packed than the church had been. Folks milling around everywhere; kids and parents trying to meet up with no clue where each other was. They might've made a plan to meet at such and such a place, but if they had, they sure forgot about it.

Anyhow, I spotted Mrs McDonald, Eddie's mom, and telling Delancey to come on, wedged my way through the mob towards her. She was pretty surprised to see us.

"Iggy! Delancey! What're you doing here?" was how she put it.

"Came to give support to Eddie," Delancey replied. "He did a good job."

She beamed. "Yes, I thought he did very well. And it was awfully nice of the two of you, coming to see him. Here he is now."

Eddie was wading through the crowd that had finally started to thin a bit. He was carrying his coat—no elbow room to put it on—and his Wise Man robe. He stopped cold when he saw us. For a second, it looked like he might bolt, and I worried it was a mistake for us to come. Then he grinned, sheepish, and came forward.

"You did a great job," Delancey said, and Eddie blushed.

"Yeah," I added. "I even sort of understood the story."

"Thanks," he managed.

It would've been nice to chat some more, but the gabble of voices made it darned near impossible for anything but a few words. So we stepped outside as Eddie slipped on his coat. Standing in the frosty air, Eddie thanked us for coming.

"If you want," Delancey said, "I can give you a lift home. You too, Iggy."

Since the night was getting pretty nippy, and there was still a touch of snow, we agreed with thanks. Delancey dropped me off first, and I wished everybody a merry Christmas. It was the end to a definitely weird December 24th.

The next day dawned bright and sunny, though a little cold. I went outside, just poking around. Eddie was late, because after all it was Christmas, and he had presents to open and breakfast to eat. No running off with a piece of toast in his mouth.

When he finally came outside, Eddie was beaming, holding his brand new sled.

"Hey, that's a peach," I told him, and he smiled so broad I thought his face would crack.

"Yep. It's just the one I wanted." Then his face darkened a bit. "I have t 'be back by eleven. My aunt and uncle are coming for Christmas dinner."

"Sure. C'mon. Let's go try out that new sled."

I had a sled of my own, and a pretty good one, but this day it was Eddie's turn to show off. He got the first ride down Taylor's Hill, of course, where a dozen other kids were trying out their new sleds and toboggans. The crisp cold air was filled with shouts and laughter. It was like the whole world decided to give trouble the day off.

Eddie's sled was the best one there, which I told him of course. But honest, it was true. The sharp red paint, the clean runners—it really was a peach. After Eddie had had a couple of tries, it was my turn, and his sled pretty much rocketed down the hard snow. Steered like a dream too.

As if by agreement, we didn't say a word about the case while we sledded. We were having too much fun. After a while though our noses felt ready to fall off, so we hightailed it to my place (Eddie's mom was too busy for us to get in her way. Besides, she might put us to work). There, Mom was still cleaning up the breakfast dishes.

"Good morning, Eddie," she said. Mom's not much for wishing Christians a merry Christmas. She has nothing against them, but the phrase means nothing to her, so she doesn't use it. Anyhow, he wished her a good morning too.

We went through the living room, exchanged greetings with my dad. I told him about Eddie's new sled (which we'd parked in the front hall because it was caked with snow) and he insisted on seeing it. When he did, Dad declared it to be the finest he'd seen, which made Eddie blush to the roots.

After that, Eddie and I went to my room, just to talk, and it was then we finally started in on the case.

"I don't know that we've got anywhere to go," I said. "I mean, we've investigated all we can, and we're still no closer to knowing who the killer is."

"I still say it could be two of 'em. That Mr Blank killed Mrs Clapham, then someone killed him. Maybe Mr Clapham found out Blank offed his missus and got his revenge."

"I guess that makes sense."

"Sure it does!"

"But how do we *prove* it, I'd like to know? We've talked to everyone involved. Delancey's on the job. The cops are back on the case since Blank got bumped off. What can we do that they can't?"

"I dunno," Eddie admitted.

For a time, we just sat on the bed, quiet. Eddie stood and walked around, pacing like Holmes on the case. He stopped cold suddenly.

"What is it?" I asked. "You got something?"

"It ain't that. Come here. And be careful while you're at it." He was near the window. I joined him quietly.

"Careful now," Eddie whispered. "That feller out there has been standing on the corner, lookin 'up at us for some time. *And* I thought I saw the same guy at the sled hill."

"You sure?"

Eddie's powers of observation are pretty good, so I wasn't doubting his abilities. If he was certain, then I would believe him.

"Yep. That ratty coat he's wearing, dark blue an 'all—I *know* the same feller was at the hill. And every so often he looks up at this window. There he goes again! Act innocent!"

I pretended to point at something on a nearby shelf. Eddie was fooled at first and looked, then nodded slightly. We would make the guy think we were just looking at something in my room. We stepped away from the window.

"What do we do?" Eddie asked.

"First thing we've gotta do is be sure he's following us. Let's go out for a bit, walk around. If he follows, then we'll split up and see who he goes with."

"Right. I'd better start heading for home anyway, or Mom'll have my hide."

"Okay. Let's go."

I told my mom I was going to walk a bit with Eddie then come back. She waved her okay, and off we went, making sure to bring Eddie's new sled along.

It didn't take long to figure out for sure that the guy was tailing us. We stopped outside a shop window to look at the Christmas decorations, and glanced to the side. There was Old Blue Coat, as Eddie took to calling him. He stopped about fifteen feet away, checking his fingernails.

"Not very good, is he?" I muttered to Eddie, who chuckled.

We walked a bit farther, then Eddie said he really had to go home. So we parted ways, eager to see which of us Old Blue Coat would follow. I guess each of us hoped we were the target.

Anyhow, the streets were pretty quiet, except for some folks heading home from church, and I took it slow on the way but made sure I was always in public with at least a few folks around… because Old Blue Coat followed me. I made it home without him trying to nab me, though.

"Did you have a good time with Eddie?" Mom asked. Now she was busy cooking dinner. I've never seen her when she isn't doing *something*.

"Yup. His sled's a peach."

"Now don't go hinting around for a new sled. Your old one is perfectly fine."

"I wouldn't, Mom. Eddie has so few nice things, I don't want to outshine him on this. He should have the best of something once in a while."

There was a pause, then Mom came over and gave me a big hug. Why, I don't know. Got flour all over my sweater.

Anyhow, it was a nice quiet day. With everything closed, we spent time as a family. I thought at first my folks had invited relatives over—they do that sometimes when shops are closed—but I was spared Aunt Gracie's voluminous hugs or Uncle David's overpowering cigar smoke. Even Uncle Fred, who had helped at the shop when Dad was sick, wasn't around. I guess he'd had enough of our family.

We played cards for a bit, chatted about this or that, and had a pretty nice time. I thought about Eddie and his raucous relation (he tells me stories you wouldn't believe). And I thought about Old Blue Coat. Even felt a little sorry for him, standing out there in the cold.

Later that afternoon, I went to my room and casually looked out the window. Old Blue Coat was nowhere to be seen.

Twenty-Six

The more I thought about this whole thing, the more my head hurt.

How does Delancey do all this? Investigate a murder, I mean. For that matter, how do the police do it? Well, I guess it helps that the cops have lots of men to help. But not Delancey. He has Beulah. And while she's pretty smart, and so is he, it's still just two of them. It just baffled me, as I thought about it. Eddie and I had spent hours pondering this case and working on it, and it was just blasted confusing.

Yet, I told myself as I lay in bed that night, we must be getting close to something. Why else would someone shove me down into that tunnel? Why would someone take pot shots at us? Why was Old Blue Coat hanging around? And why would we get kidnapped in broad daylight to get warned off? We just *had* to be getting warmer. I just couldn't figure out how.

I had no idea how to proceed. Should we just listen to what every adult was telling us, to leave it alone? That might be for the best, I decided. Just leave it be. Delancey would be sure to tell us what happened when it was over.

And yet… the cops had never found who killed Mrs Clapham. Delancey and the cops didn't seem to be making progress on Blank's murder, either. Would it really be such a bad thing to look into it some more? No, I told myself. It wouldn't. So I went back and forth. Should we or shouldn't we keep going?

Like the flu, an answer came to me in the middle of the night.

I woke up, sweating, my heart pounding. I'd been dreaming of the case, Miss Dare falling down the tunnel, the black robed people standing around, including dead Mr Blank and Mister X the kidnapper.

In my dream, Miss Dare fell down the tunnel and walked to the center of that room where the altar was, and all those people standing around. There on the altar were Eddie and me! We were tied up like Isaac, and Mr Blank, like Abraham, raised a crooked dagger, ready to plunge it into our hearts. "No!" Miss Dare cried, and I felt relieved until she said, "Allow me."

I couldn't believe it. Miss Dare was our friend! Why would she do this? As she took Blank's place at the altar, Mr Clapham was saying, "This will teach you not to snoop around where you don't belong!" I told him we promised not to do it again.

Eddie cut in, saying, "Speak for yourself, Iggy. I'd do it again in a minute."

"Just as I thought," Miss Dare replied. She raised the dagger. Just as she was about to run us both through the heart, I woke up.

That settled it. I wasn't going to get any sleep until this case was solved, and if it meant Eddie and I had to solve it, we would.

Fortunately, Eddie had the same opinion, and he even had an idea when we met up the next day, just outside his place.

"It came to me," he said, "while my boring old uncle was telling one of his war stories. How dull do you have to be, to make a big battle sound boring?"

"So what's your idea?" I asked.

"I think we should go back to Clapham's house. The robes were there. Heck, he'd even kept his wife's robe, and she's been dead for years. There has to be something else there."

"And what if he's home?" I asked. "Or even that creepy maid of his. It was different the last time—Delancey was talking with Clapham, to keep him occupied."

Eddie thought about this. "Okay. What if you go and talk to the feller while I look around?"

"*Me!* What am I supposed to talk to him about? He'll tell me to scram, and I won't be able to say anything to keep him from kicking me out. You'd be caught inside with no hope of escape."

More thinking. We were slowly walking in the direction of Clapham's house. I think Eddie thought I couldn't tell we were, but I noticed it all right.

"Well, I won't go inside until I hear you and him in the living room together, talkin'," Eddie suggested.

It still sounded like a dumb plan, but I agreed to at least give it a shot. "One problem," I said.

"What's that?"

"Old Blue Coat's back. Don't turn around! We picked him up around Seventh. So far, he won't have a clue where we're headed. But we need to lose him pretty soon." After a few more yards 'walking, I got an idea. "Into Mr Kramer's," I said.

Mr Kramer is an old German who runs a corner grocery. He's a jovial sort, the kind you see in tintype photographs hoisting frothy steins and so on. Everything but the lederhosen. Not the Kaiser's boy at all. In fact, Mr Kramer used to spit when the Kaiser was mentioned (which outraged some of his shop customers, I can tell you).

"Morning, boys," he said with a big grin. He was helping a lady reach a can of something from a high shelf. We returned the greeting. Eddie still didn't know what I was up to.

I could see Old Blue Coat standing across the street, waiting. I quickly asked Mr Kramer for three cents 'worth of licorice whips. He filled the bag with the treats, I paid, and then tugged at Eddie's sleeve.

The beauty of Mr Kramer's shop is it has two entrances—the street one, and a side door. That side door can't be seen from across the street unless you're absolutely head on, and Old Blue Coat wasn't head on. Eddie grinned, catching on, and we headed out the side door, calling goodbyes to Mr Kramer.

From that side door, we could cut across another yard to the next street, over, which we did. No sign of Old Blue Coat. Eddie started to strut. Never a good sign when Eddie struts. Means he's getting too cocky. I told him we had to hurry away from there, in case our tail caught on he'd been ditched. He stopped his strutting and we scurried off to the Clapham house.

Once we were on the quiet street where Clapham lived, I was feeling a little safer. Now we just had to get inside.

There was no sign of anyone around. Clapham had an automobile, which was not in the garage (we could peek through a window).

"Maybe at work," Eddie suggested. "He seems the type to go, day after Christmas."

Of course, both my dad and Eddie's mom were working that day, but that was out of necessity, so I said nothing about it.

"The maid might be around, though," I said. "I'd better try the front bell."

This was actually less scary than anything else we'd done. If the maid was there, I'd call the whole thing off; if she wasn't, so much the better. I rang the bell a couple times, could hear it inside—no answer. I came down from the front porch.

"Should we try the kitchen window?" Eddie asked.

"Probably best. Hopefully, they didn't figure out that's how we got in the last time."

When I think about it, I figure we were easy targets for a burglary charge. Mind you, at our age, we wouldn't get tossed in the hoosegow, but there was no better way to scare a kid than with the sheriff and a threat of reform school. Those two things petrified kids more than Santa bringing no presents.

None of that went through our heads at the time. All we cared about was finding evidence of the killings of Mrs Clapham and Mr Blank.

"Let's check on the main floor first," I whispered. "That way, if one of 'em comes home, we're upstairs and maybe can get away."

Eddie nodded.

The main floor was simple enough: the kitchen, living room, dining room, a small parlor. Eddie searched the kitchen (and came out of that room five minutes later, chewing something) while I looked through the living room. The place was really tidy, so anything hidden would have had to be hidden really well. Anyhow, we didn't find a single thing worth noting. Found out Mr Clapham read *Collier s* magazine, is about all.

Next we went upstairs. I've already described that area from our first visit, and we figured there was no sense in going over areas we'd already searched. The main item I wanted to have a look at was in a spare bedroom that we hadn't got to search thoroughly last time.

Clearly, Mr Clapham used this room as a kind of study because there was a desk and a couple of bookcases with dull books in them. While Eddie checked out the rest of the room, I sat at the desk, a roll-top affair that fortunately was unlocked.

At first, I thought it was a bust. Lots of bills, letters, receipts and so on. Might've been my dad's desk, it was that dull. That was all on the desk top and in the cubbyholes. Next it was the drawers. More of the same, only those papers were older. Finally, I checked the shallow drawer in the middle, where most folks keep pens and pencils. He had those in there, but he also had something else: a letter.

As you value your life, the letter read, *do not speak a word to the police or that detective, Delancey.*

That was all. I turned it over several times, almost as if I expected it to suddenly sprout new words. I showed it to Eddie, who got very excited about it.

"This is a big break," he declared.

"Maybe. But we've no idea who sent it."

"Don't you see, though? Clapham must know who sent it. If we show this letter to the cops, they can put the screws into Clapham, demand he tell 'em all. That should break the case open."

I shook my head. "Sure, but how are we ever gonna explain to the cops how we happened to get the letter? I mean, what we're doing ain't exactly legal."

Eddie waved it off. "Maybe not, but the cops should be impressed, and they'll want so bad to talk to Clapham, they'll drop any interest in us. Or," he added slowly, "we could take it to Delancey, instead. He's *always* doin 'stuff that's barely legal. If anyone can wiggle out of a burglary charge, it's him."

Everything Eddie said was true. Delancey has been known to get in a few scrapes with the law. Generally, his old buddy on the force, Inspector Fenrow, pulled enough strings to get him off the hook, though not always. Once, he came very close to getting tossed in the slammer for twenty years. Anyhow, I still wasn't convinced we could get the police to look the other way. Wasn't there some law against using material illegally obtained? What was called for, I thought, was an outside observer.

"I think," I said slowly, "we should hold off with the cops, or even Delancey. I think we should talk to Miss Dare."

Eddie chewed on this for a few moments, then agreed.

Little did we know, our decision would have near-disastrous consequences.

Twenty-Seven

That same day after Christmas, Beulah was back in town.

The time at her sister's had been partly good, partly awful. She enjoyed seeing her family, but there were the unending hints about her life. Two years earlier, Beulah had been happily married. Then she began to suspect her husband might be playing elsewhere. She hired Delancey (wasn't working for him at the time) to find out if it was true. No sooner had Delancey entered the picture when Mr Willows, Beulah's husband, got himself murdered.

The cops suspected Beulah, but Delancey figured out who had really done it. The two became friends (it's pretty clear that's all they are, like brother and sister, much to Eddie's relief) and Beulah suggested Delancey could do with an assistant. Delancey was barely into the business, and couldn't afford to hire anyone. No matter; Beulah's husband had left her well fixed for cash, and she agreed to work for peanuts. They've been together ever since.

Now that Beulah had been a widow for nearly two years, her family—especially her sister—was harping on at her to get married again. She was attractive (just ask my pal) and pretty well set. There was no need for her to work. Why not marry and have babies?

Beulah doesn't want to do that. Oh, I think she'd marry the right guy if he came along, and no that's *not* my best buddy, but she wasn't going to wed any Tom, Dick or Harry just so she could be married. That was the bone of contention with Beulah and her sister and the family. I guess there were a couple of aunts who were on her side, but the rest would shake their heads, tut-tut, and look at Beulah with a sad look of pity.

So it was pretty easy to see why she wanted to come home as soon as she could. Beulah got back to her apartment, unpacked, set up the cute little ceramic figurine her sister had given her for Christmas, and sat down to relax.

And immediately was bored.

Now, something Eddie and I have discovered from visiting Delancey is that the life of a private eye isn't anything like what you read about in the magazines or see in the motion pictures. Fact is, it can be pretty dull. Plenty of times, we've stopped in to say howdy and found Delancey tossing playing cards into his hat and Beulah reading a book. Even when he gets a case, it might be a simple matter of proving someone was cheating on their spouse, like what Beulah hired Delancey to do.

That day, Beulah decided going into the office had to be more exciting than sitting around twiddling her thumbs—even if that meant going through bills or typing up an invoice to a client. So she put on her coat and hat and headed out.

When she arrived, Beulah was surprised to see a light on in Delancey's office, though not in her outer office. She'd grown used to watching herself, in case someone got ticked off at something Delancey had done, so she entered cautiously.

"Delancey! What the heck are you doing here?"

"I could ask you the same thing. How was your Christmas?" Delancey was sitting at his desk, going over some old files.

"Oh," Beulah said, flopping into a chair across the desk from him, "the usual recriminations for being single."

"I get the same from my family. It's why I don't visit them." He grinned, but Beulah was serious.

"It's not the same for men, though, is it? I'm still of an age when I can have children, and some people just think it's a tragedy if I don't."

"Why do you listen to them?"

Delancey's matter of fact way of asking the question didn't please Beulah much. She balled her fists, then released them.

"Because," she said evenly, "it's family. People I love. They think they're being kind, helpful. They aren't. And anyway, I resent their suggestion that they know better than I how I should conduct *my* life." There was a pause. "How was your Christmas?"

"Quiet. I telephoned my folks, of course. Listened to a couple of Christmas programs on the radio. Oh, and Christmas Eve I went to see Eddie in his Christmas program at church."

"Oh? How was he?"

"Actually not too bad. Iggy was there too, to lend moral support. They're good kids."

"Yeah, they are."

"Even if Eddie wants to marry you some day."

Beulah shook her head. "Please don't encourage him."

"He doesn't need any encouragement. The kid's got it bad. Don't worry, it'll blow over."

"I don't want to hurt his feelings."

"You won't. In time, he'll grow up enough to latch onto a girl closer to his own age, then wonder how stupid he could've been to have such ideas."

Beulah grinned. "Sounds like you speak from experience."

Delancey shrugged. "Most boys go through it. A teacher, the mother of a friend… It's a natural occurrence. Didn't you ever have a crush on a much older man?"

"No, I've never had a crush on you, Delancey."

He shot a rubber band at her, missed by a mile, and Beulah went to her desk to get a little work done.

She wasn't sitting there five minutes when a slow tread was heard from the stairs down the hall. Beulah listened; sometimes that meant trouble. But when the walker arrived, it was only Inspector Fenrow.

Pleasantries of the season were exchanged, they asked each other how Christmas had gone. Fenrow, who's married with a couple kids just said, "Don't get me started." Then they got down to business.

"Fact is," he said, "I was wondering if you two had seen those boys."

"Who? Eddie and Iggy?" Delancey asked.

"Yeah, though we've got other names for 'em at the station, not complimentary. Pains in the asses, both of 'em. Excuse me, Beulah."

Beulah, who had heard (and said) far worse, smiled. "I thought," she said, "you had put a watch on them."

"Sure. But it's Christmas, you know? So the only guy we could get for the duty was Fustermann, who's never been more than average. He kept an eye on 'em all Christmas Day, then went home when they did. This morning, he picked 'em up again, and it all was going pretty well. Then they ditched him." Fenrow explained how we'd gone into a shop and not come out.

Delancey cracked up, shook his head. "Those kids are sharper than anyone gives them credit for. Either they didn't want him following because they're up to no good, or they thought it would be funny to get rid of him. If it's the latter, they're okay, just off somewhere. If it's the first…"

"I know, I know. So I take it neither of you have seen 'em?" Both shook their heads.` "Damn. For two pennies I'd forget 'em completely. But with their skills, I was sort of hoping they'd be cops one day."

199

"Or better yet, private detectives."

Fenrow made a rude noise. He and Delancey are friends, but Fenrow never did like it that Delancey went private. I think he hoped one day he could be Delancey's boss. Each ignored the insult to his career, and went on.

"Any ideas where they might've gone?" Fenrow asked. Delancey and Beulah looked at each other.

"Might be any of a half dozen places," Delancey said.

"Damn. I've got a murder to solve, and those two are out playing detectives. For two pennies—" He was starting to repeat himself.

Beulah cut in. "Did Mr Fustermann check any of their haunts?"

Fenrow nodded. "Yesterday, they went sledding, so he checked there— although they didn't have their sleds with 'em, so that was a waste of time. Then he checked their homes. Of course, he didn't actually knock—no sense worrying parents when they could be fine. I dunno. You don't think they'd be stupid enough to return to the church?"

"Maybe," Delancey said. "Look. Why don't you go about your business, and Beulah and I will check around. We really weren't up to much today, anyway."

Fenrow looked pleased. "You'd do that? Great. Just give me a jingle at headquarters when you find 'em. Then I can go and slap handcuffs on 'em, teach 'em a lesson."

He was only joking—a little.

As Beulah and Delancey were getting on their coats, Delancey stopped cold. "What's up?" Beulah asked. She knew the look on his face was a good sign.

"I think I have an idea who the killer is. Come on."

While this was going on, Eddie and I went to Miss Dare's house. Ditching Old Blue Coat had been fun, but now we had to get down to business, and Miss Dare would be the one to ask for help.

"She's bound t 'have ideas," Eddie said as we walked along. "I mean, she's a writer, ain't she?"

Eddie has always been in awe of writers. Never fond of writing anything at any time, he admired those who actually did it for fun, or for a living. He thought they were amazing.

We reached the door of Miss Dare's place, and knocked. No answer. We were a little puzzled because we could see her car through the garage window.

"Maybe they're at some holiday do," Eddie suggested.

"Do either of 'em strike you as the merry Christmas, eggnog and mistletoe type?"

"Not really."

"Let's go." And I started to leave.

But Eddie wasn't giving up so easily. He tried the front door and it opened. I whispered that this was not a good idea, but he ignored me, as he always does when he goes all Sherlocky on me.

Eddie peeped inside, then slipped through the door. I followed.

We were as quiet as could be. Eddie eased the door shut and we waited a second while our eyes adjusted to the dark hall.

Eddie tiptoed to the living room. No one there. The Christmas tree stood dark and forlorn in a corner. Papers were scattered all over, and at first I thought Miss Dare had been attacked, until I remembered what a slob she was.

I expected Eddie to go upstairs next. Instead, he went down the hall toward the study. I was really impressed at how catlike he was. The study was empty too, but Eddie started looking around, checking drawers and such.

"What're you doing?" I hissed. "Miss Dare is our friend!"

"I know. But I wanna look for clues anyhow."

I stood back, shaking my head. One of these days, he was going to get in big trouble. My upset didn't matter to Eddie, though—he just kept opening drawers, finding little, if anything, inside. The papers he did find were old paid bills or an odd letter related to business. He would examine each one in turn, then put it on a stack on the desk. When he finished with the drawer, the stack went back inside. I had to hand it to him: he was methodical if nothing else.

Actually, he told me later, he was just stalling, hoping Miss Dare or even Beggars would show.

So I did likewise, wandering around the room like a window-shopper.

After a minute or two, I arrived at the bookcase behind the desk, the one that had the book Delancey had pushed in. What was the book again? Oh, yes, *The Scarlet Letter*. I found it again, took it out this time.

"What'd Miss Dare say this book was about?" I asked.

He shrugged. "Idolatry or some such."

"Oh, yeah." I opened the book idly.

That was when the letter fell out.

Well, it was more of a note than an actual letter. It was folded in quarters, and fluttered to the floor. I watched as if a butterfly had emerged from the pages. Eddie paused in his search. For a moment, hearts pounding, we just stared at the paper on the floor. Then we both went into action together, and actually cracked heads, reaching for it at the same time.

Rubbing our noggins, I took up the paper and Eddie stood aside so I could spread out the letter on the desktop. The letter began:

Here is the confession of—

That was as far as I got because the next thing you know, there was a woman standing in the doorway, holding a pistol.

"I really wish you boys had left this alone," she said.

Twenty-Eight

It was Mrs Blank.

A zillion things ran through my brain at once. The primary one was: *she wants this paper*. The second thing was: *how can I stop her from getting it?*

Eddie had other thoughts.

"What's the big idea?" he demanded. "Put that gat away, sister."

Man, he could be so melodramatic at times. I just *had* to ween him off those stories he read all the time.

Mrs Blank smiled, amused in spite of the situation.

"On the contrary," she said. "I won't be putting my 'gat 'away, and you two are coming with me. Bring that letter."

Here was my opportunity. See, I didn't know exactly when she had entered the room. Had she seen the letter fall from the book? Maybe. If she had, my idea was probably doomed. If she hadn't, if she had come in as we started to read the letter, then maybe we were okay. Because one thing I'd happened to notice before Mrs Blank came in was that one of those invoices from the drawers had been missed, had fallen on the floor behind the desk. This would all be a matter of timing.

Eddie went first, as I knew he would. He's a brave man. That was hopefully the diversion I needed. He would temporarily block Blank's field of vision and allow me to perform my sleight of hand. With one quick move, I slipped the letter onto the floor and picked up the invoice. All she saw was me bending over a bit, and picking up the paper from the desk. For good measure, I used my foot to slide the real letter farther under the desk.

"Hurry up," she snapped at me, and I scurried along, following Eddie out the study door and into the hallway.

"Upstairs," Mrs Blank said, waving her pistol. Man, she was a lot nastier than when we'd talked to her the other day.

We went up, slowly. At the top, she said, "This way," and pointed us toward a disused section of the house. Three doors down on the left, she told us to stop, to go inside. I was shocked to see Miss Dare and Beggars, hands and feet tied to a chair, looking none too happy.

"Sit, you two." Mrs Blank waved us to two chairs.

"Why did you bring them?" Miss Dare demanded, as we took chairs near her. "The boys are innocent."

"Hardly that. They were always snooping about. I did my level best to discourage them—you can't deny it. But they kept at it, on and on. Even so, when they came here today, I was willing to let them leave. I figured they would get tired of waiting for you to return, and go. No, they had to go snooping." She turned our way. "But I believe this time, your snooping has proved beneficial. The paper, please."

Here it came. Would my little switcheroo work? I handed her the paper, the one I'd substituted. She took it triumphantly, looked at it. Her face went to puzzled, then angry. I figured I was done for, for sure. She crumpled it.

"Where is the paper that was in the book?" she demanded.

"That was it," I lied. "Honest."

She turned to Eddie. "You. Get over into that corner."

Oh, no, I thought. *She's gonna shoot him, and it's all my fault*! But no—she just wanted him far from the door, far from the chairs, far from her gun. I stayed sitting and she tied my hands and feet, like she had the two ladies. I was now sitting next to Miss Dare, and asked where the cook was.

"Off for the holidays," she said. From her tone I could tell that, if she ever got out of this, no one would have another day off for the rest of their lives.

"Now you," Mrs Blank said to Eddie. My buddy went obediently to a chair. Now, Eddie's pretty strong, like I've said, and probably could've overpowered her, though she looked pretty tough. But she was smart: she pointed the gun at me. If he didn't behave, I'd be the one to pay. So Eddie sat down and let himself be tied like we were. He winced a little because his arm still hurt, and being tugged backwards didn't help. But my buddy didn't say boo.

"Why're you doing all this?" I asked.

"The very question I asked," Miss Dare said.

"And I was about to answer when you two horned in. Since it won't do you any good, I'll explain."

"Crooks always like to brag," Eddie informed us.

That may have been true, but it was the wrong thing to say. She slapped Eddie, hard. "I'm no crook," she snapped. "I had perfectly good reasons to do as I did."

"Let's hear it," Miss Dare said, a little impatiently, I thought. Mrs Blank pulled up a chair and sat about six feet from us.

"I was a member of that church, the one where Mrs Clapham attended. I was even in the choir, and was at rehearsal that night."

"Your husband was director, and you helped clean up after rehearsal," I said.

"That's what made it so easy," she said with a dreamy smile, like she was remembering a nice vacation. "It was so easy to slip away from my dim-witted husband, while he finished straightening the choir loft."

I'll spare you all her side comments and just tell you her story. It seems that she was all het up about religion, and especially the group. And despite her snippy comments about him, I think she loved the guy. Why, I don't know; he certainly was no prize. She must've been lonely. Come to think of it, she wasn't exactly Theda Bara either

Then came Miss Dare's backyard party. Everyone from the surrounding area was invited, including the Claphams and the Blanks. The party, she said, was dull. Nothing to do but wander around and eat and drink. She didn't actually care for the other guests, found them stupid and boring. She lost track of Mr Blank before too long. From what she said, Blank was the life of the party. I didn't see it, but since he was the leader of their little religious group, he must've had some charisma.

About an hour in, she was puzzled to see her husband slip into the house by the study door. Maybe he was ill! That thought worried her, and she started for the door, but lo and behold, Mrs Clapham slipped into the study as well. Heart pounding, she went to investigate. She looked in the study door, couldn't see anyone, and circled around to the front of the house. Inside, she went down the hallway toward the study.

The house was empty; everyone was outside on this nice day. Mrs Blank crept along. What she heard and saw, she wouldn't tell us, I think because she thought Eddie and I were too young. Unlike some boys my age, I don't claim to understand how that whole sex thing works, but it was clear that was what she saw: Mr Blank and Mrs Clapham having sex on the desk.

Right in the middle of things, he looked up at his wife, and smiled slyly.

Mrs Blank was furious. She stormed off and wasn't seen at the backyard party for another hour.

"I remember you being gone," Miss Dare said now. "I just assumed the excitement of the day was too much," she added—sarcastically, I think.

205

Nothing was said that night, but the next morning at breakfast, Mr Blank said to her, "I hope you won't say anything about… what you saw yesterday." This made her even angrier, but she swallowed it and said okay, she'd keep her mouth shut.

No more was said, but Mrs Blank didn't forget. She plotted and planned what she would do about it. Should she tell Mr Clapham what she saw? Would he believe her? Or would he think she was just a meddlesome busybody whose husband was playing around? Anyhow, as time passed, she figured that option was out. Mr Clapham would undoubtedly ask what took her so long to say anything. No, she thought, she'd have to do something bigger.

She came to the conclusion that she had to get rid of the anger inside her, and the only way to do that was to get rid of Mrs Clapham.

"You might've thought of something a little less permanent," Miss Dare told her now.

"Bah," was all Mrs Blank replied.

She plotted and schemed until October. The plan was simple, though the timing had to be just so. After that practice, she left her husband with the clean-up and headed out the side church door, and crept through the churchyard to the gate that led into the cemetery. Along the way, she picked up a shovel that the caretaker always left outside.

Mrs Clapham was genuinely surprised to see her, standing at the cemetery door. When Mrs Blank told her she had to stay away from her husband though, Mrs Clapham just laughed. How dare she insist? Blank, after all, wanted her, not his wife. That was the last straw. Mrs

Blank swung the shovel and cracked her a good one over the head. She pulled the body (unknown whether the woman was dead then or not) through the church gate and left it there, then hurried off to join her husband. She'd planned to leave the body where it was, in the graveyard, but fate intervened.

After they were home for a bit, Mr Clapham arrived to say his wife hadn't been home from choir practice, and had they seen her? Mrs Blank faked a worried look and went with Clapham and her husband to look for the missing woman. Mrs Blank couldn't have them find the body yet because the cops would probably suspect the choir, so she volunteered to check the church. She went in the front door and out the side.

Mrs Clapham hadn't moved, and now Mrs Blank checked for vital signs. She thought there might be a weak pulse, but her own heart was beating pretty strong, and she couldn't tell whose pulse she was feeling.

Some weeks before, Mrs Blank had been shown the tunnel by her husband, who thought it might be a good place for their group. He hadn't brought it up at a meeting yet, so Mrs Blank dragged the body—and it was a body now, she was sure of it—to the tunnel entrance. With effort, she pushed Mrs Clapham's corpse through the little opening. Anyone finding the tunnel would see the body right off, but she was counting on the tunnel remaining a secret for a while yet.

The police investigation, as you know, was fruitless. Mrs Clapham was missing, and while the officials might suggest she'd met with foul play, others were quite certain she'd run off with some man.

When the heat had worn off, Mrs Blank returned to the tunnel one dark night. She'd had a little time to think about what to do. She dragged the corpse through the tunnel to the other end. Now came the tough part. She had to drape the body over her shoulder and carry it up the ladder. But Mrs Clapham was a small woman and Mrs Blank was strong, and besides she had necessity on her side. She managed to get the body up and out of the tunnel. After a short rest, she dragged the body to Miss Dare's house and deposited it in the study. Fitting, she thought, for the woman's transgression there. Then came one of those flashes of conscience that killers sometimes get. She pulled out *The Scarlet Letter* and in it she put her signed confession. Either the cops would find the paper and arrest her or she'd go free. Leave it up to God. Sort of a coward's way out, though I didn't say so just then. My Uncle Benjamin used to say that God has bigger fish to fry than make up your mind for you.

That might've been that, but for Mr Blank. After he'd shown everyone the tunnel, he puzzled over something that was in his brain but refused to be let out. You could see it in his eyes. That puzzlement would remain there, off and on, for years.

Then the body was found.

Blank, who was slow on the uptake though eventually the light dawned, told his wife of his suspicions: that she had killed Mrs Clapham. Mind you, this took a couple of years for him to figure out. He confronted her. She'd always been jealous of him and Mrs Clapham, he said, although there was nothing to be jealous about. He had no intention of leaving his wife. It was just a bit of fun. That didn't sit well with her at all. How dare he toy with women that way? It was so... un-

Christian, in her mind. Blank just laughed. This was real life, not some romantic notion from the films. Besides which, didn't Solomon have all those concubines?

The couple kept silent because Blank had no proof his wife had done it, but things were mighty frosty at their house. Still, life went on as usual, and Blank might've even forgotten what she'd done. Then Eddie and I started poking our noses in (her words, not mine).

One day, close to Christmas, Blank told his wife he'd like to discuss the matter with her, in the tunnel. That put her on her guard, and she took a knife from the church kitchen to defend herself. When she entered the tunnel though, the rest of the group were there, all dressed in their ceremonial robes.

"You must be placed on trial," Blank intoned, "by the entire group, to see if you are worthy of our allegiance. We are, after all, Christians." Which was a joke, I thought.

Anyhow, they had their 'trial'. I was surprised that Clapham was a part of it. Hadn't he wanted his wife's murderer brought to justice? When I asked that, Mrs Blank smiled and said Clapham knew his wife fooled around, and didn't miss her very much. In fact, he was one of the strongest supporters for letting the killer off the hook.

There were four jurors: Blank, the Meyers, and Mr Clapham. The vote was two to two. Clapham and Mrs Meyer voted for innocent. But Blank looked triumphant and said that, as head of the group, he had the deciding vote, and voted guilty. He beckoned her with a curled finger. "Come along," he said. "You must be made to give penance."

Mrs Blank could barely contain her anger. How dare they pass judgment on her? Still, she followed Blank down the tunnel to the entrance from the church. The rest of the group was just behind them. They trudged on, and all along she fondled the knife inside her cloak.

They had reached the entrance. Blank climbed out, then his wife. Before the others could do likewise, she took out the knife and stabbed Blank through the back. He staggered forward, and out into the chancel, where we saw him.

Mr Meyer was the next one near the entrance and had seen it happen—the others didn't—but Meyer staggered back onto the ladder and forced the rest back down. Mrs Blank followed them into the tunnel.

"Now," she told them, closing the tunnel door as she spoke, "the vote is in my favor."

"So," Miss Dare said now, "why didn't they turn you in? Surely the others now saw you for the killer you are?"

Mrs Blank looked ready to smack her, but held back, then smiled.

"They couldn't turn me in, for fear of being held complicit in the killings. Clapham and the Meyers had far too much to lose."

"Didn't you regret," Eddie said, "killing your husband?"

"Never. You see, my husband didn't stop when Mrs Clapham was gone. It was like a disease with him. He simply moved on to others."

"So what happened, then?" I asked.

"Why, so far, nothing. By agreement, the group said nothing about what happened that day—or five years ago. When Clapham was visited by that detective of yours, Delancey, he needed a little convincing, so I sent him a short note to remind him not to speak. As to Meyer, why, I sent him to warn you off."

"That was *Meyer* who forced us into his car?" I asked.

"It was. Mind you, he'd never have it in him to actually harm you. He was just supposed to scare you. He didn't hurt either of you, did he?"

Her sudden change to caring was scarier than when she was talking about murder. We shook our heads.

"And who pushed me down the tunnel?" I demanded. "And shot at us?"

"That was me, I'm afraid. The shot was just to warn you off; the tunnel… well, I panicked, seeing you there, finding the entrance. So I pushed you in. My plan was to wait and see if you made it out on your own, and if you didn't, then I would make an anonymous telephone call to the police, to let you out."

"We only have your word on that," Miss Dare said drily.

She looked hurt. "I would never hurt a child, after what happened to my own. The two adults who died knew what they were doing and deserved what they got. But a child… I might give 'em a cuff around the ear now and again, but—"

"You might've *killed* Iggy, shoving him down that hole!"

"I know, and I'm very sorry. As I said, I panicked. I wouldn't have done any of this," she waved her pistol hand at us," but you invited me here, Miss Hogwood, and I was sure you had figured it out, so I brought my gun."

"Actually, I only had a hunch," Miss Dare admitted.

"What happens now?" I asked.

All this time, Beggars was silent. It wasn't like her. Eddie was fidgeting; that was like him. Both occasionally moved around in their chairs, but I figured they were just trying to get some feeling in their hands. Mine were going a little numb from the ropes.

Mrs Blank didn't seem to notice, or if she did, she ignored them. She had the pistol, after all.

So it came as a complete shock when, after I'd barely got my question out, Beggars sprang forward at our captor. The chair was still around her ankles, but she paid it no mind. She knocked Mrs Blank to the floor. The gun went flying, but she couldn't get to it because of the chair. Right after, Eddie got his hands free too! He fiddled with the ropes while the two women fought on the floor. I thought he might go for the gun, but no, he just ran out the door and down the stairs.

Twenty-Nine

I hated to leave you hanging at the last chapter, but it's what we authors call a 'grabber'.

"That," said Mrs Blank, "was a very foolish thing to do."

She was talking to Beggars, who sat groaning on the floor. In their tussle, Mrs Blank had managed to get her gun, and clocked Beggars over the noggin with it.

Meantime, Eddie had untied his ankles in a jiffy, then looked for the gun. Problem was, the gun was lying on the opposite side of the two women wrestling on the floor, so he couldn't get past. Instead, he hightailed for the door and out. By the time Mrs Blank had recovered enough to get on her feet, gun pointing at us, the front door had banged open and shut, and Eddie was long gone.

"So what do you do now?" Miss Dare asked, which I wished she hadn't, for fear of the answer.

"Of course, this has changed my plans a little. Eddie will undoubtedly run to the police, or more likely, Delancey. Regardless, time is suddenly not on my side." She paused only a moment. Quick thinking, she was, I have to give her that.

First, she ordered Beggars back to her chair. The housekeeper was still woozy, but managed to scramble to the chair and sit. This time, Mrs Blank would make sure she was tied securely. Then she began to untie me, ankles first, then hands. "Up," she said, and I rose, though I swayed a little because the ropes had been pretty tight, and my ankle was still plenty sore.

"Where are you taking the boy?" Miss Dare demanded. "He's innocent in all this."

"Sadly, he isn't," Mrs Blank answered ominously. "Move," she told me, "and don't even think about running."

As you can guess, I couldn't have run if she'd told me to. We went out of the room and down the stairs. The front door was open a little, from when Eddie had banged it behind him. Mrs Blank headed that way, and I assumed we were going out the front, but all she wanted to do was close the door.

Then she turned and directed me to the back. All along, I figured I was done for. Of course, she could've plugged me at any time before this, so my fears maybe didn't make sense, but I was too scared to make sense.

At the back door, she grabbed a set of keys hanging nearby. Then we headed for the garage and to Miss Dare's car. "In," she commanded. By now, my legs were working properly, and I suppose I could've run for it, but you can't outrun a bullet with or without a limp, so I got in and waited till she opened the garage door. She started the car, drove out, got out to properly shut the garage door, and drove off.

For now, it's time to leave me in my predicament and return to the house, to see what Miss Dare and Beggars were up to when we'd left. Miss Dare struggled with her ropes. "How the hell did Eddie…" she started to mutter, but left it hanging. "Beggars, are you all right?" Only a groan in reply. It was no use on the ropes—too tight. All she could do was cry out in desperation.

That was how they found them about twenty minutes later—'they' meaning Eddie, Inspector Fenrow, and a uniformed officer. Eddie had run straight for Delancey's office, but he and Beulah were gone, so he tried the police station. He quickly explained, Fenrow listened. They hurried to Miss Dare's house.

Before entering, Fenrow pulled his gun, told Eddie to wait. Eddie was thrilled: this was exactly like the coppers did it in his magazines! Just as they were ready to enter, Delancey and Beulah showed up. They'd been to the Blank house first, with no answer. A quick illegal break-in, and Beulah had noticed Miss Dare's address on a notepad by the telephone.

All this, Delancey explained quickly (except for the break-in part). He joined Fenrow as they silently entered Miss Dare's house, the others behind.

At the top, Delancey turned to Eddie, who pointed to the room they'd been in. Delancey nodded, motioned the others back again, and he headed forward with Fenrow by his side. In one quick move, they entered the room, gun at the ready.

"Well!" Miss Dare said. "It's about time!"

In a few minutes, after Miss Dare informed them that Mrs Blank and I were gone, they were walking downstairs. Miss Dare was wobbly on her feet, as I had been, and insisted on a brandy (Beggars joined her) while the inspector called police headquarters. Meantime, Eddie and Beulah went to the garage to make sure the car was gone. While Fenrow was on the telephone he got the particulars of Miss Dare's car so the police could put out an alert for the vehicle. A doctor was sent for and tended Beggars's bruised noggin, much to her annoyance.

"Now," said Miss Dare, brandy in hand, when everyone was seated in her living room. "Beggars, Eddie—how on earth did you get yourselves untied? I worked my bonds till my wrists bled, and couldn't get loose."

Beulah had found some gauze and ointment in a medicine chest and tended Miss Dare's raw wrists.

Eddie grinned. "It was easy, miss. See, I read that what you do is arc your hands a bit while they're tyin 'you up. Then you bring your hands together, and the ropes are loose, see? It don't fool a real pro, but I was hopin 'Mrs Blank was no pro."

"I did likewise," Beggars said, wincing like it hurt to even talk.

"I shall have to use that in one of my stories," Miss Dare mused.

"So what was your clue that Mrs Blank was behind these murders?" Fenrow asked.

"I didn't have one. Mrs Blank was a connection between the murders, but then so was Mr Clapham, and anyone in the choir."

Delancey nodded. "I thought of Clapham, but he just didn't seem the type to get his hands dirty. The book—*The Scarlet Letter*—was a clue, and it seemed more something she would do than Clapham. Besides, if it was Clapham, why kill Blank second? I'd have thought he would get Blank first."

Talk of the book jogged Eddie's memory.

"In that book… Iggy found a note. A confession, it said. I didn't see who wrote it, or what they were confessing." He hadn't seen me shove the real note under the desk. I was pretty sneaky.

"Well," said Inspector Fenrow, "hopefully we'll get to ask Iggy in person."

Beulah asked him if there was any idea where Mrs Blank might've gone. Fenrow shrugged, but Beggars cut in.

"I might. During a choir practice… well, people yammer on so. You'd think they hadn't see one another in years. Mrs Blank was as bad as the rest, and she sometimes mentioned family in Rockford. I was only half listening, you understand."

"There's one major road headed south," Fenrow mused. "Maybe I'd better call it in."

Beulah said, "She might try side roads at first."

"Good thinking," Fenrow said, and headed for the telephone.

By now, you're probably wondering how I was faring. I don't blame you.

I was sitting next to Mrs Blank. She had the pistol in her lap, ready to grab if needed. But she told me right off: "No harm will come to you, if you don't try anything fancy."

"Where are you taking me?" I asked.

"I just need someone as hostage, in case the cops catch up to me before I'm out of the area. Once I feel in the clear, I'll let you go."

Actually, we were already out of the area. She'd headed right out of town after leaving Miss Dare's. The quickest way was due west. Once on the county roads, she'd turned south. I had no idea where we were, but I'd seen more of the countryside the past few days than I'd done in all my years previous.

"You could just let me out now," I suggested. "It would be a long time before I'd find my way back."

"I have to say," she went on, ignoring my timely suggestion, "you and Eddie are quite a team. If you weren't poking your nose into my business, I might admire you."

"Thanks."

We drove in silence. Snow and ice rimmed the road and the farm fields we passed. The roads themselves had a thin crust that made the ride bumpy, but Mrs Blank didn't seem to notice. It wasn't her car, after all. There were farmhouses and barns all along the road, but little sign of life. Milking was long over with, and no doubt the farm families were cozied up before a fire, keeping warm. Maybe still celebrating Christmas. I smiled at the thought.

Then we came to a stop, right next to a sign that read: County Line.

"Out," she said.

"What? Here?"

"Yes. You didn't think I'd take you all over Creation, did you? Out."

It's a funny thing: when we'd first driven off, I was eager to get out of the car. Now, with the heater finally working, and the desolate fields outside, I preferred to stay. But she had the gun, so I got out.

"I doubt we'll see each other again," Mrs Blank said as I got ready to shut the door. "You're a good kid, Iggy."

There wasn't any more to say. I shut the car door and she rode off.

So there I was, in the middle of nowhere again. This was getting monotonous. What made it worse this time was I was miles from any town. And we hadn't seen a single car in a good twenty minutes. So where was I supposed to go?

It was too blinking cold to debate the issue for long. With a shrug, I started back the way we'd come, heading for a farmhouse with smoke curling out of the chimney. Along the way, I wondered what the family would make of my sudden appearance. No matter how I fashioned it in my brain, the story sounded unbelievable. Still, it might be best to tell as much of the truth as needed in order to get help.

So I kept walking. The day was cold. A strong wind had picked up, and seemed to blow in my face no matter where I turned. As expected, not a single car was on the road. Was the farmhouse getting farther away as I walked? It sure seemed so.

Eventually, I made it. The farmyard was deserted as I walked up the gravel driveway to the door. It was a sturdily-built house, like its occupants, I guessed. I knocked and waited.

Before too long, the door was opened by a round, short woman with rosy cheeks and kind eyes.

"*Gott in Himmel!*" she cried. "*Ein gefrorener Junge!*"

Without a word from me, she yanked me inside and made me sit in the toasty warm kitchen.

The room was huge, and smelled of bread and roast beef. My stomach growled at the thought of it. The woman called," Emil!" and before long a wiry little man appeared, pulling up his suspenders as he entered.

"*Vas is los?*" he asked. "Who is this?"

They spoke with German accents, and I won't try to recreate them. At the man's question, they turned in my direction.

"My name is Iggy, and I was taken by a bad lady, but managed to escape. I could use your help."

The farmer and his wife looked at me, then at each other. My heart sank. They didn't believe a word of it.

"Where are you from?" the farmer asked. I named my hometown.

"Such a long way!"

It was a good thirty miles, I found out later.

"Look," I said politely. "All I really need is a telephone. I'd like to call for someone to pick me up."

Again they looked at each other.

"We have no telephone," said the farmer at last.

I didn't know many of these rural families had no use for a phone. They must've seen the disappointment in my face because they started jabbering a bit in German. Since that language isn't too far from Yiddish, which my folks can speak and I know a little of, I could pick out the odd word, but still had no idea what they were saying. Finally, they nodded.

"Have something to eat," said the woman.

"I'm not hungry," I lied.

"You must eat, while Emil puts on his town clothes. He will take you into town. There you may call."

I brightened. My stomach was happy too because I had a nice plate of hot food—some of it not kosher, but I'm sure God will forgive. Before long, the farmer was ready, and I took a large dinner roll in my pocket (with the woman's blessing) before joining him out the door.

We crossed the barnyard, and entered a shed next to the barn. There was our conveyance: a bright green tractor. It was a single seater, but the farmer showed how I could stand on the back and hang on. Probably against all sorts of traffic laws, but I wasn't about to argue. This would be great! Something to tell Eddie about when all this was over. I really wanted to drive, but would never have dreamt of making the kind farmer stand on the back.

So we headed to town, which took about thirty bone-jarring minutes. Not meant for pleasure riding, tractors. When I climbed off, my legs were numb from the bouncing. Anyhow, we went to a feed store where they knew the farmer well. He explained (in German again) my predicament.

The feed store guy looked at me suspiciously a few times and finally decided it was legitimate. He directed me to the telephone.

Now, the only number I know by heart is my home number, and that didn't seem the best. Chances are, my folks didn't even know I was missing. So instead, I asked for the sheriff's number. That turned out to be a good idea because it lent credence to my story. The feed guy relaxed a little and started chatting amiably with Emil. I had a little trouble convincing the sheriff's deputy of my story, but asked him to telephone the city police, to speak with Inspector Fenrow. I gave my name and where I was.

Then I sat back and watched the feed guy and the farmer play two games of checkers while I waited.

It was the better part of an hour, I'd say, before a police car rolled up outside. Fenrow got out, looking both steamed and relieved. He came into the feed store, spotted me, and clapped a strong hand on my shoulder.

"Good to see you're safe, Iggy. And thank you gentlemen for your help."

The two barely looked up from their checkerboard to acknowledge his thanks.

I'll spare you all the details of my homecoming. Needless to say, my folks had been informed I'd been taken hostage. I suppose they had to know. Anyhow, they were just like the inspector: relieved to see me safe but angry I'd gotten into danger in the first place. My parents threatened to keep me under lock and key, but Mom would never want to put up with me at home all the time. They also found out the name of the kind farm couple and sent them two nice presents from Dad's shop.

It had been a very interesting Christmas vacation.

Thirty

I'll start this final chapter on the last day of the year.

It was bitterly cold. The snow on sidewalks and roads had frozen so solid, people and cars and wagons slipped every which way. Anyone planning to get a little tipsy that night (not to let a little thing like Prohibition stop them) would have an interesting trek home.

Eddie and I did our share of sliding on the ice—on purpose—and had a jolly time of it. Eddie's arm was all healed and my ankle only twinged once in a while. Afterward, our cheeks red as beets and all feeling lost in our fingers and toes, we decided to head for Delancey's office. There were only a few days left of no school, and tomorrow Delancey's office would be closed.

Our detective friend and Beulah were seated in his office, playing cribbage. They play a lot of cards. They started to scramble, to hide the cards and board, in case we were potential clients, then relaxed and went on playing.

"Hi, boys," Beulah greeted us. "What's up?"

"Nothin 'much," Eddie admitted.

"Did you finish your report?"

Since I'd been released and we'd been given a talking-to by our parents, things had settled down, until the day before, when I suddenly remembered our assignment. Eddie and I had spent the better part of the previous day working on it.

"Just about," Eddie said.

Delancey muttered, "Then hop to it." He always mutters when he's losing to Beulah at cribbage.

"Aw, it's just a few mop-up things. We'll have it done. We got a couple of days yet."

This unassailable logic didn't impress Delancey, who just muttered again, something I couldn't make out, and probably not printable anyway.

For a bit, it was quiet in the room, except for the players pegging. Then the sound of footsteps on the stairs, a scuffle to hide the board and cards, and further relaxation when Inspector Fenrow walked in. Surprisingly, he'd come to see Eddie and me.

"I tried your house," he told me, "and your ma said you'd probably be here."

Another pause as Fenrow settled himself down in a chair like he just wanted to watch the cribbage game. Eddie and I stood to one side, near the radiator.

"Actually," the inspector went on, "I'm glad to have you all in one place. Save me some time. Fact is, we've caught Mrs Blank."

We all let out little expressions of relief. My mom, especially, had been at her wit's end, thinking Mrs Blank would come back and kill me. It was useless to remind Mom that Mrs Blank could have killed me when she had me in the car… or on any one of several other occasions, if it came to that. It didn't matter: Mom was scared, which made me nervous. Now she could rest easy.

"How did you do it?" Delancey asked.

"Actually, it wasn't tough. She went to her family in Illinois, like we thought. Her folks seemed to think it was just to say goodbye, because that's what she did. Said she'd be going away for a while, and would see them someday. That made 'em wonder because they hadn't seen their daughter for ages. When the state patrol car pulled into the driveway, she didn't resist at all."

"Has she confessed?" Beulah asked.

Fenrow nodded. "Basically told us everything she'd already told these two. Only difference this time was, a police stenographer was there to take it all down. She signed it and is now in a cell, waiting for her trial. Shouldn't take too long."

"Will Iggy and me have t 'testify?" Eddie asked hopefully.

A head shake. "No, Eddie. Her confession will mean no trial, just a sentencing." We were sorely disappointed.

Now for the final scene. It takes place our first day back at school. Eddie and I had worked like the dickens to finish our report the day before (editorial differences had dragged out the process), and were certain ours would be the best. When Miss Postlethwaite asked for volunteers to give the first report, Eddie's arm shot up so fast and hard I thought it would fly out of his shirt. No good—Miss P called on two others before she got around to us.

Finally, she gave the signal that it was our turn. Eddie was at his best, laying the groundwork, telling about the mysterious mummified body in the study. Miss P grew impatient so I took over and read the short article that had started everything.

"Perfectly ghastly," shuddered our teacher.

"Thanks, Miss Postlethwaite," said Eddie, beaming.

And so our report went on. Eddie, who isn't fond of reading—even stuff we ourselves had written—went off the script and prattled on about how our investigations had taken us to Miss Hogwood's place, and the mysterious church group, and so on. I had to get a word in edgewise, to tell about my shove down into the tunnel. Eddie slipped in the part about us getting shot at, though his sling had come off a couple of days before. It was riveting.

The story of Mrs Blank's killings and how she'd been caught in another state—all that had been in the papers, but our parents had insisted our names be left out of the story which was a huge disappointment, naturally. The police mostly obliged, though there was a vague reference to a boy being kidnapped by the fleeing murderess. All in all, it had been a letdown. Eddie and I had been all set to clip out the articles to hang on our walls.

Anyhow, Miss P had read the papers and never come across our names, so when we finished, she had stern words.

"Eddie, Iggy, I'm surprised at you. The story you chose was bad enough, but then to fabricate this entire tale of what happened to you! It's very disappointing. Especially you, Iggy. I expect more from you."

Which was an insult to Eddie, of course, but he was more insulted that she thought we were lying about it all. No amount of our insistence that it was true (if embellished a bit) would sway her. She simply tapped her toe, which meant nothing but trouble. Eddie glanced at me, because I *had* suggested we have Delancey read the story and sign it to the effect that it was true. Now, we retreated to our desks in shame, amid the smirks and whispers of our classmates. Miss P called for order, and the next report was begun.

And there it might have stood, with Eddie and me barely getting a passing grade on our report. Except for something that happened later that afternoon.

We were sitting quietly, doing our arithmetic, when a knock came. Everyone looked up. Whoever it might be, was a welcome interruption to arithmetic. Imagine my shock when Inspector Fenrow himself entered!

"Excuse me, miss. Your principal said it would be all right—"

In fact, our principal, a sweaty bald guy named Mr Bludgeon (or was that just what we called him? I forget—he's retired now) entered right after the inspector, looking very nervous. He gave a quick nod to Miss P, assuring her it was all right.

"My name is Inspector Fenrow, of the city police." He flashed his badge, which made everyone ooh and ahh. Miss P called for order. (She calls for order a *lot*.) She politely asked the inspector what he wanted.

"Well," said Fenrow, a slight twitch to his mouth but keeping serious overall, "I've been given the honor by our mayor, to bestow the city's award for merit to Eddie—that is, to Edwin McDonald—and Ignatz Silver. Boys?"

He curled a finger in our direction, and we stood. I haven't asked Eddie, but I was more nervous then than any time during our adventure. We walked to the front of the class and Inspector Fenrow took two parchments from his inner coat pocket, tied with red ribbon, the whole shebang. He unrolled one.

This is to certify, he read, *that Edwin McDonald, with his friend, Ignatz Silver*—"The other certificate has the names reversed," he assured us—*are hereby awarded the Certificate of Merit for our City, for their exhibition of bravery and daring, in regard to the recent outrages, most notably the murders of Mrs Millicent Clapham and Mr Henry Blank, and the subsequent absconding by the perpetrator of said crimes. Such resourcefulness and daring are excellent examples of boyhood, to which our nation should aspire.* "And it's signed and dated today, by the mayor himself."

Inspector Fenrow handed us our parchments, shook our hands, and congratulated us. Spontaneous applause broke out, and we returned to our seats, red-faced but triumphant. Miss P tried to look proud. I guess maybe she was because she applauded too.

On the way back, Eddie muttered to me," I bet we still only get a B."